Catherynne M. Valente is a *New York Times* bestselling author of fantasy and science fiction. She began writing September's adventures in installments on the Web. She lives on a small island off the coast of Maine with her husband, six chickens, two dogs, one enormous cat, a red accordion, a spinning wheel with ulterior motives, a bookshelf full of folktales and the *Oxford English Dictionary*. *The Girl Who Circumnavigated Fairyland in a Ship of Her Own Making* won the Andre Norton Award for YA literature in 2011.

The Girl Who Circumnavigated Fairyland in a Ship of Her Own Making

CATHERYNNE M. VALENTE

A Corsair book

Constable & Robinson Ltd
55–56 Russell Square
London WC1B 4HP
www.constablerobinson.com

First published in the US by Feiwel and Friends,
an imprint of Macmillan, 2011

First published in the UK by Corsair,
an imprint of Constable & Robinson Ltd., 2012

A copy of the British Library Cataloguing in Publication Data is available from the British Library

ISBN 978-1-78033-833-0 (paperback)
ISBN 978-1-78033-862-0 (ebook)

Printed and bound by CPI Group (UK) Ltd, Croydon, CR0 4YY

3 5 7 9 10 8 6 4 2

For all those who walked this strange road with me,
and held out their hands when I faltered.
This is a ship of our own making.

Dramatis Personae

SEPTEMBER, a Young Girl

HER MOTHER

HER FATHER

THE GREEN WIND, a Harsh Air

THE LEOPARD OF LITTLE BREEZES, His Steed

HELLO, a Witch

GOODBYE, her Sister, also a Witch

MANYTHANKS, their Husband, also a Witch, but Additionally, a Wairwulf

A-THROUGH-L, a Wyvern

LYE, a Golem

GOOD QUEEN MALLOW, Former Ruler of Fairyland

CHARLIE CRUNCHCRAB, a Fairy

SEVERAL GLASHTYN

THE MARQUESS, Current Ruler of Fairyland

IAGO, the Panther of Rough Storms

SATURDAY, a Marid

CALPURNIA FARTHING, a Fairy

PENNY FARTHING, her Ward

NUMEROUS VELOCIPEDES

DOCTOR FALLOW, a Spriggan

RUBEDO, a Graduate Student, also a Spriggan

CITRINITAS, an Alchemical Genius, a Spriggan as Well

DEATH

TWO LIONS, Both Blue

MR MAP, the Royal Cartographer

NOR, a Nasnas

AN UNFORTUNATE FISH

A SHARK (Actually a Pooka)

HANNIBAL, a Pair of Shoes

GLEAM, a Lamp

CHAPTER I

Exeunt on a Leopard

In Which a Girl Named September Is Spirited Off by Means of a Leopard, Learns the Rules of Fairyland, and Solves a Puzzle

Once upon a time, a girl named September grew very tired indeed of her parents' house, where she washed the same pink-and-yellow teacups and matching gravy boats every day, slept on the same embroidered pillow, and played with the same small and amiable dog. Because she had been born in May, and because she had a mole on her left cheek, and because her feet were very large and ungainly, the Green Wind took pity on her and flew to her window one evening just after her twelfth birthday. He was dressed in a green smoking jacket, and a green carriage-driver's cloak, and green jodhpurs, and green snowshoes. It is very cold above the clouds in the shantytowns where the Six Winds live.

'You seem an ill-tempered and irascible enough child,' said the Green Wind. 'How would you like to come away with me and ride upon the Leopard of Little Breezes and be delivered to the great sea, which borders Fairyland? I am afraid I cannot go in, as Harsh Airs are not allowed, but I should be happy to deposit you upon the Perverse and Perilous Sea.'

'Oh, yes!' breathed September, who disapproved deeply of pink-and-yellow teacups and also of small and amiable dogs.

'Well, then, come and sit by me, and do not pull too harshly on my Leopard's fur, as she bites.'

September climbed out of her kitchen window, leaving a sink full of soapy pink-and-yellow teacups with leaves still clinging to their bottoms in portentous shapes. One of them looked a bit like her father in his long coffee-colored trench coat, gone away over the sea with a rifle and gleaming things on his hat. One of them looked a bit like her mother, bending over a stubborn airplane engine in her work overalls, her arm muscles bulging. One of them looked a bit like a squashed cabbage. The Green Wind held out his hand, snug in a green glove, and September took both his hands and a very deep breath. One of her shoes came loose as she hoisted herself over the sill, and this will be important later, so let us take a moment to bid farewell to her prim little mary jane with its brass buckle as it clatters on to the parquet floor. Goodbye, shoe! September will miss you soon.

'Now,' said the Green Wind, when September was firmly seated in the curling emerald saddle, her hands knotted in the Leopard's spotted pelt, 'there are important rules in Fairyland, rules from which I shall one day be exempt, when my papers have been processed at last and I am possessed of the golden ring of diplomatic immunity. I am afraid that if you trample upon the rules, I cannot help you. You may be ticketed or executed, depending on the mood of the Marquess.'

'Is she very terrible?'

The Green Wind frowned into his brambly beard. 'All little girls are terrible,' he admitted finally, 'but the Marquess, at least, has a very fine hat.'

'Tell me the rules,' said September firmly. Her mother had taught her chess when she was quite small, and she felt that if she could remember which way knights ought to go, she could certainly remember Fairy rules.

'First, no iron of any kind is allowed. Customs is quite strict on this point. Any bullets, knives, maces or jacks you might have on your person will be confiscated and smelted. Second, the practice of alchemy is forbidden to all except young ladies born on Tuesdays—'

'I was born on a Tuesday!'

'It is certainly possible that I knew that,' the Green Wind said with a wink. 'Third, aviary locomotion is permitted only by means of Leopard or licensed Ragwort Stalk. If you find yourself not in possession of one of these, kindly confine yourself to the ground. Fourth, all traffic travels widdershins. Fifth, rubbish takeaway occurs on second Fridays. Sixth, all changelings are required to wear identifying footwear. Seventh, and most important, you may in no fashion cross the borders of the Worsted Wood, or you will either perish most painfully or be forced to sit through a very tedious tea service with several spinster hamadryads. These laws are sacrosanct, except for visiting dignitaries and spriggans. Do you understand?'

September, I promise you, tried very hard to listen, but the rushing winds kept blowing her dark hair into her face. 'I . . . I think so . . . ,' she stammered, pulling her curls away from her mouth.

'Obviously, the eating or drinking of Fairy foodstuffs

constitutes a binding contract to return at least once a year in accordance with seasonal myth cycles.'

September started. 'What? What does that mean?'

The Green Wind stroked his neatly pointed beard. 'It means: Eat anything you like, precious cherry child!' He laughed like the whistling air through high branches. 'Sweet as cherries, bright as berries, the light of my moony sky!'

The Leopard of Little Breezes yawned up and farther off from the rooftops of Omaha, Nebraska, to which September did not even wave goodbye. One ought not to judge her: All children are heartless. They have not grown a heart yet, which is why they can climb tall trees and say shocking things and leap so very high that grown-up hearts flutter in terror. Hearts weigh quite a lot. That is why it takes so long to grow one. But, as in their reading and arithmetic and drawing, different children proceed at different speeds. (It is well known that reading quickens the growth of a heart like nothing else.) Some small ones are terrible and fey, Utterly Heartless. Some are dear and sweet and Hardly Heartless at all. September stood very generally in the middle on the day the Green Wind took her, Somewhat Heartless, and Somewhat Grown.

And so September did not wave goodbye to her house or her mother's factory, puffing white smoke far below her. She did not even wave goodbye to her father when they passed over Europe. You and I might be shocked by this, but September had read a great number of books and knew that parents are only angry until they have discovered that their little adventurer has been to Fairyland and not the corner pub, and then everything is all right. Instead, she looked straight into the clouds until the wind made her eyes water. She leaned into the Leopard of Little Breezes, whose pelt was rough and bright, and listened to the beating of her huge and thundering heart.

'If you don't mind my asking, Sir Wind,' said September after a respectable time had passed, 'how does one get to Fairyland? After a while, we shall certainly pass India and Japan and California and simply come round to my house again.'

The Green Wind chuckled. 'I suppose that would be true if the earth were round.'

'I'm reasonably sure it is . . .'

'You're going to have to stop that sort of backward, old-fashioned thinking, you know. Conservatism is not an attractive trait. Fairyland is a very Scientifick place. We subscribe to all the best journals.'

The Leopard of Little Breezes gave a light roar. Several small clouds skipped huffily out of their path.

'The earth, my dear, is roughly *trapezoidal,* vaguely *rhomboid,* a bit of a *tesseract,* and altogether grumpy when its fur is stroked the wrong way! In short, it is a *puzzle,* my autumnal acquisition, like the interlocking silver rings your aunt Margaret brought back from Turkey when you were nine.'

'How did you know about my aunt Margaret?' exclaimed September, holding her hair back with one hand.

'I happened to be performing my usual noontime dustup just then. She wore a black skirt; you wore your yellow dress with the monkeys on it. Harsh Airs have excellent memories for things they have ruffled.'

September smoothed the lap of her now-wrinkled and rumpled orange dress. She liked anything orange: leaves; some moons; marigolds; chrysanthemums; cheese; pumpkin, both in pie and out; orange juice; marmalade. Orange is bright and demanding. You can't ignore orange things. She once saw an orange parrot in the pet store and had never wanted anything so much in her life. She would have named it Halloween and fed it butterscotch. Her mother said butterscotch would make a bird sick and, besides, the dog would certainly eat it up. September never spoke to the dog again – [illegible]

'The puzzle is not unlike those rings,' said the Green Wind, tipping his gaze over his green spectacles. 'We are going to unlock the earth and lock it up again, and when we have done it, we shall be in another ring, which is to say, Fairyland. It won't be long now.'

And indeed, in the icy-blue clouds above the world, a great number of rooftops began to peek out. They were all very tall and very rickety: cathedral towers made of nailed boards, cupolas of rusted metal, obelisks of tattered leaves and little more, huge domes like the ones September had seen in books about Italy, but with many of their bricks punched out, broken, turned to dust. Just the sorts of buildings where wind howls hardest, whistles loudest, screams highest. The tips and tops of everything were frozen – including the folk that flew and flittered through the town, bundled up tight much like the Green Wind himself, their jodhpurs and jackets black or rosy or yellow, their cheeks puffed out and round, like the cherubs blowing at the corners of old maps.

'Welcome, September, to the city of Westerly, my home, where live all the Six Winds in nothing at all like harmony.'

'It's . . . very nice. And very cold. And I seem to have lost one of my shoes.'

The Green Wind looked down at September's toes, which were beginning to turn slightly purple. Being at least a bit of a gentleman, he shuffled off his smoking jacket and guided her arms into it. The sleeves were far too big, but the jacket had learned a drop or two of manners in its many travels and adjusted itself around September's little body, puffing up and drawing in until it was quite like her own skin.

'I think I look a little like a pumpkin,' whispered September, secretly delighted. 'I'm all green and orange.'

She looked down. On her wide, emerald velvet lapel, the jacket had grown a little orange brooch for her, a jeweled key. It sparkled as though made out of the sun itself. The jacket warmed slightly with bashfulness and with hoping she'd be pleased.

'The shoe is a very great loss, I won't lie,' clucked the Green Wind. 'But one must make sacrifices if one is to enter Fairyland.' His voice dropped confidentially. 'Westerly is a border town, and the Red Wind is awfully covetous. Terribly likely your shoe would have been stolen eventually, anyway.'

The Green Wind and September entered Westerly smoothly, the Leopard of Little Breezes being extra careful not to jostle the landing. They strode down Squamish Thoroughfare, where big-cheeked Blue and Golden Winds went about their grocery shopping, piling their arms with tumbleweeds for rich, thorny salads. Clouds spun and blew down the street the way old paper blows in the cities you and I have seen. They were heading for two spindly pillars at the end of the Thoroughfare, pillars so enormous that September could not see right away that they were actually people, incredibly tall and thin, their faces huge and long. She could not tell if they were men or women, but they were hardly thicker than a pencil and taller than any of the bell towers and high platforms of Westerly. Their feet went straight down through the clouds, disappearing in a puff of cumulus. They both wore thin circular glasses, darkened to keep out the bright Westerly sun.

'Who are they?' whispered September.

'That's Latitude, with the yellow belt, and Longitude, with the paisley cravat. We can't get very far without them, so be polite.'

'I thought latitude and longitude were just lines on maps.'

'They don't like to have their pictures taken. That's how it is with famous folk. Everyone wants to click, click, click away at you. It's very annoying. They made a bargain with the Cartographers' Guild several hundred years ago – symbolic representations only, out of respect, you understand.'

September felt very quiet in front of Latitude and Longitude. Being young, she was used to most people being taller than she was. But this was of another order entirely, and she hadn't eaten anything since breakfast, and travel by Leopard is very tiring. She didn't think she ought to curtsy, as that was old-fashioned, so she bowed from the waist. The Green Wind looked amused and copied her bow.

Latitude yawned. The inside of his mouth was bright blue, the color of the ocean on school maps. Longitude sighed in a bored sort of way.

'Well, you wouldn't expect them to speak, would you?' The Green Wind looked slightly embarrassed. 'They're celebrities! They're very private.'

'I thought you said there would be a puzzle,' said September, catching Latitude's yawn. The Green Wind picked at his sleeve, as though miffed that she was not more impressed.

'When you solve a jigsaw puzzle,' he said, 'how do you do it, pumpkin-dear?'

September shuffled her cold foot on the smooth blue stone of the Thoroughfare. 'Well . . . you start with the corners, and then you fill in the edges to make a frame, and then work inward until all the pieces fit.'

'And, historically, how many winds are there?'

September thought back to her book of myths, which had been bright orange and therefore one of her favorite possessions.

'Four, I think.'

The Green Wind grinned, his green lips curling under a green mustache. 'Quite so: Green, Red, Black and Gold. Of course, those are roughly family designations, like Smith or Gupta. And actually there is also Silver and Blue, but they've made trouble off the coast of Tunisia and have had to go to bed without supper. So the fact remains: Today, we are the corners.' He gestured at the placid Latitude and Longitude. 'They are the edges. And you, September' – he gently pulled a strand of September's hair free of her brooch – 'are the middle pieces, all funny shaped and stubborn.'

'I don't understand, Sir.'

'Well, it's all in the verbiage. One of the pieces is *a girl hopping widdershins on one foot, nine revolutions*. One is *wear motley colors*. One is *clap hand over one eye*. One is *give something up*. One is *have a feline in attendance*.'

'But that's easy!'

'Mostly easy. But Fairyland is an old place, and old things have strange hungers. One of the last pieces is: *There must be blood*. The other is: *Tell a lie*.'

September bit her lip. She had never been fond of jigsaw puzzles, even though her grandmother loved them and had glued one thousand pieces all over her house as a kind of wallpaper. Slowly, trying to remember it all, she clapped one hand over her eye. She raised one foot and hopped in what she hoped was widdershins around the Leopard of Little Breezes. Her orange dress flapped against the green jacket shining in the sun. When she stopped, September unfastened the jeweled orange key from her lapel and pricked her finger sharply with its pin. Blood welled up and dripped on to the blue stones. She laid the key gently at the feet of the impassive Latitude and Longitude and drew a deep breath.

'I want to go home,' she lied softly.

Latitude and Longitude turned smoothly toward each other, as though they were on pedestals. They began to bend and fold like staircases, reaching out for each other and interlocking, hand into hand, foot on to knee, arms akimbo. They moved mechanically in their strange circus dance, jerkily, joints swinging like dolls'. The street shook a little and then was still. Ever so briefly, Latitude and Longitude kissed, and when they parted, there was a space between their mouths just large enough for a Leopard carrying a Harsh Air and a little girl. All September could see on the other side were clouds.

Solemnly, the Green Wind held out his gloved hand to the girl in orange.

'Well done, September,' he said, and lifted her on to the Leopard's emerald saddle.

One can never see what happens after an exeunt on a Leopard. It is against the rules of theatre. But cheating has always been the purview of fairies, and as we are about to enter their domain, we ought to act in accordance with local customs.

For, you see, when September and the Green Wind had gone through the puzzle of the world on their great cat, the jeweled key rose up and swooped in behind them, as quiet as you like.

CHAPTER II

The Closet Between Worlds

In Which September Passes Between Worlds,
Asks Four Questions and Receives Twelve Answers,
and Is Inspected by a Customs Officer

By the time a lady reaches the grand, golden evening of her life, she has accumulated a great number of things. You know this – when you visited your grandmother on the lake that summer you were surprised to see how many portraits of people you didn't recognize hung on the walls and how many porcelain ducks and copper pans and books and collectible spoons and old mirrors and scrap wood and half-finished knitting and board games and fireplace pokers she had stuffed away in the corners of her house. You couldn't think what use a person would have for all that junk, why they would keep it around for all this time, slowly fading in the sun and turning the same shade of parchmenty brown. You thought your grandmother was a bit crazy, to have such a collection of glass owls and china sugar bowls.

That is what the space between Fairyland and our world looks like. It is Grandmother's big, dark closet, her shed out back, her basement, cluttered with the stuff and nonsense of millennia. The world didn't really know where else to put it, you see. The earth is frugal; she doesn't toss out perfectly good bronze helmets or spinning wheels or water clocks. She might need them one day. As for all the portraiture: When you've lived as long as she has, you'll need help remembering your grandchildren, too.

September marveled at the heaps of oddities in the closet between worlds. The ceiling was very low, with roots coming through, and everything had a genteel fade to it, the old lace and code-breaking machines, the anchors and heavy picture frames, the dinosaur bones and orreries. As the Leopard proceeded through the dimly lit passageway, September looked into the painted eyes of pharaohs and blind poets, chemists and serene philosophers. September could tell they were philosophers because they had on drapey clothes, like curtains. But most of the portraits were just people, wearing whatever they had liked to wear when they were living, raking hay or writing diaries or baking bread.

'Sir Wind,' September said, when she had recovered herself and her eyes had adjusted to the darkness, 'I want to ask you a question, and I want you to answer me seriously and not call me any pretty names or tease me.'

'Of course, my . . . September. And you can call me Green. I feel we're becoming very well acquainted.'

'Why did you take me out of Omaha? Do you take very many girls? Are they all from Nebraska? Why are you being so nice to me?'

September could not be sure, but she thought the Leopard of Little Breezes laughed. It might have been a snort.

'That's rather more than one question. Therefore, I think it's only fair I give you rather more than one set of answers.' He cleared his throat dramatically. 'One: Omaha is no place for anybody. Two: No, my schedule keeps me quite busy enough. Three: See above. Four: So that you will like me and not be afraid.'

Up ahead, there was a line of folk in long, colorful coats,

moving slowly, checking watches, smoothing hair under hats. The Leopard slowed.

'I said no teasing,' said September.

'One: I was lonely. Two: I have been known to spirit a child or two away, I shan't lie. It is the nature of winds to Snatch and Grasp at things, and Blow Them Away. Three: Nebraska does not grow many of the kinds of girls who ought to go to Fairyland. Four: If I were not nice, and did not know the way to Fairyland, and did not have a rather spectacular cat, you would not smile at me or say amusing things. You would tell me politely that you like teacups and small dogs and to please be on my way.'

They came up short and took their place in line. Everyone towered above September – the line might have been long or short; she could not tell. September leapt off of the Leopard and on to the dry, compact dirt of the closet between worlds. The Green Wind hopped lightly down beside her.

'You said I was ill-tempered! Was that really why?'

'One: There is a department in Fairyland entirely devoted to spiriting off young boys and girls (mostly orphans, but we have become more liberal in this late age), so that we may have a ready supply of a certain kind of story to tell when winter comes and there is nothing to do but drink fennel beer and peer at the hearth. Two: See above. Three: Dry, brown places are prime real estate for children who want to escape them. It's much harder to find wastrels in New York City to fly about on a Leopard. After all, they have the Metropolitan Museum to occupy them. Four: I am not being very nice at all. See how I lie to you and make you do things my way? That is so you will be ready to live in Fairyland, where this sort of thing is considered the height of manners.'

September curled her fists. She tried very hard not to cry.

'Green! Stop it! I just want to know—'

'One! Because you were born in—'

'If I am special,' finished September, halfway between a whisper and a squeak. 'In stories, when someone appears in a poof of green clouds and asks a girl to go away on an adventure, it's because she's special, because she's smart and strong and can solve riddles and fight with swords and give really good speeches, and . . . I don't know that I'm any of those things. I don't even know that I'm as ill-tempered as all that. I'm not *dull* or anything, I know about geography and chess, and I can fix the boiler when my mother has to work. But what I mean to say is: Maybe you meant to go to another girl's house and let *her* ride on the Leopard. Maybe you didn't mean to choose me at all, because I'm not like storybook girls. I'm short and my father ran away with the army and I wouldn't even be able to keep a dog from eating a bird.'

The Leopard turned her prodigious spotted head and looked at September with large, solemn yellow eyes.

'We came for you,' she growled. 'Just you.'

The big cat licked the child's cheek roughly. September smiled, just a little. She sniffed and wiped her eyes with the sleeve of the green jacket.

'NEXT!' boomed a deep, severe voice that echoed all over the closet. It was so strong that they were blown back into the folk who had silently joined the line behind them. The party in front of them, all pink eye-shadow and spangled, spiky hair, exploded past a tall podium in a flutter of papers and luggage.

At the top of the podium loomed an enormous gargoyle, its face a mass of bronze and black rock, waggling stone eyebrows and a stern metal jaw. Its lolling eyes burned red flames. Its heavy arms clicked and whirred, greasy pistons pumping. The creature's chest was plated in gnarled, knuckled silver, half open along a thick seam, showing a thudding, white-violet heart within.

'Papers!' the gargoyle thundered. Portraits rattled along the earthen walls. Its breath was smoky and hot, and in its mechanical jaw, a steel tongue rattled. September shrank against the Leopard, the force of the gargoyle's breath pushing at her face.

'Betsy Basilstalk you come out of there this second!' the Green Wind hollered back, though not quite so loud, having no leather-bellow lungs to help him along.

The iron gargoyle paused. *'No,'* it bellowed.

'You're not impressing anyone, you know,' sighed the Green Wind.

'She's impressed. Look, she's all shaking and things,' replied the gargoyle.

'Betsy, I will thrash you a good one, and you know I can. Don't forget who whipped the Lord of Leafglen and rode him about like a dog. I am not a tourist. I will not be treated like one,' said the Green Wind.

'No, you're not a tourist,' growled a thick, phlegmy but much quieter voice. A little woman – no bigger than September and, perhaps, a bit smaller – hopped out of the gargoyle and up on to the podium. The gargoyle's eye-flames snuffed out, and its great shoulders sagged. The little woman's muscled chest was shaped like a bear's, her legs thick and knobbly, her short hair sludged up and spiked along her scalp, sticking up in knifepoints. She chewed on a hand-rolled cigarette; the smoke smelled sweet, like vanilla and rum and maple syrup and other things not terribly good for you. 'You're not a tourist,' she repeated in a grumbly, gravelly voice. 'You're *greenlist,* and that means *no-good scoundrel,* and that means *No Entry Allowed,* Orders of the Marquess.'

'Betsy, I filed my immigration request with the stamps of the Four Clandestines weeks and weeks ago. I even have a letter of reference from the Seelie Parliament. Well, the clerk. But it's on official letterhead and everything, and I think we all know that stationery makes a *statement,*' the Green Wind said defensively.

Betsy quirked a hairy eyebrow at him and hopped back into the gargoyle-puppet, quick as a blink. It roared to life, all fiery eyes and clanking arms.

'GO AWAY. OR SEE WHO GETS THRASHED.'

'Green,' whispered September, 'is she . . . a gnome?'

'Too right I am,' grumbled Betsy, squeezing out of the puppet again. It slumped in her absence. 'And very perceptive of you, that is. What gave it away?'

September's heart still hammered all over the place from the yelling of the gargoyle. She held her trembling hand a little above her head.

'Pointy,' she squeaked, and cleared her throat. 'Gnomes have . . . pointy hats? I thought . . . pointy hair is as good as a hat, maybe?'

'She's a regular logician, Greeny. My *grandmother* wears a pointy hat, girl. My *great-grandmother.* I wouldn't be caught dead in one any more than you'd like to wear a frilly bonnet. Gnomes are *modern* now. We're better than modern, even. Just look, you,' and Betsy flexed an extremely respectable bicep, the size of an oilcan. 'None of this flitting about in gardens and blessing thresholds for me. I went to trade school, I did. Now I'm a customs agent with my own great hulking hunk of heave here. What have you got?'

'A Leopard,' answered September quickly.

'True,' considered Betsy. 'But you haven't got papers or both shoes, and that's a trouble.'

'Why do you need that thing?' September asked. 'None of the airports back home have them.'

'They do. You just can't see them right,' Betsy Basilstalk said with a grin. 'All customs agents have them, otherwise, why would people agree to stand in line and be peered at and inspected? We all live inside the terrible engine of authority, and it grinds and shrieks and burns so that no one will say, *lines on maps are silly*. Where you live, the awful machinery is smaller, harder to see. Less honest, that's all. Whereas Rupert here? He's as honest as they come. Does what it says on the box.'

She scratched the hulking shell behind what might have been an ear. It remained still and dark.

'Then why *tell* me it's all puppets and engines? Don't you want me to let you peer at me?' asked September.

Betsy beckoned her closer, until they stood nose to nose and all September could smell was the vanilla and rum and maple syrup of her cigarette, which was all through the gnome's skin, too.

'Because when humans come to Fairyland, we're supposed to trick them and steal from them and whap them about the ears – but we're also supposed to hex them up so that they can see proper-like. Not everything, just enough so as to be dazzled by mushroom glamours, and not so much that we can't fool you twice with Fairy gold. It's a real science. Used to be done with ointment. It's in the rule book.'

'Are you going to put something very foul in my eyes, then?'

'I told you, kid. Gnomes are modern now. I have personally picketed the Hallowmash Pharmacy. There's other ways of opening your thick head. Like Rupert. He's great with thick heads. Most people, I show them Rupert, they see anything I tell them to. Now, *papers,* please.'

The Green Wind looked sidelong at September and then at his feet. September could swear he was blushing, blushing green through his beard. 'You know very well, Betsy,' he whispered, 'that the Ravished need no papers. It's in the manual, page 764, paragraph six.' The Green Wind coughed politely. 'The Persephone clause.'

Betsy gave him a long look that plainly said, *So that's what's afoot, you old bag of air?* She blew her sweet, thick smoke up into his face and grunted.

September knew she could not have been the only one.

'Don't answer for you, though, tall thing. All right, she can go, but you stay.' Betsy chewed her cigarette. 'And the cat, too. I'm not violating the Greenlist for the likes of you.'

The Green Wind stroked September's hair with his long fingers.

'Time for us to part, my acorn love. I'm sure my visa will come through soon . . . maybe if you put in a good word for me with the embassy. In the meantime, remember the rules, don't go swimming for an hour after eating and never tell anyone your true name.'

'My true name?'

'I came for you, September. Just you. I wish you the best that can be hoped for, and no worse than can be expected.' He leaned in close and kissed her cheek, courtly, gentle, dry as desert wind. The Leopard licked her hand passionately.

'Close your eyes,' he whispered.

September did. She felt a warm, sunny wind on her face, full of the smells of green things: mint and grass and rosemary and fresh water, frogs and leaves and hay. It blew her dark hair back, and when she opened her eyes, the Green Wind and the

Leopard of Little Breezes had gone. In her ear floated his last airy sigh: *Check your pockets, my chimney-child.*

Betsy waved her hands in the air as if to disperse an unpleasant perfume. 'He's such a lot of bother. You're better off – theatrical folk are nothing but a bundle of monologues and anxiety headaches.'

The gnome pulled a little green leather book and a polished ruby-handled stamp from behind the podium. She opened the book and began stamping with a vicious delight.

'Temporary Visa Type: Pomegranate. Housing Allotment: None. Alien Registry Category: Human, Ravished, non-changeling. Size: Medium. Age: Twelve. Privileges: None, or As Many As You Can Catch. Anything to declare?'

September shook her head. Betsy rolled her red-rimmed eyes.

'Customs Declaration: One shoe, Black. One dress, Orange. One smoking jacket, Not Yours.' The Gnome peered down from her podium. 'One kiss, Extremely Green,' she finished emphatically, stamping the book hard and handing it down to September. 'Off you go now, don't hold up the line!'

Betsy Basilstalk grasped September by her lapels and hauled her off her feet, past the podium, toward a rooty, moldy, wormy hole in the back wall of the closet between worlds. At the last moment, she stopped, spat out a Fairy curse like a wad of tobacco, and pulled a little black box out of her pocket. She slid a red rod out of it, and the lid snapped open. It was filled with a vaguely golden jelly.

'Pan's hangover, kid.' Betsy cursed again. 'Old habits die hard.' She dug her greasy finger into the stuff and flung it at September's eyes. It dripped down her face like yolk.

The gnome looked profoundly embarrassed. 'Well,' she mumbled, looking at her toes, 'what if Rupert fell down on the job and you got there and all you could see was sticks and grasshoppers and a lot of long, empty desert? It's a long way to go for desert. Anyway, I don't have to explain myself. On your way, then!'

Betsy Basilstalk gave the girl a hard shove into the soft, leafy wall of the closet. With a wriggle, a squeeze, and a pop, September slid backward through to the other side.

CHAPTER III

Hello, Goodbye, and Manythanks

In Which September Nearly Drowns, Meets Three Witches (One a Wairwulf), and Is Entrusted with the Quest for a Certain Spoon

Salt water hit September like a wall. It roared foamily in her eyes, snatched at her hair, dragged at her feet with cold, purple-green hands. She gasped for air and got two lungfuls of freezing, thick sea.

Now, September could swim quite well. She had even

won second medal at a tournament in Lincoln. She had a trophy with a winged lady on it, though she had always wondered what use a flying girl would have for swimming. The lady should have had webbed feet, September was sure. But in all her after-school practices her coaches had never impressed upon her the importance of practising her butterfly stroke while being dropped from a great height without any ceremony at all into an ocean. With Fairy ooze in one's eyes. *Really,* September thought, *how could they leave something like that out?*

She floundered and dipped beneath the giant waves, only to bob up again, spluttering, gulping air. She kicked hard, struggling to get her legs properly under her and orient herself toward the shore – if there was a shore – so that the waves would carry her toward land – if land there was – and not away from it. Riding the crest of a horrid wave sickeningly upward, she turned her head as fast as she could and glimpsed through the last, stubborn streaks of ointment a fuzzy, orangish strand off to the west. Against the will of the water, she hauled her body around until she was more or less pointed at it and stroked as fast as she could on the swell of the next wave, letting it push her and punch at her and drag her – whatever it liked, as long as it was closer and closer to land. September's arms and legs burned and her lungs were seriously considering giving the whole thing up, but on she went, and on and on until quite unexpectedly her knees knocked on sand, and she fell face-first as the last waves slid up past her on to a rose-colored shore.

September coughed and shook. On her hands and knees, she threw up a fair bit of the Perverse and Perilous Sea on to the beach. She squeezed her eyes shut and shivered until her heart stopped beating quite so fast. When she opened her eyes, she was steadier but elbow-deep in the beach and sinking fast. Thick red rose petals, twigs, thorny leaves, yellowish chestnut husks, pine cones, and rusty tin bells littered the shoreline as far as she could see. September scrambled and tripped and waded through the strange, sweet-smelling rubbish, trying to find some solid ground beneath the blackberry brambles and robins' eggshells and wizened, dried toadstools. The land was not very much more solid than the sea, but at least she could breathe – in sharp, jerky gulps, as the brambles pricked at her and the twigs pulled at her hair.

I have not been in Fairyland nearly long enough to start crying, September thought, then bit her tongue savagely. That was better; she could think, and the flotsam of the beach did seem to get shallower as she pushed through the wreckage. Finally, the wreckage was only knee-deep, and she could trudge through it like so much heavy snow. At the far edge of the shore were tall silvery cliffs, spotted with brave, stubborn little trees that had found purchase on the rocks and grew straight out sideways from the cliffside. At their tops, great birds wheeled and cried, their long necks glowing bright blue in the afternoon light. She stood alone on the beach, breathing heavily. She rubbed her eyes to get the last of the gnome ointment out, where it had hardened like sleep dust. When September's eyes were clean of salt and gnome, she looked back down the beach in the direction she had come from. Suddenly, the beach didn't look like rose petals and sticks and eggshells at all. It glittered gold, real gold, all the way down to the violet-green water. Doubloons and necklaces and crowns, pieces of eight and plates and bricks and long, glittering sceptres. These shone so brightly September had to shade her eyes. No matter how she walked, to the left or right, the shore stayed firmly golden now.

September shivered. She was terribly hungry and dripping rather dramatically. She wrung out her hair and the skirt of her orange dress on to a huge golden crown with crosses on it. The jacket, mortified that it had been so distracted from its duties by a mere momentary drowning, hurriedly puffed out, billowing in the sea wind until it was quite dry. *Well,* September thought, *it's all certainly very strange, but the Green Wind is not here to explain it anymore, and I can't stay on the beach all day like a sunbather. A girl in want of a Leopard still has feet.* She looked out at the rolling purple-green waves of the sea once more. A stirring that she could not name fluttered within her – something deep and strange, to do with the sea and the sky. But deeper than the stirring was her hunger and her need to find something that bore fruit or sold meat or baked bread. She folded up the stirring very carefully and put it away at the bottom of her mind. Tearing her eyes from the stormy waves, she began to walk.

After a moment, she prudently knelt down and gathered up a particularly jewel-encrusted sceptre. *You never know,* she thought, *I might have to ransom things, or bribe folk, or even buy something.* September was not prone to stealing, but neither was she entirely stupid. She began to walk up the beach, using the sceptre as a walking stick.

The going was not easy. Gold is very slippery to walk on and insists on sliding all over the place. She found that her bare foot was actually a bit more suited to the task than the shod one, as she could grasp at the gleaming ground with her toes. Nevertheless, every step set off a little cascade of coins. By afternoon, September thought she had probably stepped on the collective national worth of Finland. Just as this rather grown-up thought crossed her mind, a long, peculiar shadow fell across her path.

In Omaha, signposts are bright green with white writing, or occasionally white with black writing. September understood those signs and all the things they pointed to. But the signpost before her now was made of pale wind-bleached wood and towered above her: a beautiful carved woman with flowers in her hair, a long goat's tail winding around her legs, and a solemn expression on her sea-worn face. The deep gold light of the Fairyland sun played on her carefully whittled hair. She had wide, flaring wings, like September's swimming trophy. The wooden woman had four arms, each outstretched in a different direction, pointing with authority. On the inside of her easterly arm, pointing backward in the direction September had come, someone had carved in deep, elegant letters:

TO LOSE YOUR WAY

On the northerly arm, pointing up to the tops of the cliffs, it said:

TO LOSE YOUR LIFE

On the southerly arm, pointing out to sea, it said:

TO LOSE YOUR MIND

And on the westerly arm, pointing up to a little headland and a dwindling of the golden beach, it said:

TO LOSE YOUR HEART

September bit her lip. She certainly didn't want to lose her life, so the cliffs were right out, even if she thought she could climb them. Losing her mind was not too much better, and besides, there was nothing about with which to fashion a seagoing vessel, unless she wanted to sink promptly on a raft of gold. She had already lost her way, walking for miles in this direction, and anyway, if one's way is lost one cannot get anywhere, and she definitely wanted to get *somewhere,* even if she didn't know where *somewhere* was. Somewhere mainly involved food and a bed and a fireplace, whereas here had only Fairy gold and a roaring, cold sea.

Only the heart was left.

You and I, being grown-up and having lost our hearts at least twice or thrice along the way, might shut our eyes and cry out, *Not that way, child!* But as we have said, September was

Somewhat Heartless, and felt herself reasonably safe on that road. Children always do.

Besides, she could see smoke off in the distance, wafting upward in thin curlicues.

September ran off toward the spiraling smoke. Behind her, the beautiful four-armed woman who pointed the way closed her eyes and shook her birch-wood head, rueful and knowing.

'Hello!' called September as she ran, tripping over the last of the gold bricks and sceptres. 'Hello!'

Three figures hunched blackly around a large pot, a cauldron, really – huge and iron and rough. They were dressed very finely: two women in old-fashioned high-collared dresses with bustles, hair drawn back in thick chignons, and a young man in a lovely black suit with tails. But what September chiefly noticed were their hats.

Any child knows what a witch looks like. The warts are important, yes, the hooked nose, the cruel smile. But it's the hat that cinches it: pointy and black with a wide rim. Plenty of people have warts and hooked noses and cruel smiles but are not witches at all. Hats change everything. September knew this with all her being, deep in the place where she knew her own name, that her mother would still love her even though she hadn't waved goodbye. For one day, her father had put on a hat with golden things on it and suddenly he hadn't been her father anymore, he had been a soldier, and he had left. Hats have power. Hats can change you into someone else.

These hats were not Halloween witch hats, made out of thin satin or construction paper and spangled with cheap glitter. They were leather, heavy and old, creased all over, their points slumped to one side, being too majestic and massive to be expected to stand up straight. Old, knotted silver buckles gleamed malevolently on their sides. The brims jutted out, sagging a little, the kind of brim you might expect cowboys to have, the kind that isn't for show, but to keep out wind and rain and sun. The witches hunched a little under the weight of their hats.

'Hello?' September said, a little more politely – but only a little.

'What?' snapped one of the women, looking up from her muttering. She held a beaten black book in one hand, heavily dog-eared.

'I said, "Hello!"'

'Yes, that's me.'

'What?' said September, confused.

'Are you very dull or very deaf?' said the other woman, flinging an alarmed lizard into the cauldron.

'Oh!' cried the young man. 'A little deaf child! How

sweet! We should adopt her and teach her to write symphonies. She'll be all the rage in town. I'll buy her a powdered wig and a tricorne!'

'I'm not deaf,' said September, who was very cross when she was hungry. 'Or dull. I said, "Hello", and you said nothing sensible at all.'

'Manners, child,' said the woman with the book, her cruel witch's smile curling up the corners of her lips. 'If you haven't got your manners, you might as well toss it all and become a witch.' She peered at the cauldron and after a moment's disapproving stare, spat into it. 'My name is Hello,' she continued as if nothing had happened. 'So you see the confusion. This is my sister Goodbye and our husband, Manythanks.'

'He's married to both of you? How odd!' Suddenly their eyes narrowed, and they stood very straight. September hurried to correct herself. 'I mean – my name is September. How do you do?'

'We do perfectly well,' said Goodbye coldly, pinching off one of the black pearl buttons at her throat and tossing it into the brew. 'It all works out very nicely, really. My sister and I are very close, and very different, and when we were young, it seemed like a great waste of time for us both to go through the tiresome nonsense of courtship and blushing behind curtains and love potions and marriage. So we went through it once, together. We estimate that we saved each other two full years of living. And besides, all witches must keep up a certain level of deviance in their personal lives, or we should be expelled from the union.'

Hello smiled as demurely as a witch can manage. 'We chose Manythanks for his many virtues, and because, besides being a wonderful cook and a superb mathematician, he is also a wairwulf.'

'Really? A real werewolf? And you turn into a wolf when the moon is full?'

Manythanks grinned.

'No, dear,' said Hello, 'a *wairwulf*.' She rolled her *r* a little, otherwise it seemed quite the same word to September. 'It's quite different. Twenty-seven days a month, my love is a fine wolf, with a great powerful jaw and a thumping tail. During the full moon, he becomes human, as he is now. My husband is the wolf, hers is the man.'

'That doesn't seem quite fair,' said September. 'She gets a lot more husband.'

'Oh, we agreed upon it long ago. I don't like men to talk too much, and she doesn't like them too much underfoot,' Hello said with a laugh. Goodbye smiled at her husband with a deep fondness.

'Aren't you . . . afraid of the wolf?' asked September, who secretly felt she might get over such a fear, if the wolf would love her and guard her and not get mud on the covers.

'I'm quite civilized, I promise,' Manythanks sniffed, smiling. 'Wairwulves are cultured. We have choirs and charity races and rotary clubs. It's when we're human that you must take care.'

'Now what is it you want, child? As you can see, we're quite busy.' Goodbye sniffed deeply at the pot.

Be bold, thought September. *An ill-tempered child should be bold.* 'I . . . I hoped you might have something for me to eat. I've only just gotten here and . . . well, I'm not lost, because I haven't any idea where to go that I might get lost on the way to.' Even to September that did not sound quite right. 'I'd *like* to get lost, because then I'd know where I was going, you see. But the Green Wind wasn't terribly clear about what to do once I got here, only what not to do, so getting lost would be making very good headway, all things considered. But I don't know where I am and the beach was full of garbage, and then it wasn't—'

'Fairy gold,' interrupted Manythanks. 'It lies about, waiting for a Fairy to pick it up on her way to the human world. You must have had some gnome ointment gobbed on you or you wouldn't be able to see it at all. Some things any old ravished child can see. Some things are only meant for locals.'

'Yes, Betsy . . . she showed me Rupert, but then she threw that stuff at me, too.' September clutched her sceptre a little tighter.

'She must have taken a shine to you. I assume Rupert was very terrible and frightening? A good scare will knock your eyeballs sideways enough to see a few brownies. But not enough for Fairy gold and other things besides. Else playing tricks on tourists would not be half as fun.' The wairwulf sighed heavily. He had little wrinkles at the corners of his eyes. 'But there's rationing these days, and gnomestuff is precious. Have you got any left?' Manythanks peered at her eyes and sighed in disappointment. September did not like being examined so closely.

'I'm very hungry, Sir Wulf,' she whispered hopefully. 'Is that soup?'

'Don't you dare!' breathed Goodbye. 'It's our spell, and you can't have any.'

September brightened a little. This was what she had come for: witches and spells and wairwulves. 'What sort of spell?'

All three looked at her as though she had asked what color a carrot is.

'We're *witches,*' said Hello.

Manythanks pointed meaningfully at his hat.

'But witches do all kinds of spells—'

'That's sorceresses,' corrected Goodbye.

'And magic—'

'That's wizards,' sighed Hello.

'And they change people into things—'

'That's thaumaturgists,' huffed Manythanks.

'And make people do things—'

'Enchantresses,' sneered Goodbye.

'And they do curses and hexes—'

'Stregas,' hissed both sisters.

'And change into owls and cats—'

'Brujas,' growled Manythanks.

'Well . . . what *do* witches do, then?' September refused to feel foolish. It was hard enough for a human to get into Fairyland. True stories must be nearly impossible to get out.

'We look into the future,' grinned Goodbye. 'And we help it along.'

'Why do you need lizards and buttons for that? And such nice clothes?'

'Look who's a witch now?' mocked Hello, snapping her book shut. 'What could you know about it? The future is a messy, motley business, little girl.'

'We have to dress well,' whispered Goodbye, 'or the future will not take us seriously.'

Manythanks put his hands out to his wives. 'She's just a child. We were once children. She knows nothing of the future. Be kind. We can afford to be kind to this one when there is so much ahead of her.' Manythanks reached into his pocket and took out a fat bundle wrapped in wax. He unwrapped it corner by corner, slowly, as if revealing the vanished dove at the end of a magic trick.

Inside was a thick slice of deeply red cake, so moist it wet the paper, slathered with rich red icing. It glowed in the slight gloam of the seaside. The wairwulf bent down to her, the black tails of his suit whipping in the wind, and offered it, balanced delicately on one flat hand.

September tried not to snatch it too fast. She swallowed it in three wulfish bites, so starving was she. But hadn't the Green Wind said something about eating Fairy food? *Well,* reasoned September, *this isn't the same thing at all. It's witch food.*

'I don't suppose,' gulped September, when the cake had settled in her belly, 'that you would tell me what was ahead of me, so I could look out for it.'

'Hello, I believe we have an utterly unique specimen on our hands: a child who listens,' Goodbye said, laughing. Goodbye laughed a lot.

Manythanks shook his head. 'That's really more a seer's business, love—'

'I'd be happy to show you your future, little one,' interrupted Hello, but her voice was dark. The witch dipped her bare hand into the gurgling, boiling soup of the cauldron. She hauled out a handful of lumpy muck, the color of bruises and jam gone off. She flung it at the earth, where it steamed and wriggled and reeked. All three witches peered at the gob intently. Mankthanks poked at it with a neatly trimmed fingernail. It quivered. The sisters looked meaningfully at one another. September tried to peer as well but did not feel she had the hang of it.

'My future looks lumpy,' she said uncertainly.

Goodbye broke ranks with her family and swooped around the great cauldron, kneeling before September. The witch suddenly looked very beautiful, her pale hair swept back, her eyes dark and bright. September did not remember her looking so beautiful before, when she was stirring the pot. But now, Goodbye's face fairly glowed, her lips perfectly rose-colored, her cheeks high, aristocratic, even blushing a little. 'September,' she breathed. Her voice was pure honey-wine, warm and deep and sweet. 'That's what you said your name was, yes? I prefer October, myself, but it's *such* a pretty name. Your parents must have loved you very much, to give you a name like that. Do you like my name? It's unusual, like yours.'

'Y . . . yes.' September felt odd. She wanted to please Goodbye very much – but more, she wanted Goodbye to like her, to love her even and tell her more about how much they were alike. The witch laughed again. But now it was a long rippling laugh full of notes, almost a song.

'My sister has no shame at all, September,' Goodbye continued. 'That's a very secret thing she did – right in front of you! You see, the future is a kind of stew, a soup, a vichyssoise of the present and the past. That's how you get the future: You mix up everything you did today with everything you did yesterday and all the days before and everything anyone you ever met did and anyone they ever met, too. And salt and lizard and pearl and umbrellas and typewriters and a lot of other things I'm not at liberty to tell you, because I took vows, and a witch's vows have teeth. Magic is funny like that. It's not a linear thinker. The point is if you mash it all up together and you have a big enough pot and you're very good at witchcraft, you can wind up with a cauldron full of tomorrow. That lump of greasy, slimy goop is a prophecy, and my sister cast it for you.'

'What does it say?'

Goodbye smiled like a sun rising. 'Oh, so many things,

September, if you know how to look. Would you like to know how? Would you like to be able to divine the meaning of that blob there, the color of mashed potatoes, or that vein of jelly? Would you like to be a witch?'

'Witchery is a life of wonder,' said Hello, 'all the wheeling stars at your command, all the days of the future laid out before you, like dolls in bronze armor!'

'And a really top-notch hat,' added Manythanks.

'The Marquess has a fine hat, too,' said September, shaking her head to clear Goodbye's sudden perfume. 'I've been told.'

Their faces darkened a little.

'Well, I'm sure we'll all be wearing tweed trousers by fall,' Goodbye snapped sarcastically. She shut her eyes and shook her head. When she opened them again, they were once more pools of deep violet, glistening with promises. 'But we were discussing your prospects, my dear. For as much as I would like to bring you into my coven this very day, something bars me from accepting such a charming, polite, *intelligent* young ward. For a witch is nothing without her Spoon, and the Marquess stole mine years ago, because she is capricious and selfish and a brat.'

Hello and Manythanks drew back from Goodbye as though the Marquess might appear that very moment and punish the brazen witch soundly.

Goodbye hurried on. 'But if some intrepid, brave, *darling* child went to the City and got it back for me, well, a witch would be grateful. You'll know it right away: It's a big wooden spoon, streaked with marrow and wine and sugar and yogurt and yesterday and grief and passion and jealousy and tomorrow. I'm sure the Marquess won't miss it. She has so many nice things. And when you come back, we'll make you a little black bustle and a black hat and teach you to call down the moon gulls and dance with the Giant Snails that guard the Pantry of Time.'

September's stomach hurt. She found it terribly hard to speak. 'I've only just gotten here, Miss Goodbye. I . . . I don't think I want to be anything but myself just yet. It would be like deciding on the spot to become a geologist back home. What if I don't like rocks when I'm older? Witchery sounds very nice now, but I'm sure I should take better care with my . . . my prospects.'

'But the future, child! Just think of it! If you see something you don't like – pop! In go leek and liquorice, and you can change it. What could be better?'

'Does it really work that way? Can you really change the future?'

Manythanks shrugged. 'I'm sure it's been done once or twice,' he said.

September wrenched her eyes away from Goodbye's loveliness. Her head cooled and cleared and smoothed itself out. 'Miss,' she said, 'don't you really just want your Spoon back?'

Goodbye stood up abruptly and brushed off her black dress. The perfume was gone, and she shrank a bit, still a somewhat handsome woman, but the glow, the perfect colors of her, were muted and usual again.

'Yes,' she said curtly. 'I can't get it, the Marquess has lions.'

'Well . . . you don't have to shine at me and offer me a bustle, you know. I . . . I could get it for you. Maybe I could get it for you. Anyway, I could try. What did I come to Fairyland for, after all? To wander around on the beach like my grandfather, looking for dropped wedding rings?' September laughed for the first time since leaving Omaha, picturing her grandfather in his patched jacket waving his metal detector over the beach of Fairy gold. *A quest,* she thought, excitement rising in her like bread, *a real quest like a real knight, and she doesn't even see that I'm short and I don't have a sword.*

'Well . . . how *gallant* of you, child,' said Hello. 'She didn't mean to offend with her *shining* . . . it's only that the Marquess is fearful and fell. Long ago, she hunted witches. She rode out on a great panther and wielded her iceleaf bow against us. She broke our mother's Spoon across her back and killed our brothers Farewell and Wellmet. Fine witches in the prime of their craft, all pierced with her arrows, laid out in the snow. And all because we would not give her what she wanted.'

'What did she want?'

Goodbye answered, her voice thick and ugly. 'A single day. She commanded us to simmer for her a single day, the day of her death, so that she could hide from it. And we would not serve her.'

September let go a long-held breath. She stared into the roiling black-violet soup, thinking furiously. The trouble was, September didn't know what sort of story she was in. Was it a merry one or a serious one? How ought she to act? If it were merry, she might dash after a Spoon, and it would all be a marvelous adventure, with funny rhymes and somersaults and a grand party with red lanterns at the end. But if it were a serious tale, she might have to do something important, something involving, with snow and arrows and enemies. Of course, we would like to tell her which. But no one may know the shape of the tale in which they move. And, perhaps, we do not truly know what sort of beast it is, either. Stories have a way of changing faces. They are unruly things, undisciplined, given to delinquency and the throwing of erasers. This is why we must close them up into thick, solid books, so they cannot get out and cause trouble.

Surely, she must have suspected the shape of her tale when the Green Wind appeared in her kitchen window. Certain signs are unmistakable. But now she is alone, poor child, and there do not seem to be too terribly many fairies about, and instead of dancing in mushroom rings, she must contend with very formal witches and their dead brothers, and we must pity her. It would be easy for me to tell you what happened to her – why, I'd need only choose a noun and a few verbs and off she goes! But September must do the choosing and the going, and you must remember from your own adventuring days how harsh a task lies before her at this moment.

But a machinist's daughter can be shrewd and practical. And can't there be snow and enemies *and* red lanterns *and* somersaults? And at least one mushroom ring? That would be the best thing, really, if she can manage it.

There must be blood, the girl thought. *There must always be blood. The Green Wind said that, so it must be true. It will all be hard and bloody, but there will be wonders, too, or else why bring me here at all? And it's the wonders I'm after, even if I have to bleed for them.*

Finally, September stepped forward and, quite without knowing she meant to do it, dropped to one knee before the witch Goodbye. She bent her head to hide her trembling and said, 'I am just a girl from Omaha. I can only do a few things. I can swim and read books and fix boilers if they are only a little broken. Sometimes, I can make very rash decisions when really I ought to keep quiet and be a good girl. If those are weapons you think might be useful, I will take them up and go after your Spoon. If I return' – September swallowed hard – 'I ask only that you give me safe passage back to the closet between worlds, so that I can go home when it is all over and sleep in my own bed. And . . . a favor . . .'

'What sort of favor?' said Goodbye warily.

September frowned. 'Well, I can't think of anything good just now. But I will think of something, by and by.'

The moon peered over the clouds at them. With great solemnity, Hello and Goodbye spat into their hands and shook on the bargain.

'What about the lions?' Goodbye said fearfully.

'Well, I have some experience with big cats. I expect lions are no more fearsome than Leopards,' answered September, though she was not quite so sure as she sounded. 'Only, tell me, where does the Marquess live? How can I get there?'

As one, the three witches pointed west at a cleft in the cliffs. 'Where else?' said Manythanks. 'The capital. Pandemonium.'

'Is it very far?'

They all looked shamefacedly at their feet. *More than 'very', then,* thought September.

'Good-bye,' said Hello.

'Many thanks,' said Goodbye.

'Farewell,' said Manythanks, and kissed her very lightly on the cheek. The wairwulf's kiss joined the Green Wind's there, and the two of them got along very well, considering.

The full moon shone jubilantly as September strode up over the dunes and into the interior of Fairyland with her belly full of witch-cake. She smelled the sweet, wheat-sugar scent of sea grass and listened to distant owls call after mice. And then she suddenly remembered, like a crack of lightning in her mind, *check your pockets*. She laid her sceptre in the grass and dug into the pocket of her green smoking jacket. September pulled out a small crystal ball, glittering in the moonlight. A single perfectly green leaf hung suspended in it, swaying back and forth gently, as if blown by a faraway wind.

CHAPTER IV

The Wyverary

In Which September Is Discovered by a Wyvern, Learns of a Most Distressing Law, and Thinks of Home (but Only Briefly)

September woke in a meadow full of tiny red flowers. She had walked through the night, watching the moon slowly fall down into the horizon and all the dark morning stars turn in the sky, like a silver carousel. It was important, she reasoned, not to fall asleep in the dark where deviant things might carry her off. No matter how tired she was, or how sore her bare foot, she would wait till morning, when she could be assured of the sun to keep her warm while she dreamed. And the sun had pulled up a warm blanket of her light over the little girl, tucking her in with gentle beams. September's long hair had dried on the meadow-grass. Her orange dress was only a little stiff now from the salt of the sea. She yawned and stretched.

'What happened to your shoe?' said a big, deep, rumbling voice. September froze in mid-stretch. Two blazing, flame-colored eyes danced before her. A dragon was staring at her with acute interest, crouching like a cat in the long grass. His tail waved lazily. The beast's lizardish skin glowed a profound red, the color of the very last embers of the fire. His horns (and these horns led September to presume the dragon a *he*) jutted out from his head like a young bull's, fine and thick and black. He had his wings tucked neatly back along his knobbly spine – where they were bound with great bronze chains and fastened with an extremely serious-looking lock.

'I . . . I lost it,' said September, holding herself utterly still so as not to spook either the dragon or herself, her arms still stuck out into the air. 'It fell into the sink as I was climbing on to a Leopard.'

'That's not losing it,' the beast rumbled sagely. 'That's leaving it.'

'Um,' said September.

'Don't wear shoes myself,' the dragon haroomed. 'Tried

when I was a wee thing, but the cobblers gave me up for lost.' He rose up on heavily muscled hind legs and, balancing carefully on one of them, flexed one enormous three-toed scarlet foot. His black claws clicked together with a sound like typewriter keys clacking. 'You're very quiet! Why don't you say something? Why don't you do a trick? I'll be impressed, I promise. Start with your name, that's easiest.'

September put down her arms and folded them in her lap. The dragon hunched in close, his smoky-sweet breath flaring huge red nostrils. 'September,' she said softly. 'And . . . well, I'm very scared, and I don't know if you're going to eat me or not, and it's hard to do tricks when you're scared. Anyway, where I come from, it's a known fact that dragons eat people, and I prefer to be the one doing the eating if *eating* is to be done. Which it hasn't been since last night. I don't suppose you have cake? I think dragon food would be all right, it's only Fairy food I'm to watch out for.'

'How funny you are!' crowed the beast. 'First off, I am not a dragon. I don't know where you could have gotten that idea. I was very careful to show you my feet. I am a Wyvern. No forepaws, see?' The Wyvern displayed his proud, scaled chest, the color of old peaches. He balanced quite well on his massive hindquarters, and the rest of him rose up in a kind of squat S-shape, ending in the colossal head, which bore many teeth and a thick jaw and snapping bits of fire-colored whiskers. 'And you must have very rude dragons where you come from! I've never heard the like! If people show up to a dragon's mountain yelling about sacrifices and O, YE, FELL BEAST SPARE MY VILLAGE this and GREAT DRAGON, I SHALL MURDER THEE that, well, certainly, a fellow might have a chomp. But you oughtn't judge any more than you judge a lady for eating the lovely fresh salad that a waiter brings her in a restaurant. Secondly, no, I don't have any cake.'

'Oh. I didn't mean any offence.'

'Why should I be offended? Dragons are a bit more than cousins, but a bit less than siblings. I know all about them, you see, because they begin with D.'

'What is your name, Wyvern? I should have been more polite.'

'I am the Honorable Wyvern A-Through-L, small fey. I would say, "at your service", but that's rather fussy, and I'm not, you see, so it would be inaccurate.'

'That's a very funny name for . . .' – September considered her words – 'such a fine beast,' she finished.

'It's a family name,' A-Through-L said loftily, scratching behind one horn. 'My father was a Library. So properly speaking, I am a Lyvern, or . . . a Libern? A Wyverary? I am still trying to find the best term.'

'Well, I think that's *very* unlikely,' said September, who preferred *Wyverary*.

'However unlikely it may seem, it is the truth and, therefore, one hundred percent likely. My sainted mother was the familiar of a highly puissant Scientiste, and he loved her. He polished her scales every week with beeswax and truffle oil. He fed her sweet water and bitter radishes grown by hand in his laboratory and, therefore, much larger and more bitter than usual radishes. He petted her, and called her a good Wyvern, and made a bed for her out of river rushes and silk batting and old bones. (They didn't come from anyone he knew, so that was all right, and a Wyvern nest has to have bones, or else it's just not home.) It was quite a good situation for my mother, even if she hadn't liked him a great deal and thought him very wise. As all reptiles know, the bigger the spectacles, the wiser the wearer, and the Scientiste wore the biggest pair ever built. But even the wisest of men may die, and that is especially true when the wisest of men has a fondness for industrial chemicals. So went my mother's patron, in a spectacular display of Science.'

'That's very sad,' sighed September.

'Terribly sad! But grief is wasted on the very roasted. Without her companion, my mother lived alone in the ruins of the great Library, which was called Compleat, and a very passionate and dashing Library indeed. Under the slightly blackened rafters and more than slightly caved-in walls, my mother lived and read and dreamed, allowing herself to grow closer and closer to Compleat, to notice more and more how fine and straight his shelves remained, despite great structural stress. That sort of moral fortitude is rare in this day and age. By and by, my siblings and I were born and romped on the balconies, raced up and down the splintered ladders, and pored over many encyclopedias and exciting novels. I know just everything about everything – so long as it begins with A through L. My mother was widowed by a real estate agent some years ago, and I never finished the encyclopaedia. Anyway, Mother told us all about our father when we were yearlings. We asked, "Why do we not have a Papa?" And she said, "Your Papa is the Library, and he loves you and will care for you. Do not expect a burly, handsome Wyvern to show up and show you how to breathe fire, my loves. None will come. But Compleat has books aplenty on the subject of combustion, and however odd it may seem, you are loved by two parents, just like any other beast."'

September bit her lip. She did not know how to say it gently. 'I had a friend back home named Anna-Marie,' she said slowly. 'Her father sold lawn mowers all over Nebraska and some in Kansas, too. When Anna-Marie was little, her daddy ran off with a lady from Topeka with the biggest lawn in the county. Anna-Marie doesn't even remember her daddy, and sometimes when she's sad, her mother says she didn't have one, that she's an angel's daughter and no awful lawn mower salesman had a thing to do with her. Do you think, maybe . . . it could have been like that, with your mother?'

A-Through-L looked pityingly at her, his blazing red face scrunched up in doubt. 'September, *really*. Which do you think is more likely? That some brute bull left my mother with egg and went off to sell lonemozers? Or that she mated with a Library and had many loved and loving children? I mean, let us be realistic! Besides, everyone says I look just like my father. Can't you see my wings? Are they not made of fluttering vellum pages? If you squint you can even read a history of balloon travel!'

A-Through-L lifted his wings slightly, to show their fluttering, but the great bronze chain kept them clamped down. He waggled them feebly.

'Oh, of course. How silly of me. You must understand, I am new to Fairyland,' September assured him. But really, his wings were leathery and bony, like a pterodactyl's, and not like vellum at all, and there was certainly nothing written there. September thought the creature was a little sad, but also a little dear.

'Why are your wings chained up?' she asked, eager to change the subject. A-Through-L looked at her as though she must be somehow addled.

'It's the law, you know. You can't be so new as all that. *Aeronautic locomotion is permitted only by means of Leopard or licensed Ragwort Stalk.* I think you'll agree I'm not a Leopard or made of Ragwort. I'm not allowed to fly.'

'Whyever not?'

A-Through-L shrugged. 'The Marquess decreed that flight was an Unfair Advantage in matters of Love and Cross-Country Racing. But she's awfully fond of cats, and no one can tell Ragwort to sit still, so she granted special dispensations.'

'But surely you're bigger than the Marquess. Couldn't you say no? Squash her or roast her or something?'

A-Through-L marveled. His mouth dropped open a little. 'What a violent little thing you are! Of course, I'm bigger, and, of course, I could say no, and, of course, in the days of Good Queen Mallow, this would never have happened and we're all very upset about it, but she's *the Marquess*. She has *a hat*. And muscular magic, besides. No one says no to her. Do you say no to your queen?'

'We don't have a queen where I live.'

'Then I'm sorry for you. Queens are very splendid, even

when they call themselves Marquesses and chain up poor Wyverns. Well, very splendid and very frightening. But splendid things are often frightening. Sometimes, it's the fright that makes them splendid at all. What kind of place did you come from, with no queens and bad fathers and Anna-Marees?'

'Just one Anna-Marie. I come from Nebraska,' September said. Home seemed very far away now, and she did not yet miss it. She knew, dimly, that this made her a bad daughter, but Fairyland was already so large and interesting that she tried not to think about that. 'It's very flat and golden, and my mother lives there. Every day, she goes to a factory and works on airplane engines because everyone's father left for the war, and there was no one left to make airplanes. She's very smart. And pretty. But I don't see her much anymore, and my father went away with all the others. He said he would be safe, because he would be mainly learning things about other armies and writing them down, not shooting at them. But I don't think he's safe. And I don't think my mother does, either. And the house is dark at night, and there are howling things out on the prairies. I keep everything as clean as I can so that when she comes home she'll be happy, and tell me stories before bed, and teach me about boilers and things that she knows.' September rubbed her arms to keep warm in a sudden breeze that kicked and bucked through the field of little red flowers. 'I don't really have many friends back home. I like to read, and the other kids like to play baseball or play with jacks or curl their hair. So when the Green Wind came to my window, I knew what he was about, because I've read books where things like that happen. And I didn't have anyone to miss, except my mother.' September wiped her nose a little. 'I didn't wave goodbye to her when we flew away. I know I ought to have. But she goes to the factory before I'm awake in the morning and just leaves biscuits and an orange on the table, so I thought maybe I wouldn't say goodbye to her, since she doesn't say goodbye to me. I know it was vicious of me! But I couldn't help it. And, really, she leaves little notes with the biscuits and sometimes funny drawings, and I didn't leave her anything, so it's not fair at all. But I don't want to go home, either, because there aren't gnomes and witches and wyveraries at home, just nasty kids with curly hair and a lot of teacups that need washing, so I will say I'm sorry later, but I think it's better to be in Fairyland than not in Fairyland on the whole.'

A-Through-L carefully put his claw around her shoulders. His talons quite dwarfed her. She wrapped her arms around one and leaned against it, the way she might have leaned against an oak trunk back home.

'Except . . . things are not all well in Fairyland, are they? The witches' brothers are dead, and they've no Spoons, and your wings are all chained and sore – don't say they aren't, Ell. I can see where they've rubbed the skin away. And can I call you Ell? A-Through-L is so very many syllables. Things are not right here, and I haven't even seen a proper Fairy at all, with glittering wings and little dresses. Just sad folk and no food. And that's more than I've said to anyone in forever, even the Green Wind. I do wish he had been allowed to come with me. I believe I am sick to death of hearing what is and is not allowed. What is the purpose of a Fairyland if everything lovely is outlawed, just like in the real world?'

'How poor you are, September. You make my heart groan. I know about Homesickness. It begins with H. What will you do?'

September sniffed and straightened up. She was not one to feel sorry for herself for long. 'Mainly, I am going to Pandemonium, to steal the Spoon that belongs to the witch Goodbye, so that she can cook up the future again and not feel so sad.'

A-Through-L sucked in his breath. 'That's the Marquess's Spoon,' he whispered.

'I don't care if it is! What a dreadful person the Marquess must be, with her ugly chains and her bow and her silly hat! I shan't feel at all bad about stealing from her!'

The Wyverary drew his huge foot back and settled down

on his haunches just exactly like a cat, so that his face was on a level with September's. She saw now that his eyes were kindly, not fearsome at all – and a beautiful shade of orange.

'I am going to the City myself, human girl. After my mother was widowed, my siblings and I went each our separate ways: M-Through-S to be a governess, T-Through-Z to be a soldier, and I to seek our old grandfather – the Municipal Library of Fairyland, which owns all the books in all the world. I hope that he will accept me and love me as a grandson and teach me to be a librarian, for every creature must know a trade. I know I have bad qualities that stand against me – a fiery breath being chief among these – but I am a good beast, and I enjoy alphabetizing, and perhaps, I may get some credit for following in the family business.' The Wyverary pursed his great lips. 'Perhaps we might travel together for a little while? Those beasts with unreliable fathers must stick together after all. And I may be a good deal of help in the arena of Locating Suppers.'

'Oh, I would like that, Ell,' said September happily. She did not like to travel alone, and she missed the Leopard and her Green Wind fiercely. 'Let us go now, before the sun gets low again. It is cold in Fairyland at night.'

The two of them began to walk west, and the chains around the Wyverary's red wings jangled and clanked.

September was not even so tall as his knee, so after a little while, he let her climb the chains and ride upon his back, sliding her sceptre through the links. September could not know that humans riding Marvelous Creatures of a Certain Size was also not allowed. A-Through-L knew, but for once he did not care.

'I shall amuse you along the way,' he boomed, 'by reciting all of the things I know. Aardvark, Abattoir, Abdication, Adagio, Alligator, Araby . . .'

CHAPTER V

The House Without Warning

In Which September Measures the Distance to Pandemonium, Receives a Brief Lecture in History, Meets a Soap Golem, and Is Thoroughly Scrubbed

September bit into a fat, juicy persimmon. Well, something like a persimmon. Rather larger, greener, and tasting of blueberry cream, but it looked terribly *like* a persimmon, and so September had resolved to call it that. A Through-L still worried a poor tree, which was so tall and stubbornly thick that no small girl could ever have hoped to climb it, even if she had known that there was fruit up there in its yellowy-silver branches. *Still, if a dragon – a Wyvern – brings it to me,* September thought, *it's dragon food and not fairy food at all, and no one should blame me for breakfast.* September insisted she was full between peals of laughter, but the Wyverary seemed to delight in charging the tree with a cheerful snarl and smacking into it full force until the helpless fruit gave up and came tumbling down. After each blow, A-Through-L sat back on his enormous haunches and shook his head, sending his whiskers a-flying. The sight of it kept September laughing helplessly, her skirt tumbling-full of oozing, green-orange, blueberryish persimmons.

The sun hitched up her trousers and soldiered on up into the sky. September squinted at it and wondered if the sun here was different than the sun in Nebraska. It seemed gentler, more golden, deeper. The shadows it cast seemed more profound. But September could not be sure. When one is traveling, everything looks brighter and lovelier. That does not mean it *is* brighter and lovelier; it just means that sweet, kindly home suffers in comparison to tarted-up foreign places with all their jewels on.

'How far is it to Pandemonium, Ell?' yawned September. She stretched her legs, flexing the bare toes of her left foot.

'Can't say, small one.' The beast thwacked into the tree

again. 'Pandemonium begins with P, and, therefore, I don't know very much about it.'

September thought for a moment. 'Try "Capital" instead. That starts with C. And Fairyland stars with F, so you could, well, cross-reference.'

A-Through-L left off the nearly persimmon tree and cocked his head to one side like a curious German shepherd. 'The capital of Fairyland is surrounded by a large, circular river,' he said slowly, as if reading from a book, 'called the Barleybroom. The city consists of four districts: Idlelily, Seresong, Hallowgrum, and Mallowmead. Population is itinerant, but summer estimates hover around ten thousand *daimonia* – that means spirits – '

'And *pan* means all,' whispered September, since the Wyvern could not be expected to know, on account of the *p* involved. In September's world, many things began with *pan. Pandemic, Pangaea, Panacea, Panoply.* Those were all big words, to be sure, but as has been said, September read often, and liked it best when words did not pretend to be simple, but put on their full armor and rode out with colors flying.

'The highest point is Groangyre Tower, home of the Royal Inventors' Society (Madness Prerequisite), the lowest is Janglynow Flats, where once the Ondines waged their algae wars. Common imports: grain, wishing fish, bicycle parts, children, sandwiches, brandywine, silver bullets—'

'Skip to the part where it says, "I Am This Many Miles Away from a Girl Named September," ' suggested the girl helpfully.

A-Through-L grimaced at her, curling his scarlet lips. 'All books should be so accommodating, butler-wise,' he snorted. 'As you might expect, the geographical location of the capital of Fairyland is fickle and has a rather short temper. I'm afraid the whole thing moves around according to the needs of narrative.'

September put her persimmon down in the long grass. 'What in the world does that mean?'

'I . . . I *suspect* it means that if we *act* like the kind of folk who would find a Fairy city whilst on various adventures involving tricksters, magical shoes and hooliganism, it will come to us.'

September blinked. 'Is that how things are done here?'

'Isn't that how they're done in your world?'

September thought for a long moment. She thought of how children who acted politely were often treated as good and trustworthy, even if they pulled your hair and made fun of your name when grown-ups weren't around. She thought of how her father acted like a soldier, strict and plain and organized – and how the army came for him. She thought of how her mother acted strong and happy even when she was sad, and so no one offered to help her, to make casseroles or watch September after school or come over for gin rummy and tea. And she thought of how she had acted just like a child in a story about Fairyland, discontent and complaining, and how the Green Wind had come for her, too.

'I suppose that is how things are done in my world. It's hard to see it, though, on the other side.'

'That's what gnome ointment is for,' winked the Wyvern.

'Well, we'd better be at it, then,' said September. 'At least I shall have no trouble with the shoes.' She kept a persimmon or two for a late lunch – the pockets of her smoking jacket were quite full, yet the jacket was quite sensitive about its figure and did not bulge in the slightest. A-Through-L squirmed down to the ground to allow her to climb up onto the bronze lock, where September sat pertly, clutching the wiry red stripe of fur that ran down the Wyverary's long neck. She drew her sceptre from the belt of the smoking jacket and extended it to the horizon like a sword. Blue mountains rose on either side of their path, shining and faceted like lumps of sapphire.

'Onward, noble steed!' she cried loudly.

Nothing much happened. A few birds catcalled and trilled.

As the two of them travel along, I shall take a moment's pause, as is my right. For it deserves remarking that if one is to obtain a monstrous companion, a Wyvern – or a Wyverary – is really a top-notch choice. Firstly, they rarely tire, and their gait is remarkably even, considering the poultry-like disposition of their feet. Secondly, when they do tire, they snore, and no ravening bandit would dare to come near. Thirdly, being French in origin, they have highly refined tastes and are unlikely to seek out unsavory things to eat, such as knights' gallbladders or maidens' bones. They much prefer a vat or two of truffles, a flock of geese, and a lake of wine, and they will certainly share. Lastly, their mating seasons are brief and infrequent, and the chances of experiencing one is so small as to be beyond the notice of any native guidebook or indeed the concern of any small girl with brown hair who might be utterly innocent of such things. Truly, the latter hardly bears mentioning.

September knew none of this. She knew only that A-Through-L was huge and warm and kind and smelled like roasting cinnamon and chestnuts and seemed to know simply everything. The rest of the alphabet held considerably less charm once she saw the world from her perch on his back.

A-Through-L walked late into the afternoon. The alpine grass full of little red flowers gradually turned into a wide, wet valley, full of rich chocolate mud and bright iridescent flowers nodding on pearly stalks taller than September. September tried very hard to look intrepid on her beast's back, and Ell tried on a look of grim determination. It did not seem to be moving Pandemonium any closer to them. After a long while, she tucked the sceptre between two links of chain and laid her cheek against Ell's back. *Perhaps a city takes a long time to rouse in the morning when it has not had its breakfast yet,* she thought. *Or perhaps it has other young girls to tend to first.*

And then, suddenly, a house rose up before them, as though it had been crouching in wait for hours and sprang out when it thought it might scare them most. It looked much like a Spanish mosque – if a giant had firmly stepped on it. All the curly door frames and tiled mosaics were broken and leaning, each blue-green wall propping up the other. Fragrant red wood lay about in rough piles, and pools of seeping black mud dotted the halls. Moss covered every shattered pillar. September and her Wyverary stood before a beautifully carved archway leading into a little courtyard, where a shabby fountain gurgled valiantly. The arch read:

The House Without Warning

'What is this place?' breathed September, climbing down the Wyverary's red flank. She was becoming quite agile at it.

A-Through-L shrugged. 'Too many W's,' he whispered. 'If only my brother were here!'

'It is my mistress's house,' came a thick, wet voice behind them.

September turned to see a most curious lady standing serenely on a patch of tile depicting a great blue rose. The woman stood in the precise center of the rose. A rich, clean perfume surrounded her in a light pinkish haze, for the woman was carved entirely from soap. Her face was a deep olivey-green castile, her hair a rich and oily Marseille, streaked with lime peels. Her body was patchwork: here strawberry soap with bits of red fruit showing through, there saffron and sandalwood, orange and brown. Her belt was a cord of hard, tallowy honey soap, her hands plain-blue bathing soap, and her fingernails smelled like daisies and lemons. Her eyes were two piercing, faceted slivers of soapstone. On her brow someone had written TRUTH in the kind of handwriting teachers always have: clear and curling and lovely.

'My name is Lye,' the soap-woman said. A few bubbles escaped her mouth. She was utterly still. No soapy muscle trembled. 'It is my part to welcome you, to show you to the baths, to tend to you and to all weary travelers, until my mistress returns, which will not be long now, I'm sure.'

'Why does it say "truth" on your forehead?' asked September shyly. She could be quite brave in the presence of a Wyverary, but tall and lovely ladies made her shy, even if they were made of soap.

'I am a golem, child,' answered Lye calmly. 'My mistress wrote it there. She was marvelous clever and knew all kinds of secret things. One of the things she knew was how to gather up all the slips of soap the bath house patrons left behind and arrange them into a girl shape and write "truth" on her forehead and wake her up and give her a name and say to her: "Be my friend and love me, for the world is terrible lonely and I am sad."'

'Who was your mistress, Lye?' said A-Through-L, settling into the courtyard as best he could, his feet crunched up against a broken pillar. 'She sounds like someone who spends a lot of time in libraries, which are the best sorts of people.'

Lye sighed – her bayberry soap shoulders rose and fell abruptly, as though no one had really taught her how to sigh before. 'She was a beautiful young girl with hair like new soap and big green eyes and a mole on her left cheek and she was a

Virgo and she liked a hot bath first and then a very cold one right after and she always went barefoot and I miss her. I am sure she did spend a lot of time in libraries, for she was always reading books, little ones she could hang from her belt and regular ones with garish covers and big ones, too, so big she'd lie on her stomach in their spines to read them. Her name was Mallow, and she has been gone for years and years, but I am still here, and I keep going, and I never stop because I don't know how to stop because she said I'd never have to stop.'

'Mallow!' cried the Wyverary, his scaly red eyebrows shooting up. '*Queen* Mallow?'

'I am sure she could have been queen if she wanted to. She was marvelous clever, as I said.'

'Who is Queen Mallow?' asked September, who felt quite left out of the excitement. 'You mentioned her before. And why is there a Marquess now if there was a Queen before? It seems to me that if you want to mess about with monarchy, you might, at least, get your traditions straight.'

'Oh, September, you don't understand!' said Ell, curling his tail down around her. 'Before the Marquess came with her lions and her great old panther with his ivory collar, Fairyland dwelt in the eternal summer of Good Queen Mallow, the Bright and the Bold. She loved us and governed with rhyming songs and cherries for all on Sundays. When she rode out on holidays, she wore a crown of red pearls the selkies gave her, and all the pookas did gymnastics just to make her laugh. Every table groaned with milk and wheat and sugar and hot chocolate. Every horse was fat. Every churn was full. Queen Mallow danced in circles of silver mushrooms to bring on the spring and apparently, before she became queen, ran a bath house.'

'But Mallow begins with M. How do you know so much about her?' asked September.

'*Everyone* knows about Good Queen Mallow,' replied the Wyverary, shocked that September did not.

'Master Wyvern, if you please, where has my mistress gone? It has been many years, and I have drawn many baths, but she has never come back to me, and I cannot sleep or eat because she didn't teach me how to sleep or eat, and it is dark at night and bits of me slough off in the rain.'

'Oh, darling Lye,' cried the Wyverary. 'How I wish I could bring you good news! But late in the golden reign of the Queen, the Marquess arrived and destroyed her. Or made her sit in a corner. Reports vary. And now there are complicated proclamations, and the lamentations of the hills and my wings are locked down to my skin, and no one has access at all. Some of us hope that in the dungeons of the Briary, the Queen is still alive, and playing solitaire to pass the years, waiting for a knight to release her, to repeal the Marquess's laws, and restore cocoa to Fairyland kettles.'

A single liquid tear melted the cheek of the soap golem. 'I suspected,' she whispered thickly. 'I suspected when the place began to break down and crumble and cry big dusty tears at night. I suspected, because I am not very good company. Why stay with a silly golem when you can be Queen? Even if she said I was her friend.'

'I'm sure she meant to come back,' said September, trying to comfort the great, kindhearted golem. 'And we are going to Pandemonium to steal back a part of what the Marquess has taken away.'

'A girl with green eyes, perhaps?'

'Well, no, a Spoon.' September suddenly felt her lovely quest was a bit small and shabby. But it was hers. 'Do you know how far it is from here to Pandemonium?'

'What an odd question,' said Lye.

'I'm not from these parts, you see,' September said demurely. She was beginning to feel she ought to have that stitched on her jacket.

'Wherever you are, child, the House Without Warning lies between you and Pandemonium. However you turn, you cannot get to the City without passing through the House, without being cleaned and prepared, without having the road washed from you and your feet made soft and your spirit thoroughly scrubbed. I thought all cities were like that. How could they bear to have a great lot of filthy, exhausted folk milling around inside them, grumpy and nervy and dingy?' The soap golem extended her long, stiff arm, her skin a spiral of buttery greens. September took it. 'When you leave this place, human child, you will find Pandemonium. The two are tied together, like a ship and a pier. Like my mistress and I, once, years and years ago.'

The soap golem led them to the center of the House Without Warning, which was not really a house at all but many small rooms connected by long tiled halls and courtyards, which would once have been charming but were now covered in slime and green with age, falling apart, morose. Lye thoughtfully led A-Through-L to a great waterfall whose pool would accommodate him but drew September farther into the depths of the House. The soft smacking sounds of her soapy heels against the floor were pleasant, lulling. No one else seemed to be about. Everything was quiet – but not frighteningly so. The place seemed to be, well, *napping*. Finally, they entered the largest courtyard yet. In the midst of copper statues and fountains caked with verdigris rested three huge bathtubs. The floor showed two winged hippogriffs rampant in cobalt and emerald. The tubs covered their hooves like great horseshoes.

Lye pulled at September's jacket and she wriggled out of it – but when the golem tugged at her orange dress as well, September quailed.

'What's wrong?'

'I . . . don't like to be naked. In front of strangers.'

Lye thought for a moment. 'My mistress used to say that you couldn't ever really be naked unless you wanted to be. She said, "Even if you've taken off every stitch of clothing, you still have your secrets, your history, your true name. It's quite difficult to be really naked. You have to work hard at it. Just getting into a bath isn't being naked, not really. It's just showing skin. And foxes and bears have skin, too, so I shan't be ashamed if they're not." '

'Did Mallow tell you her true name?' September asked.

Lye nodded slowly. 'But I won't tell you. It's a secret. She told me and then cut her finger and mine and blood came out of her and liquid soap came out of me and they mingled and turned golden and she kissed the place where I'd been wounded and told me her name and not to tell, not ever. So I won't. She already knew mine.' The soap golem pointed shyly to the word written on her forehead.

'The Green Wind told me not to tell anyone my true name. But I don't know of any name truer than September, and if I didn't tell anyone that was my name, what would they call me?'

'It cannot be your true name, or you would be in awful trouble, telling everyone like that. If you know someone's true name, you can command them, like a doll.' Lye stopped uncomfortably, as though the subject caused her pain. 'It's very unpleasant.'

'Can't you call Mallow back then, if you know her name?'

Lye sobbed a little, a terribly awkward noise at the back of her throat, like snapping a bar of soap in half. 'I've tried! I've tried! I've called and called and she won't come so she must be dead! And I don't know what to do except keep the baths full.'

September took a step back from the force of the golem's grief. She slowly pulled off her orange dress – which to tell the truth had become rather filthy – and her precious remaining shoe. In the cooling evening, she stood naked before the many-colored golem, uncomplaining. 'The baths smell very nice,' she whispered. She only wanted the golem to stop being sad.

A breeze came sighing along the courtyard and picked up her clothes and her shoe, shaking them and soaking them in the fountain water to get the seawater and beach grime out.

The green smoking jacket spluttered and wrinkled, most upset.

Lye lifted September up suddenly and put her down in the first tub, which was really more like an oak barrel, the kind you store wine in, if you need to store rather a lot of wine, for it was enormous. September's head ducked immediately under the thick, bright gold water. When she bobbed up, the smell of it wrapped her up like a warm scarf: the scent of fireplaces crackling and warm cinnamon and autumn leaves crunching underfoot. She smelled cider and a rainstorm coming. The gold water clung to her in streaks and clumps, and she laughed. It tasted like butterscotch.

'This is the tub for washing your courage,' Lye said, her voice as even and calm as ever, performing her task, grief packed away for the duration of a bath.

'I didn't know one's courage needed washing!' gasped September as Lye poured a pitcher of water over her head. *Or that one needs to be naked for that sort of washing,* she thought to herself.

Lye poured a bucketful of golden water over September's head. 'When you are born,' the golem said softly, 'your courage is new and clean. You are brave enough for anything: crawling off of staircases, saying your first words without fearing that someone will think you are foolish, putting strange things in your mouth. But as you get older, your courage attracts gunk and crusty things and dirt and fear and knowing how bad things can get and what pain feels like. By the time you're half-grown, your courage barely moves at all, it's so grunged up with living. So every once in a while, you have to scrub it up and get the works going or else you'll never be brave again. Unfortunately, there are not so many facilities in your world that provide the kind of services we do. So most people go around with grimy machinery, when all it would take is a bit of spit and polish to make them paladins once more, bold knights and true.'

Lye broke off one of her deep blue fingers and dropped it into the tub. Immediately, a creamy froth bubbled up, clinging to September's skin and tickling.

'Your finger!' she cried.

'Don't fear, little one. It doesn't hurt. My mistress said: "Give of yourself, and it will return to you as new as new can be." And so my fingers do, when the bathers have gone.'

September looked inside herself to see if her courage was shining up. She didn't feel any different, besides the pleasure of a hot bath and clean skin. A little lighter, maybe, but she could not be sure.

'Next tub!' said Lye, and lifted her up, still covered with golden foam, out of the oak barrel and into a shallow, sloping bronze tub, the kind noble ladies in films used. September loved the movies, though they could not afford to go often. In her most private moments, September thought her mother was prettier than any of the girls on the screen.

The water of the bronze tub gleamed icy and green, redolent of mint and forest nights and sweet cakes, hot tea and very cold starlight.

'This is for washing your wishes, September,' said Lye, breaking off another of her fingers with a thick snap. 'For the wishes of one's old life wither and shrivel like old leaves if they are not replaced with new wishes when the world changes. And the world always changes. Wishes get slimy, and their colors fade, and soon they are just mud, like all the rest of the mud, and not wishes at all, but regrets. The trouble is, not everyone can tell when they ought to launder their wishes. Even when one finds oneself in Fairyland and not at home at all, it is not always so easy to remember to catch the world in its changing and change with it.'

Lye dropped in her finger, which did not foam this time, but melted, like butter in a pan, over the surface of the green water. September sank under and held her breath, as she often did at home, practising for a swimming meet. *I used to wish my father would come home and my mother would let me come sleep with her like when I was a baby. I used to wish I had a friend at school who would play games and read books with me, and then we would talk about what wonderful things had happened to the children in the books.* But all that seemed far away now. *Now I wish . . . I wish the Marquess would leave everyone alone. And that I could be a . . . a paladin, like Lye said. A bold knight and true. And that I will not cry when I get afraid. And that Ell really is part library, even though I know he probably isn't. And that my mother will not be angry when I get home.*

September's hair floated up above her head in drifting curls. Lye scrubbed her, even under the water, with a rough brush until her skin tingled. Abruptly, the soap golem lifted her up and dropped her into the next tub, a silver claw-foot filled with creamy hot milk. It smelled of vanilla and rum and maple syrup, just like Betsy Basilstalk's cigarette. Lye stroked September's hair in the new bath and lifted several pitchers of it over her head. She broke off her thumb and swirled it three times through the bath, counterclockwise. *All traffic travels widdershins,* September thought, giggling. The golem's thumb fizzed and sparkled, showering the surface with blue sparks.

'Lastly,' Lye said, 'we must wash your luck. When souls queue up to be born, they all leap up at just the last moment, [illegible] the [illegible] of the world for their [illegible]. Some jump high and can seize a great measure of luck; some jump only a bit and snatch a few loose strands. Everyone manages to catch *some.* If one did not have at least a little luck, one would never survive childhood. But luck can be spent, like money; and lost, like a memory; and wasted, like a life. If you know how to look, you can examine the kneecaps of a human and tell how much luck they have left. No bath can replenish luck that has been spent on avoiding an early death by automobile accident or winning too many raffles in a row. No bath can restore luck lost through absentmindedness and overconfidence. But luck withered by conservative, tired, riskless living can be plumped up again – after all, it was only a bit thirsty for something to do.'

Lye pushed September down into the milk again. She shut her eyes and sank into the warm cream, enjoying it, flexing her aching toes. She did not know whether her luck was even then growing more robust, but she found she did not much care. *Baths are marvelous whether or not,* she thought, *and Fairy baths best of all.*

The soap golem pulled September at last from the luck-bath and began drying her with long, flat, stiff banana leaves, baked brown by the sun. She tousled her clean, wet hair. When September was beginning to feel quite dry and happy, the Wyverary ducked into the courtyard, shaking his scales like an indignant cat. He tried to shake out his wings, but the chain stopped him short, and he winced. September's sceptre jangled against the padlock.

'Brrr!' he boomed. 'I suppose I'm clean, if it matters. Books don't judge one for being a touch well-traveled.'

The soap golem nodded. 'And ready for the City to take you in.'

The little breeze returned September's clothes, crisp and clean and dry, scented lightly with a bit of water from the baths of courage and wishing and luck. She could not be sure, but she thought the breeze might have purred a bit, rather like a Leopard.

'If you see her,' said Lye softly, almost whispering. 'My mistress. If you see her, tell her I am still her friend, and there are ever so many more games to play . . .'

'I shall, Lye, I promise,' said September, and reached up suddenly to hug the golem, though she hadn't meant to. Lye slowly enfolded her soap-arms around the child. But when September reached up to kiss the golem's brow, Lye drew back sharply before her lips could touch the word written there.

'Careful,' Lye said. 'I am fragile.'

'That's all right,' said September suddenly, feeling the warm cinnamon courage of her bath bubble up inside her, fresh and bright. 'I'm not.'

The House Without Warning was possessed of a small door nestled beside a marble statue of Pan blowing his horn – if only September knew that Pan is also a god, and not merely a prefix! Well, never mind. It was too late for warnings now, as the House well knew. The door straightened up and opened gallantly for the Wyverary and the girl. Seagulls cried from inside, and many voices jangled together, but all was dark within. Slowly, they stepped through into the black.

'Ell,' said September as they crossed the threshold, 'what sort of tubs did you wash in?'

The Wyverary shook his great head and would not speak.

CHAPTER VI
Shadows in the Water

In Which September Crosses a River, Receives a Lesson in Evolution, and Loses Something Precious but Saves a Pooka

The Barleybroom River roared and splashed as September and the Wyverary stepped through the bath-house door on to a rich, wet, green bank. At least, September presumed it was the Barleybroom. Something colorful and hazy floated in the center of the river as it foamed along around it in a great circle. September almost tripped for gawking. Folk surrounded them, pushing, laughing, shouting, all laden with every kind of suitcase and traveling pack, from brass-banded steamer trunks to green handkerchiefs tied around knotty sticks of hawthorn. September tried to look as though she belonged there, back straight, eyes ahead. Black river mud squelched between the toes of her one bare foot.

Every sort of creature jostled for position, trying gamely to get to a long, pale pier first: Centaurs and Satyrs and Brownies and Will-o'-the-wisps, Birds with girls' legs and girls with Birds' legs, Trolls with splendid epaulets and Dwarves in velvet trousers and waistcoats, Hobgoblins plying violins as they walked, Mice taller than September, and a great number of human-seeming ladies and lords and children. September caught the eye of one of them, a little girl in a neat hazelnut-husk dress. She had red columbines tangled up in her blonde hair. She danced around her mother, teasing and pulling at her skirt. The girl clapped her gaze on September in mid-leap. She winked wickedly and shivered her shoulders – and suddenly the girl was a sleek black jackal pup, with a gold stripe down her back. Now, jackals are not the wicked creatures some irresponsible folklorists would have children believe. They are quite sweet and soft, and their ears are clever and enormous. Such a lovely creature the little girl had become. Only her narrow blue eyes were the same. Her great tall ears twitched, and she continued on pestering her mother with yips and nips.

'Did you know,' said the Wyverary happily, snuffling the fresh air with his huge nostrils, 'that the Barleybroom used to be full of tea? There was an undertow of tea leaves, flowing in from some tributary. It used to be, oh, the color of brandy, with little bits of lemon peel floating in it and lumps of sugar like lily pads.'

'It's not tea now, at least, I've never had tea colored indigo.'

'Well, the Marquess said that sort of thing was silly. Everyone knows what a river looks like, she said. She got the Glashtyn to dam the tributary and drag along nets to catch all the leaves and eat up all the lemon peels and sugar cubes. They cried while they did it. But you see now, it's a nice, normal blue color.' The Wyverary scowled. 'Proper, I guess,' he sighed. The jackal-girl chased her tail.

'What is that girl, Ell?'

'Mmm? Oh, just a Pooka, I suspect. Starts with P. None of mine, you know.'

Finally, the procession fanned out before a great, gnarled pier of driftwood and ropy yellow vines. A great barge tiered like a black cake moored there. Green paper lanterns swung from its ledges and arches; fell designs had been long ago carved into its wood. All along the top were old men leaning against monstrous poles. Ribbons and lily strands streamed from the pole-tips. The whole effect was very gay and festive, but the old men were haggard and salty and grim.

'The Barleybroom ferry!' crowed the Wyverary. 'Of course, never was a need for it before when a body could fly into Pandemonium as quick as you like. But progress is the goal of all good souls.'

September stared openmouthed as they slowly inched nearer to the gangplank. She tugged at the tip of A-Through-L's wing.

'It's a Fairy,' she whispered.

'Of course, it is, girl! What did I just say?'

'No, not a ferry, a *Fairy*.'

The toll man was ancient and hunched, his gray hair caught up in several wild pigtails around two barnacled goat horns. He had rheumy eyes and glasses as thick as beer-mug bottoms and three gold hoops in one ear. He wore a thick Navy peacoat with brass buttons and sailcloth trousers – and two iridescent wings jutted out of the back of his tailored coat, rimmed in gold, glittering as the sunlight made spinning violet prisms inside them. They were bound with a delicate iron chain, thin but enough to keep them flat and useless against the old ferryman's back.

'Fare,' he growled as their turn came.

The Wyverary cleared his prodigious throat. September

started. 'Oh!' she cried. 'I suppose I'm the one with the purse strings.' She pulled her sceptre from the links in Ell's chain. *I knew I might need such a thing!* September felt quite pleased with herself for displaying such excellent foresight. With the end of one of Ell's claws, she chipped two rubies from the bulb of the sceptre and held them out proudly.

''E's too big,' sniffed the ferryman. 'Have to pay double for Excessive Baggage.'

'I am not *baggage,*' gasped the Wyverary.

'Dunno. She keeps her shiny whatnot on ya. Might be Baggage. Sure, and you're Excessive. Double fare, anyhow.'

'It's fine!' hushed September, and chipped a third gleaming red stone from the sceptre. All three glittered on her palm like pricks of blood. 'Easy come, easy go. I certainly shan't be going without you!'

'On with it,' gruffed the ferryman, waggling his caterpillary eyebrows and scooping up the gems.

The Wyverary gave one giant leap and settled gracefully on the top level of the great black ferry. September walked with her head straight, up the plank and around the spiral staircase to join him. Perhaps it was Lye's bath, but she felt quite bold and intrepid and, having paid her own way, quite grown-up. This inevitably leads to disastrous decisions, but September could not know that, not then when the sun was so very bright and the river so blue. Let us allow her these new, strange pleasures.

No?

Very well, but I have tried to be a generous narrator and care for my girl as best I can. I cannot help that readers will always insist on adventures, and though you can have grief without adventures, you cannot have adventures without grief.

Chaise longues in blue and gold dotted the sunny deck of the ferry. Lithe blue women and great pale trolls lay out, bathing in the light. A-Through-L snorted happily along with the creaking and groaning sounds of the ferry uncoupling from the pier.

'Isn't it lovely to be on our way,' he said, sighing, 'to be near the City? The great City, where everyone has some hope of becoming marvelous!'

September did not answer. A shadow fell over her as she thought of how often she had heard older girls in her school bathrooms talk about how they would go one day to a place called Los Angeles and be stars, be beautiful and rich, marry the men from the movies. A few said they might chuck California and go to New York, where they would also be beautiful and rich, but instead of movie stars, they would be dancers and photographers' models and marry great writers. September had been dubious. She had not wanted to go to either city. They seemed awful and huge and too crammed with marriageable men. She did not want to think that Pandemonium could be like that. She did not want Fairyland to be full of older girls who wanted to be stars.

'Look sharp, girl,' grumbled the ferryman, who had come up to take his place at the pole. He did not take it up, however, and yet the ferry sailed smoothly through the water. He just leaned against it and squinted at the distant City. 'Small'ns who daydream are like to fall off, and you'dn't want that.'

'I can swim,' said September with mild indignation, recalling her adventure in the ocean.

'Sure, and you can. But the Glashtyn have run of the Barleybroom, and they swim better.'

September wanted to ask about the Glashtyn, but her mouth ran away from her.

'Are you a Fairy, Sir?'

The ferryman gave her a withering look.

'Well, I mean, I *think* you are one, but I'd rather ask. I wouldn't like someone to assume I'm something I'm not! And what I mean to say is, if you *are* a Fairy, then could you tell me what a Fairy *is,* taxonomically speaking, and why you're the only one I've seen.' September was glad for her pronunciation of *taxonomically,* which she had had as a spelling word not terribly far back.

'*Scientifick'ly* speaking, a Fairy – what I am – is not much different'n a human. Your lot evolved from monkeys. We evolved . . . well, it's not talked on in polite circles, but there never was a polite circle with a human in it. Fairies started out as frogs. *Amphibianderous,* right? Well, being frogs was no kind of fun, so we went about and stole better bits – wings from dragonflies and faces from people and hearts from birds and horns from various goats and antelope-ish things and souls from ifrits and tails from cows – and we evolved over a million million minutes, just like you.'

'I . . . I don't think that's how evolution works . . .' said September softly.

'Oh? Your name Charlie Darwin all sudden-true?'

'No, it's just—'

'It's Survival of Them Who's Best at Nicking Things, girl!'

'I mean to say, humans didn't evolve like that—'

'That's your trouble, then. Don't you go striping my facts with your daft babbling. I say, let them as wants to evolve do it and soak the rest. As for why we're not exactly thick on the ground, that's none of yours, and I'll thank you not to pry into family business.' The ferryman fished a corncob pipe out of his pocket and snapped his fingers. Smoke began to trail out of the basket, smelling mostly like a wet cornfield.

‘’Course, if you want to keep evolving your own self, I’d advise you get stowing away down below.’

‘What? Why?’

‘I’m not supposed to say. Whole point is your’n don’t know what day the tithe comes calling.’ The ferryman winked, his eyes twinkling with a sudden dim glee, rather more like September expected from a Fairy. ‘Now, look there,’ he said with a grin. ‘I’ve gone and spilt it.’

September might well have run, but she could not abandon her scaly red friend and, despite being quite able to use the word *taxonomically* in a sentence, was somewhat fuzzy on the meaning of *tithe*. Thus it was that September was caught with her mouth hanging open when the ferry ground splashily to a halt in the middle of the roaring river.

‘Told you, but ears like a cow you’ve got,’ sighed the ferryman, and stuck his pole to meet the six tall men climbing six ropes, pirate-like, over the top of the deck.

Each of the men stood naked but for silver gauntlets and greaves and had black regal horse’s heads where their human heads ought to have been. The leader, a big brass ring in his silky nose as if he were a bull, called out in a deep echoing voice, ‘Charlie Crunchcrab, the Glashtyn come to claim our tithe by Law and Right of Fair Trade!’

‘I hear ya, old nag,’ grumbled the ferryman. ‘Not so dense

as all that. Got the summons this morning and everything. Needn't be so formal.'

The Fairy folk gathered on the top deck and quailed and clung together in silent terror. They stared fixedly at the floor, trying desperately not to look the horse-men in the eye. September looked across the throng at Ell, who shook his great head and tried to hunker down and become, improbably, invisible.

'Bring the children up!' bellowed one of the horse-men.

Rough hands grabbed September's arms and dragged her, along with dozens of other small ones, to stand before the Glashtyn, whose eyes flashed blue-and-green fire. September looked down and saw the little Pooka girl beside her, trembling, her jackal-ears appearing and disappearing nervously. September took the child's hand and squeezed it comfortingly.

'Not me,' the girl whispered. 'Please let it not be me.'

The Glashtyn walked down the line, staring each of the children in the eye. The leader glared hard at September, and yanked her chin upward to check her teeth. But finally, he passed her by. The horse-heads conferred.

'That one!' cried the leader, and a ripple of relief passed through the crowd. For a moment, September's breath stopped, sure he was pointing directly at her.

But it was not her.

The little Pooka girl screamed in utter, animal terror. She shivered into a jackal and clambered around September's legs, clawed up her back and on to her shoulders, wrapping her tail around her throat.

'No! No!' the Pooka wept, shrieking and clinging to September.

'What's happening?' September choked, stumbling under the weight of the panicked jackal-girl.

'She's the tithe – and nothing to be done,' said the ferryman Charlie Crunchcrab. 'Might as well be grown-up and dignified about it. The ferry pulls on through Glashtyn territory. They have a right to their fare, too. No one knows what day it will come, or who they will choose, but, well, you all have to get to the City, one way or any way, is true?'

'No! Not me! I don't want to go! Mama, please! Where's my mama?'

But September could see her mother, near one of the chaises, a long black jackal with golden ears, lying on her side, paws over her face in grief.

'That's the worst thing I've ever heard!' The girl clung to September

'That's evolution, love. Take as taking can.'

'What are they going to do to her?'

'None of your business,' snapped the Glashtyn leader.

The Pooka wailed, 'They'll eat me! And drown me! And lash me to the ferry and make me pull it back and forth under the river!'

'It's good enough for us,' growled one of the other Glashtyn. September saw for the first time that each of them clutched reins and ugly, cruel bits in their fists.

'Please, please, please,' sobbed the child. She shivered back and forth from girl to jackal to girl with alarming speed, the whites of her eyes showing. September reached up to pet her and pried her slowly loose, the claws from her hair, the tail from her throat. She cradled the jackal pup awkwardly, for she was not a very little creature. Her snout flashed into a mouth and back into a muzzle as she wept.

'Isn't there anything else you could take?' September said wretchedly. 'Does it have to be a child?'

'There must be blood,' answered the Glashtyn quietly. 'Do you offer yourself as replacement? That is certainly traditional.'

To her credit, September considered this for a moment. She was a strong swimmer and would likely not drown, and they hadn't said, exactly, that they meant to eat anyone. Being only Somewhat Heartless, she could not cradle a trembling child in her arms and not feel sorry for it and want to keep it from being tossed overboard. But she did not want to be a tithe, and she did not want to die, even a little bit, and she did not even want to brush shoulders with the smallest chance of it.

'No,' she whispered. 'I can't. Isn't there anything else? I have rubies. . . .'

The horse-man snorted. 'Dead rocks.'

'I have a jacket and a shoe.'

They stared at her.

'Well, I haven't anything else! But I can't let you have her – she's just a kid, poor thing! How can you frighten her like this?'

The Glashtyn's stare bored into her. The blue fire in his eyes was calculating.

'You have a voice,' he said slowly, 'and a shadow. Choose one, and I will take it instead of the skin-shrugger.'

You might think that is no kind of choice. But September was suspicious. No bargain in Fairyland could be that easy. And yet— she could not lose her voice, she could not! How would she talk to Ell? How would she sing? How would she explain to her mother where she had gone? And she could not let the girl, whose arms were clutched even now around her neck, go down into the dark river. Even if they did not drown her and eat her, the girl didn't want to go, and September could get very cross about that sort of thing.

'My shadow,' she said. 'Take it. Though it hasn't any blood, you know.'

She set the Pooka down. And the child bolted to her mother, shivering fully into a pup midway across the ferry deck. The two jackals licked each other's faces and whined. The Glashtyn held out his hand to Charlie Crunchcrab. The Fairy unbuckled an ugly, rusted, serrated knife from his belt and passed it over.

September had time to think, *Oh, this will hurt,* before the Glashtyn seized her, spun her around, and sawed the knife back and forth along her spine. She felt cold and faint. The knife made noises like shredding silk and grinding bone. She thought she might topple over, the pain was so terrible, running up and down her back. Still, she refused to cry. Finally, there was a sickening *crack,* and the Glashtyn pulled away with a scrap of something in his hand. A single drop of September's blood dripped from the knife to the bleached wood of the deck.

The Glashtyn set the scrap of something down before him. It pooled darkly, shining a little, and then stood up in the shape of a girl just September's height, with just September's eyes and hair, all of black smoke and shadow. Slowly, the shadow-September smiled and pirouetted on one foot. It was not a gentle smile or a kind one. The shadow extended her hand to the Glashtyn, who took it, smiling himself.

'We shall take her below and love her and put her at the

head of our parades,' he said. 'For she was not taken but given – and thus our only true possession.'

The shadow curtsied. To September, the curtsy seemed somewhat vicious, if a curtsy could be vicious. September was unsure that she had done the right thing now – surely, she would miss her shadow, and surely, the Glashtyn meant to make mischief with it of some sort or another. But it was too late: The Glashtyn leapt overboard as one, with the shadow-September riding on the leader's shoulders. The Fairy throng stared at her, amazed. No one would speak to her. A-through-L finally strode across the deck to gather her up. He smelled so good and familiar, and his skin was so warm. She hugged his knee.

'Did I do the right thing, Charlie?' September asked the ferryman softly.

He shook his mad gray head. 'Right or blight, done is dusted.'

September looked across the water at the gleaming City rising up, all towers and shine. Then she looked down into the Barleybroom.

Six dark horse heads glided through the water at the head of the ferry, bits clamped in their teeth. Over their backs, a shadow girl leapt and danced, her ghostly laughter all but eaten up by the waves.

The Key and its Travels

In Which We Turn Our Attention to a Long-Forgotten and Much-Suffering Jeweled Key

Being careful and clever readers, you must now wonder if your woolgathering narrator has completely forgotten the jeweled key that so loyally followed September into Fairyland. Not so! But a key's adventuring is of necessity a quieter thing than a girl's, more single-minded and also more fraught with loneliness.

For the Key slipped between Latitude and Longitude and tumbled briefly – oh so briefly! – through the starry dark behind the screen of the world. It landed unceremoniously on the shimmering jacket of a hobgoblin in transit from Brocéliande to Atlantis. The Key blended into the other glittery bits of folly that bedecked the jacket and went unquestioned by Betsy Basilstalk or Rupert the Gargoyle.

Good-naturedly illiterate, the Key had no wish to visit the blue-crystal universities of Atlantis and unhooked its clasp just in time to tumble through the rooty, moldy, wormy passage to Fairyland. It caught an updraft of sea air and soared over the fleecy clouds, playing tag with the blue-necked gillybirds.

It passed over the witches and narrowly avoided a sucking vortex of the events of next week that threatened to pull it down into the cauldron.

It flew over the field full of little red flowers, but no Wyverary – or even a Wyvern – appeared to accompany it or explain how anything worked or was in the days before today.

The Key, too, found the House Without Warning, long after a nicely scrubbed September had passed through. Under Lye's gentle eye, the Key primly dropped into a tiny tub and soaked until it gleamed.

The Key missed the ferry September rode into Pandemonium and was forced to sleep on the grassy shore, where it was picked up by a delighted bamboo child. The girl squealed piercingly and pinned the Key to her little green-gold breast. Her mother admonished her not to pick up strange treasures that surely were not hers, but no one can listen to a banshee shriek in indignation for long without giving in. So it was that the Key boarded the ferry and passed into Pandemonium, three days after September had left the city behind.

The Key cursed its slowness. It wept an orange tear, slightly rusted.

The Key remembered being part of a green smoking jacket. It remembered wanting to please. It remembered, a little, being born out of a lapel, the sudden rush of air over facets and gold. It recalled with sorrow being torn from its mother, the jacket, and the taste of a young girl's blood under its needle. It shuddered at the memory of her blood, at night.

What the Key knew was that it was connected to September, that the purpose of its whole being was to be with her, just to rest near her skin. The Key had been created to make her smile. It could not stop wanting to make her smile, any more than you can stop walking on two legs or start breathing with your liver instead of your lungs. What if September needed the Key? What if the world became dark and frightening and it was not there to comfort her? The Key knew it must fly faster.

It was only that the girl kept *running,* so far and so fast, almost as if she didn't know that the Key was trying as hard as it could to keep up.

CHAPTER VII
Fairy Reels

In Which September Enters Pandemonium at Last and Is Discovered by the Marquess While A-Through-L Enjoys a Lemon Ice

'Go on,' said the Wyverary, nudging the girl in the orange dress with his great red nose. 'Ask.'

September squinted dubiously. The brass face before her [illegible]

In fact, it was a brass face hoisted up on a tower of tangled brass hands that seemed to be frozen in the acts of pleading, praying, beseeching, orating, pointing, prodding. They wound around each other until five of them fanned out in a kind of finger-fringed flower that held the face aloft. The burnished face had swollen, puffy cheeks, a pursed mouth, and eyes squeezed tightly shut. Its ears flared enormous, larger than its head. Behind the post rose a huge, bustling, and walled city. The sounds from within rumbled indistinctly, as bustle will do. The wall did not look terribly sturdy – it was patchwork, motley-colored, a dozen kinds of brocade and stiff silk and satin and broadcloth, all sewn together with gnarled, ropy yarn the color of squash, thicker than tree trunks.

They stood at a goat-hide gate. The Switchpoint, for that's what Ell called it, made a kissing face at them. All around them well-kept lawns wound down to the lapping Barleybroom, full of gentle little paths and sedate violets nodding pleasantly. A sundial spun its shadow slowly around clusters of yellow peonies. Not at all what you might expect from a place called Pandemonium, really, especially the bird-baths and commemorative benches. It looked much more like Hanscom Park in Omaha than the outskirts of a Fairy City.

The Switchpoint still pursed its lips at them. A sparrow landed on one of its oversize ears and flew away again, as though the brass burned its feet. Ell insisted that this was the way in.

'What shall I ask?' said September, shuffling her feet.

'Well, where do you want to go?' Ell stretched his long neck, uncoiling it and yawning, then coiling it up again.

'I expect to wherever the Marquess lives.'

'That's the Briary.'

'But then . . . thieves work at night, mostly, and I ought to start acting like a thief if I mean to steal something. So we ought to wait until nightfall, you know. It's easier to be sneaky in the dark.'

'September, queen among thieves, you will never get into Pandemonium this way. You must have a Purpose. You must have Business Here. Loiterers, Lackadaisicals and other Menaces might do well in other cities, but they are allergic to Pandemonium, and it is allergic to them. If you do not have Business Here, you must at least pretend you do with a very firm expression, or else learn to eat violets and converse with sundials.'

'We could go to the Municipal Library, see your . . . grandfather.' September was still deeply unsure about Ell's theory on his parentage.

A-Through-L blushed, going all orange in the face. 'I . . . I'm not ready!' he cried suddenly. 'I haven't had a brushup on my smiles! I haven't had my horns waxed or my credentials calligraphed or anything! Tomorrow, we can go tomorrow or maybe next week!'

'Oh, Ell, don't worry,' September sighed. 'I think you look fine as you are! And you're quite the smartest beast I've ever known.'

'But how many beasts have you known?'

'Well, there's you . . . and the Leopard and the wairwulf. I'm only twelve! I think three is a very respectable number.'

'Not what you'd call a statistical sampling, though. But it's no matter. Today we ride on the rails of your quest, not mine. I'm not ready. I'm just not.' A-Through-L's eyes turned pleading. Tears welled up, bright turquoise, glittering.

'Oh! It's all right, Ell! Don't cry!' September stroked his leathery knee. She turned to the Switchpoint and took a deep breath, speaking as loudly and sternly as she could.

'Listen, Mr Brass-Ears! I should like to find a place that is cool and shady, somewhat near the Briary, but not too near, where we can rest and laugh and see something wonderful of Pandemonium while we wait for the sun to set.'

'And lemon ices,' whispered Ell.

'And where they serve lemon ices,' finished September firmly.

The Switchpoint exhaled with a long, high whistle, its cheeks deflating like spent balloons. Its eyes opened and its ears fluttered. All the hands of the post flexed, made fists, and relaxed again.

'Papers,' the Switchpoint said in a faint, airy voice. Its eyes were hard brass balls, glinting with judgment.

September fished the little green book that Betsy Basilstalk had given her out of the inner pocket of the smoking jacket. The jacket was deeply pleased to have kept it safe for her. She held it up so the cherubic little face could examine it. It clucked imperiously.

'Ravished, eh? Haven't seen one of you in a while.' The Switchpoint looked dubiously at A-Through-L, who scratched at the grass with one enormous claw.

'He's my . . . companion. My Wyvern,' said September hurriedly. She hoped he would not be too offended at being called *hers*.

'Do you have a Deed for him?'

The Wyverary drew himself up to his full height, which was considerable. 'True servitude,' he said gently, 'can only be voluntary. Surely, you know that. Surely, you once chose to stand here and frown at those who wish only to enter the city. Surely, you once did something else – sold gloves or frightened children at festivals – and chose this instead.'

The Switchpoint squinted up at him. 'Were a soldier, we were,' he grumbled.

The great goat-hair gate drew back like a theatre curtain. Four of the hands at the base of the Switchpoint post began to work furiously, so fast the fingers blurred so that September could not even see them moving. Slowly, a deep scarlet scrap began to spread out from the post, weaving itself as it went, a little brass thumb sliding back and forth like a shuttle. It flowed on, raw, shimmering silk, under September's shadowless feet and through the gate, stopping there, as if to beckon them onward.

September took a step forward. The hands blurred into industry again, and the scarlet path wove swiftly on into Pandemonium.

'It's all right,' said Ell confidentially as they passed through the gate. 'I know you didn't mean it, about my being yours.' The great beast flicked his red tail. 'But I can be. And you can be mine! And what lovely games we shall have!'

'Isn't it wonderful?' sighed A-Through-L happily as September gaped. 'Queen Mallow built it this way, years and years ago.'

Pandemonium spread out around her, a city of cloth. Bright storefronts ran on ahead of them, built with violet crinoline and crimson organdy. Towers wound up in wobbly twists of stiff, shining brocade. Memorial statues wore felt helmets over bombazine faces. High, thin, fuzzy houses puffed out angora doors; fancy taffeta offices glimmered under the gaze of black-lace gargoyles. Even the broad avenue they stood on was a mass of ropy, pumpkin-colored grosgrain. And there! That crooked, creased, ancient leather obelisk must be Groangyre Tower! The warm wind filled a coppery satin balloon at the tip-top of the tower and blew it up into a fine cupola.

The woven scarlet path at their feet waited patiently, indulging their country gawking.

'She couldn't have done it all by herself!' gasped September.

A-Through-L shrugged. 'Fierce was her needle, and she wore it like a sword. Wielded it, too! Brandished, even! Woven things are so warm, she said, so kind and home-like. But all that was so terribly long ago. The Marquess would like to change it, of course, turn it all to stone tied up in brambles, but all the brick-wights long ago learned to spin thread and knit alleyways and forgot their old trades, and even Marquesses cannot have their way in all things.'

A little sound rustled up from the patient path, something like a cough, if fabric that wove itself could cough. In fact, September noticed, a great number of linen paths wound out in front of folk as they hurried past, all of different colors, cobalt and ochre and silver and rose, busily weaving through side streets and thoroughfares, dodging carriage traffic, buskers squeezing accordions with four arms, barkers advertising roasted melons and fresh fennel bouquets for the discerning lover. Pedestrians – hoofed and web-footed and eight-legged and more – confidently ran after their paths. And on each burlap street corner, a smaller version of their own Switchpoint worked busily away.

Their little red path grew even redder as September and Ell embarrassed it by standing still.

September laughed and ran ahead, grinning into the Pandemonium sun. The path leapt up and wove swiftly on, barely missing a lavender crepe streetlight and barreling right through a pair of imps haggling over a bar of green algae. A-through-L thundered after her, squashing the linen as he bounded down the street (which possessed the name Onionbore) while all and sundry hurried to get out of his way.

The scarlet path led them more or less north-ish, and though September loved the chase and the smell of broiling maple blossoms and brewing lime liquor, she could not help but notice that every alley and avenue they sped through seemed to point directly at a small unassuming building covered in wide, fluttering golden flowers – not silk flowers but real ones that covered walls and fences of green briars and black thorns. The only house in Pandemonium that grew and lived and was not sewn. Something about it glowed strange and baleful. September did not like to look at it. Ell could not help looking. But mercifully, the scarlet path stopped short and began unraveling itself backward, the way they had come, neatly balling up its excess thread as it went.

A rose-colored jacquard building leaned over them, its walls embossed with fine flowers and paisleys and curlicues. A great sign arched over the doorway. In flashing green lights it read, THE SILVER SHUTTLE NICKELODEON.

One of the green bulbs guttered a little.

'Are those *electric* lights?' asked September.

'Of course,' said Ell softly, as if in awe of the flickering glow. 'Fairyland is a Scientifick place.'

'I suppose the Marquess did that, too.'

'No; in fact, she abhors electricity. The Royal Inventors' Society did it. A terrible racket went up for days out of Groangyre. The lightning sylphs were complicit somehow. They made a mysterious sort of bargain with the glass ghouls and voilà – *electricks*! Modernity is certainly a fascinating thing. The Marquess said it was wicked, but if we wanted to engage in such un-Fairy-like behavior, it was our funeral. This is still a brave place, September. In the shadow of the Briary, it defies her.' Ell peered into the cool, shadowy lobby, rich with velvet and plush and brass banisters. 'And they serve lemon ices.'

September chipped off another pair of her sceptre's rubies to gain admission to a film called *The Ifrit and the Zeppelin*. She passed them over to a friendly young dryad in a red uniform and a smart bellhop's cap. September knew she was a dryad because her hair was all of shiny green needles like a pine tree's, sticking out bushily from beneath her cap. Also because *dryad* begins with D and Ell greeted her by praising the distant forest. The dryad's eyes shone silver. She had very plump cheeks and smiled both when September asked for tickets and when she paid her rubies.

Shyly, September said, 'If you are a dryad, where is your tree? Are you terribly unhappy here, so far from the forest?'

The ticket dryad laughed, and the sound of it was a little like rain falling on leaves. 'Didn't you know, little love? Film is made with camphor, which *is* a tree. In the cinnamon family, to be exact, which is large and boisterous and gossipy. I run the projector, and my trees run through my fingers all day long! Just because a thing is transparent and silvery and comes in big reels, doesn't mean it's not a tree.'

Thankfully, the theatre was generous and the ceiling high, soaring up like the inside of a cathedral. Ell settled comfortably in the rear row and daintily licked his lemon ice. The lights lowered. September leaned forward, munching popped pomegranate seeds from a little striped box. *It's dryad food, really,* she thought. *I shall certainly be all right.*

At home, she loved the movies. She loved sitting in the

dark, waiting for something wonderful to begin. Especially, the tragic and frightening movies in which ladies fainted dead away and monsters roared up out of the dark. Like in that cartoon her mother had taken her to see when she was very small, in which the dark-haired princess ran away into the terrible forest and the owls flew at her and pecked at her hands. *That* was wonderful – because the world was suddenly alive and excited and wanted things just the way September herself sometimes wanted things. Even if the world seemed mainly not to want a princess bothering it. September had not liked the princess so much, either, as she had a high, breathy voice she found deeply annoying. But the owls and the mines and the flashing eyes in the wood – *that* she had liked. And now she was in the woods, really and truly, with the flashing eyes all around her. What could Fairy movies possibly be like?

'*The Associated Pressed Fairy Moveable Gazette* Proudly Presents: *News from Around Fairyland!*' announced a pleasant female voice as the screen flickered into life. *Oh, jeez,* thought September. *A newsreel. This is what happens when grown-ups run the movies. Can we not skip straight to a dark-haired princess being beset by things?*

'The wedding of Ghiyath the Jann and Rabab the Murid was celebrated with much pomp on the magnetized Arctic shores Tuesday,' continued the smooth, sweet announcer.

'Witches present brewed a bouillabaisse of a long and interesting marriage: five children (one a mermaid), a friendly sort of unfaithfulness for all involved, and an early death for Ghiyath, followed by an extended and scandalous widowhood for Rabab.'

A huge man with skin like desert sand embraced a woman passionately, one flaming hand on her foaming hair, one arm around her sea-slick waist. She wore a dress of anemones that opened and closed. A few similarly wet folk reclined on clouds, applauding, polite and bored. The scene was in black and white, and September slumped back in her chair, impatient for the Ifrit and her zeppelin.

'An exhibit of artifacts from the moon opens Sunday at the Municipal Museum. Scientists have discovered the moon is, in fact, made of pearl and are even now investigating the method by which it is attached to the firmament and what benefits lunar research might reveal for Fairies like you.'

A proud-looking spriggan with a thin, curved nose demonstrated how a piece of moon rock could be dissolved in a mysterious solution. He dropped the stone into a crystal beaker with a three-fingered claw and drank down the draught completely. The scene cut away before any effect might be seen.

'The Changeling Recital at Dandydown Hall went off splendidly last week, featuring an orchestra of violins, oboes, one piano, a nickelstave, two tubas, a lorelei, and a full grummellphone section. The children played Agnes Buttercream's famous *Elegy for Reindeer and Roc's Egg in D Minor.* The conductor unwisely chose a rousing encore of *Ode to Queen Mallow's Third Fingernail,* however, and riot police were called to the scene.'

A host of children in prim black clothing played their instruments furiously on a stage shaped like a huge oak leaf. They all wore identical shoes, which seemed painfully small and tight on their little feet: mary janes very much like September's. A little piece of sad, gentle music played, sashaying into something brighter and livelier, before two unhappy-looking kobolds lifted the conductor unceremoniously off of the stage. The goblins seemed far too strong for their slight height.

'The performance culminated in the righteous punishment of several greenlisted musicians, who certainly deserved whatever they got.'

The same kobolds – or near cousins – hauled several terrified-looking Satyrs onto the flickering gray stage and made them stomp their pan-pipes underfoot. A man in a top hat and mustache brandished a whip menacingly before the scene went dark.

'And finally, our beloved Marquess has concluded a treaty

with the Island-Country of Buyan, bringing prosperity and order to both. We here at the AP extend our praise and adulation to the Lovely Monarch.'

Onscreen, a young girl vigorously shook hands with a large bear. She was tall, but she could not have been a day older than September herself. She wore an ornate suit made for her small frame, an embroidered jacket over a fringed bustle. At her neck was a thin dark tie, like September's father once wore. The girl's hair shone thick and silver in the flickering film, falling to her shoulders in great sausage curls. Most of all, however, September noticed her hat. It was black – or some color that appeared black in the old-fashioned film. It looked a bit like a cake that had fallen over to one side under the weight of peacock and pheasant feathers and chains of jewels that cascaded down from a silk rosette on its flat top. Ribbons, bows, and satin ropes made delicate tiers like icing on its body, and the brim was so crisp and perfect it seemed deathly sharp.

The bear wrinkled his muzzle. He did not look pleased.

September trembled a little. The Marquess seemed so awfully real. She smiled broadly at the bear and laughed silently as the announcer nattered on about the treaty.

And suddenly, without warning, the Marquess onscreen turned toward the camera, her hand still clutched in the bear's paw. She cocked her head to one side like a curious bird. She blinked and leaned forward, looking directly out into the theatre – at September.

'You,' said the Marquess in the announcer's voice. The other patrons twisted to look at September, who froze in terror. 'It's you.'

Ell moved his claw around September's seat protectively.

'September,' said the movie Marquess slowly, as if pulling each letter from a stubborn cabinet. 'You shouldn't be sitting in a theatre on such a lovely day. Why don't you go out and play?'

'I . . .'

'Hush. Listening is tiresome for me. September, if you do not come to the Briary right this very instant, I shall become cross with you. I am a very pleasant Marquess if you are tractable and sweet.'

September could not move. Her hand clutched the bag of pomegranate seeds so tightly they began to spill out of the top. She felt as though she had been caught doing something awful and black. But she hadn't done anything! Not yet! How could the Marquess know her? Where could she hide?

'Right *now,*' snarled the Marquess, 'you *wicked little thief.*' She beckoned horribly with her ringed finger. The screen crackled and flicked. Silver sparks flew for a moment, and then the Marquess's face disappeared in a little burnt ring, and the theatre went suddenly dark.

CHAPTER VIII

An Audience With The Marquess

In Which September Meets the Marquess at Last, Argues Several Valid Points but Is Pressed into Royal Service Anyway, Being Consoled Only by the Acquisition of a Spoon and a New Pair of Shoes

Somewhere, under all those brambles, there was probably a building.

A palace even. Certainly September could make out towers, a portcullis, even a moat of floating golden flowers. Not golden in the darling little way folk in our world call buttercups or certain girls' hair golden: These flowers were genuinely gold, burnished, glowing, deep. Yet they were soft. A pleasant wind crinkled their petals as they drifted along on a lazy current, spinning and gently colliding. But the briars tangled up everything else, great vines – thicker than September herself – whose thorns were awfully sharp and angry looking. They braided each other, ran up and down the walls, snarled in great knots. Here and there were clutches of pale gold berries, their skin so thin that September could see the juice sloshing inside them. But neither she nor the Wyverary could glimpse even an inch of masonry. It was as though the Briary had just *grown* that way and had never been any different.

No guards flanked the door – if it were a door. Large flowers bloomed aggressively through an arch in the brambles in a sort of door-like fashion. Their centers were clotted with glistening pollen. September reached out her hand to touch one, and A-Through-L cried out a wordless warning! But the flower simply soaked her hand in pollen and closed its petals over her fingers, searching and suckling with its silken blossom. Satisfied, it wrinkled away and aside to allow September to duck into a hall hung with dim, sun-dappled shadows.

The flowers drew closed again sharply, keeping the

Wyverary outside. A-Through-L bellowed, and the bellowing of any Wyvern is terrible to hear. He struck the flower; it remained, tough and unyielding as bronze. The brambles writhed a little as if in silent, viny laughter.

September walked through the grand hall, trying not to make noise on the beautiful polished floor. A giant, heart-shaped double staircase ran up to a bank of windows. There was a neat rack on which to place one's shoes and umbrellas. A kind of light drifted in between the bramble-vines, falling on a grandiosely framed painting of a tall, lovely woman with long golden hair tied back with a velvet bow. Her hand rested on a Leopard's head, and in her other, she held a simple wooden hunter's bow. She wore an ivory crown and a smile so wide and kind September felt she could love that lady all the days of her life and never feel cheated, even if the lady never looked twice at such a poor, shabby soul as September. In the painting, she seemed to glow. *That is what a grown-up looks like,* thought September. *Not like the grown-ups in my world who look sad and disappointed and grimy with work and bored with everything. What do the storybooks say?*

'In the fullness of her strength.'

'Did you come all the way here with only one shoe?' came a sweet, wondering voice.

September whirled away from the painting. In the center of the heart-shaped staircase sat a little girl, holding her chin in her hands. She had thick cherry-purple hair that hung in old-fashioned sausage curls to her shoulders and that magnificent, terrible hat poised on her head like a cake tipping to one side. The hat was black, September could see now, as she had guessed when this child had shaken hands with the bear on-screen. The feathers shone blue and green and red and cream-colored. The jewels glittered dark and violet. Next to her, a huge Panther purred languidly and watched September out of one green eye.

'That must have been just *awfully* painful,' the child simpered. 'How brave of you!'

The Marquess ran one hand luxuriously along the Panther's spine, winding her fingers in his fur – and drew up a pair of exquisite black shoes, like September's, if September's shoe had grown up, gone to a great many balls and theatrical to-dos, and found a dashing mate. They had little heels and black crystal lilies on the toes, with bits of ribbon looping and whorling all around, speckled with garnets and tiny black pearls. She held them out to September, whose bare foot, truthfully, ached and throbbed with cold and blisters. She wanted to take them, she did, but taking gifts from wicked Queens, even if they are called Marquesses, even if they are very pretty children not big enough to hurt anyone, is a dangerous business, and September knew it.

She shook her head with much sadness. The shoes were so beautiful.

'I am only trying to help you, child,' said the little girl. She set the shoes gently on the gleaming floor and ran her hand along the cat's spine again. This time, the Marquess drew up a silver plate piled high with wet red cherries, a wedge of black cake crusted with sugar, swollen raspberries and strawberries, several lumps of dark, dusty chocolate, and a tall goblet of steaming hot cider.

'You must be *so* hungry. You've come so far!'

September swallowed. Her throat was dry, her stomach empty. But this was certainly Fairy food. The worst kind, the kind that never let you go if you even taste it once. 'Is that Queen Mallow?' she said instead, nodding toward the portrait and forcing her voice to be friendly.

The Marquess looked up at the great painting and scowled. Her curls shivered and went deep blue, the color of the sea. She sighed and snapped her fingers. The rich plate disappeared.

'You would think that new management would have the right to redecorate. But some magic never bends, not even if you tear at it with your own teeth. No matter how I tear, the portrait stays. She was never that beautiful, though. The painter must have been a loyalist.' The Marquess turned away from Queen Mallow's sweet gaze and focused on September again. She smiled. 'But she *is* dead, my child. I promise you that. Dead as autumn and last year's apple jam. But we haven't come all this way to dish gossip about ancient history. How have you been enjoying Fairyland, September?'

'How do you know my name?'

'You filed papers, of course. You have a visa. What in the world do you think all that is for, if not to make certain that I know everything?'

September didn't say anything.

'Well, I do hope everyone has been nice to you and hospitable in every way they can think of. It's important to me, September, that you're treated well.'

'Oh, yes! Everyone has been terribly helpful and kind – except the Glashtyn, I suppose. I had heard that Fairies were nasty and tricky and cruel, but they're not, not really.'

'Oh?' said the Marquess with arch amusement. She stroked the Panther with her small hands. Her fingers were covered in jeweled rings. 'But they *are,* truly, September. Just the worst sort of folk. You'd never believe how wicked! They're nice because I *make them* nice. Because I *punish them* if they are not nice. Because I put them on the Greenlist if they are not nice. Before I came, Fairyland was a dangerous place, full of brownies spoiling milk and giants stomping on whomever they pleased and trolls telling awful punning riddles. I fixed all that, September. Do you have any idea how difficult it was to invent bureaucracy in a world that didn't even know what a ledger was? To earn their submission, even to the point of having their wings locked down? But I did it. I fixed it for children like you, so that you could be safe here and have lovely adventures with no one troubling you and trying to steal your soul away. I do hope you didn't think you had charmed them all with your sparkling personality, child.'

'Why do you keep calling me a child? You're no older than I am.'

'Really, September. You're going to have to be a bit more discerning than that if you expect to get along here. I suppose I shouldn't expect any better from a Midwesterner. They teach you such frightful things about the world.' The Marquess paused. The tips of her hair grew silver and shining. 'Do you like my Panther? He is called Iago. I love him very much and he loves me. I used to have a Leopard, but she ran off some time ago. Could not change with the times, I suppose.' The Marquess nodded toward the portrait of Queen Mallow, whose hand still rested on a Leopard's head. 'That sort of thing is so tragic, don't you think? I do so prize adaptability.' The Panther Iago growled at the mention of his predecessor.

Could she mean my Leopard? thought September. *The Leopard of Little Breezes?* She did not like to think of the Marquess riding her Leopard, even for a little while.

'Cats are temperamental,' offered September softly. 'I have heard you have lions, too.'

'Too true!' cried the Marquess, her hair wholly silver now, gleaming like true metal. 'On both counts! Lions sleep a great deal, for it is from their dreams that their strength chiefly comes. They are closeted in their chambers, snoozing away on lacy coverlets. Now, I believe you wanted to steal a Spoon from me?'

September bit the inside of her lip. This was not precisely how she had thought her adventure would go. How could she be brave for the sake of the witch Goodbye if she were found out before she could even try?

'Don't be ashamed, my love. I would not be a very good Marquess if I could not tell when troublesome little Ravished children are incoming with poor intentions toward me and my belongings. After all, the Ravished are *always* trouble. Any ruler of Fairyland must learn to watch out for them particularly, as they have a nasty habit of dethroning one and undoing decades of hard work.'

'But . . . Miss Marquess. The Spoon is not one of your belongings. You took it from the witch Goodbye. That's stealing. So it's not really very wicked of me at all to want to steal it back – stealing things back is hardly stealing at all.'

The Marquess cocked her head to one side and smiled. Somehow her smile was worse than her frown. The Panther licked his black paws nonchalantly. 'Is that what she told you? That I stole it? What a dreadful misunderstanding! I shall have her to tea immediately to apologize. You must appreciate my position, September: I was under the impression that all things in my realm belong to me, and Goodbye was under the impression that Good Queen Mallow would arrive at any moment to save her. You can see how things got terribly confused!'

'Where . . .' September cleared her throat. Her hands shook. 'Where I come from, if a person has a Spoon, no one can come and take it just because they're the governor or something.'

'I think that's very naive of you, September.' The Marquess put her finger on her delicate chin as if an extraordinary idea had just occurred to her. 'Tell me, what does your father do?'

September felt her face flush. 'Well, he was a teacher. But now he's a soldier.'

'Oh! Iago, did you hear that? You mean to say that one day the governor or something came and took your father even though you were quite sure he was yours and yours alone? Well, that is certainly different. A Father is nowhere near as valuable as a Spoon! I can see why you prefer your sensible, logical world.'

'Well, they didn't kill anyone in the process!'

'No, September. They wait until little girls like you are out of sight first. War must always be done out of sight, or it shocks people and they stop immediately.' The Marquess's hair slowly deepened to the color of blood.

September squeezed back tears. 'Why did you kill Goodbye and Hello's brothers?' she cried wretchedly.

'Because, child. They were not *nice*. They defied me. But I do not wish to talk about them, or anyone else dead and, therefore, not useful. We were speaking of your parents. I do wish children could pay attention!' Her voice got very hard all of a sudden, no longer bright and full of teatime conversation, but keen and deadly interested. 'What about your mother, September?'

'She . . . she builds engines.' September did not think she ought to mention airplanes in Fairyland – visions of fleets of bombers belonging to the Marquess flooded her mind.

The Marquess stood suddenly. She was wearing a short blackberry-colored dress with violet stockings, all lace and stiff magenta petticoats. She rushed down the stairs to stare

September directly in the eye – they were precisely the same height. The Marquess's blue eyes were full of interest. The Panther slowly descended the stairs behind her, unconcerned.

'What if I told you that I would give you the Spoon? That thievery need never be mentioned between us? You can take it back to Goodbye and her silly sister or use it to stir soups of your own, whatever you like.' The Marquess was very close, as close as kissing. She smelled like beautiful, dying flowers. 'I can be nice, September,' she whispered. 'It is only right that I behave as I require my people to behave. I can help you and pet you and give you lovely presents. I can be a faithful guide.'

September felt much as she had when Goodbye had tried to convince her to be a witch. But there was no glamour. The Marquess was not a witch. It was only that she was so terribly strong and so terribly close. 'But not for nothing,' September whispered. 'Never for nothing.'

'Never for nothing.' The Marquess wavered back and forth like a snake charmer. 'But it is such a little thing, and such fun to get, that I'm sure you will leap at the chance. You want to have fun, don't you? And marvelous adventures? That's why you came to Fairyland, isn't it? To have adventures?'

'Yes . . .'

'Well! What is the use of ruling Fairyland if one cannot make little children happy? There is a place, September, oh, very far from Pandemonium. A place where it is always autumn, where there is always cider and pumpkin pie, where leaves are always orange and fresh-cut wood is always burning, and it is always, just *always* Halloween. Doesn't that sound splendid, September?'

'Yes . . .'

'And in that place is a thing I need, closed up in a glass casket in the heart of the Worsted Wood.'

'But the Green Wind said the Worsted Wood was forbidden—'

'Government has its little privileges.'

'He said it was dangerous—'

'Posh! What does he know? He is not *allowed* here. And never will be, whatever he told you. The Worsted Wood is just *wood*. No more or less dangerous than any other wood. If there are ravening beasts, well, they have every right to live and eat, don't they? If there are spells, they have a right to weave. All you must do is go there and eat candy and have a wonderful time with the spriggans and jump in leaf piles and dance in the moonlight – and before you leave, with a full belly and the first whisper of snow blowing through your hair, open the casket and bring me whatever it is you find there. Even if it is ridiculous, even if it seems useless and small. That isn't so much to ask, is it? In exchange for a Spoon that tells the future?'

'What . . . what is in the casket?'

'That's none of your worry, beautiful child. Your pretty head needn't trouble itself with that.'

September bit the inside of her cheek, but the Marquess was so *close*. She tried to think of the Green Wind, of his pleasant green smell and the clouds whisking by as they flew over Westerly. She felt calmer – a little calmer. Not terribly much calmer.

'Why can't you get it yourself? You can go anywhere . . .'

The Marquess rolled her bright blue eyes. 'If you must know, it's a cranky casket, and if I were to go . . . well, let us say, it would not give me the same gift it would give you, who are innocent and sweet and gentle of spirit.'

'I'm not . . . I'm ill-tempered and irascible . . .'

'Now, who told you that?' The Marquess caressed September's face softly. Her hand was hot, like fire. September flinched beneath her blazing touch. 'How rude of them. You are quite the sweetest child *I've* ever met.'

'I *can't*. I just can't do what you want unless I know what it is. Everyone is afraid of you, and when folk are afraid of a person, it usually means the person is cruel in some way, and

I think you are cruel, Miss Marquess, but please don't punish me for saying it. I think you know you're cruel. I think you like being cruel. I think calling you cruel is the same as calling someone else kind. And I don't want to run errands for someone cruel.'

'I will never be cruel to you, September. You remind me so much of myself.'

'I don't know why you would say something like that when you are a Marquess and I am a nobody, and no one anywhere is afraid of me,' September said, and really, it was quite brave of her. 'Still, I can't.' September blinked several times, trying to clear her head. In her pocket, she clutched the glass ball the Green Wind had given her. 'Unless you tell me the truth,' she said as firmly as she could. 'And give me the Spoon now, not later, when I've returned.'

The Marquess looked at September appraisingly. Her blood-colored hair was slowly lightening to a gentle pink, like candy floss.

'How strong you are, child. You must have eaten your spinach and Brussels sprouts all up and drunk all your milk, once upon a time. Now, let us think! What would a beautiful monarch send you for? Oh, I know! The glass casket contains a magical sword. It is so powerful that it doesn't have a name. It is no spoiled, painted dilettante like Excalibur or Durendal.

Naming a sword like this one would only cheapen it and make it tawdry. But the casket is also old, and also opinionated, and were I to stand in the forest and cut its fastenings . . . well, it would not give me the true sword.'

'But you would use it . . . to kill more witches' brothers, I think . . .'

'September, I swear to you, here and now, in the presence of Iago, Queen Mallow, and your single, solitary shoe, that I will never use that sword to harm a soul. Little unpleasantries are necessary when one rules wicked, tricksterv folk. But I would not soil such a sword by using it for simple, everyday murdering. I intend something much grander.'

September wanted to ask. She burned to ask.

'Ah, but that I will not tell you, little one. You are not ready to know. And loose lips sink *glorious* new worlds. Fairyland is still so beautiful for you. You would not believe me if I told you how sour it can go. Suffice it to say that I shall find the source of this sourness, and with the blade of the sword you bring me, I will cut it out. Will you get it for me? Will you take Goodbye's Spoon and go to the Autumn Provinces in my name?'

September thought of the poor, angry, lost witches, peering into their cauldron while the sea pounded away. She thought of the wairwulf and his kindness to her. She thought of her Wyverary and his chafed, locked wings.

'No,' she squeaked. Blood beat against her brow. She felt dizzy. 'I will do nothing in your name.'

The Marquess shrugged. She bent and kissed the Panther's ears. 'Well, then I shall have your deluded, ridiculous cut-rate dragon rendered into glue and perfume.'

'No!'

Iago growled softly. The Marquess seized September's hand and crushed her fingers in her burning grip. 'I think that's just about enough *nos* out of you, young lady,' she hissed. 'Whom do you think you're talking to? Some country witch? I do not ask favors. I do not beg indulgences from spoiled brats. Only occasionally do I make bargains. I offered you a good one, a fair one! If you do not want to play fair, you cannot expect me to. Iago, go and fetch the Wyvern.'

'No! Please don't! I'll go! I'll go. Just so long as you promise it's not for hurting anyone.'

The Marquess's hair flushed with pleasure, turning a deep pumpkiny orange, just September's favorite shade. She pressed September's hand to her lips – but still she squeezed it, painfully. 'I just knew we would be friends!' she crooned. 'Now that you've stopped being stubborn, let's get that bedraggled old shoe off of you!'

Numbly, automatically, September let the Marquess toss

away her loyal, honest mary jane and slipped the black, beribboned shoes on to her feet. They fit perfectly. Of course, they fit perfectly.

Patting her arm, the Marquess led her to the door of the Briary. September suddenly realized that she had seen nothing at all of the house, knew nothing of the Marquess's powers, knew little more than when she had arrived. She had been *handled* – and with ease.

'Still,' she whispered, her one small defiance. 'I'll take the Spoon now.'

'Of course. I can be so reasonable, when I am obeyed.' The Marquess stroked Iago again. The Panther arched his back, relishing her hand. She drew up a long wooden spoon, much stained, its handle wrapped in leather. September took it and stuck it through the sash of the green smoking jacket.

The Marquess stood on her toes and kissed September's forehead. Her lips alone were cold. When she pulled away, her hair was a deep, dark green.

'Iago will show you out. When we meet again, things between us will have progressed very far, I think.'

Iago took September's mashed hand gently in his mouth and tugged her toward the flower-door.

'Safe travels, September,' called the Marquess brightly. She smiled again, from the bottom of the heart-shaped stair, the sweetest smile September had ever seen on a child. 'And if you do not bring my sword in seven nights' time, I shall have that Spoon back – and your head on a thorn in my garden.'

CHAPTER IX

Saturday's Story

In Which a Wyverary Makes a Sacrifice While September Engages in Wanton Destruction of Lobster Cages and Meets a New Friend

Dazed, trembling, September stumbled out of the Briary, led by the jaws of the Panther. The flower door rustled closed behind her. A-Through-L was gone – he hadn't waited for her. Of course, he hadn't waited. He had known she was weak, that she would give in as soon as the Marquess behaved kindly toward her. He had known her for a rotten, cowardly child. She cursed herself, that she was not braver, not more clever. What is a child brought to Fairyland for if not to thwart wicked rulers? Ell had known she wasn't good enough. September yanked her hand from the cat's mouth and knelt in the grass, staring through growing tears.

'Good grief,' sighed Iago. 'You oughtn't waste time feeling sorry for yourself.'

'I should have said no. A braver girl would have said no. An ill-tempered one.'

'Temperament, you'll find, is highly dependent on time of day, weather, frequency of naps, and whether one has had enough to eat. The Marquess gets what she wants, little girl. There's no shame in being unable to defy her.' The Panther sniffed and scratched at his nose with a black paw. 'And precious little satisfaction in denying her, well do I know.'

'Oh, ho! September!' called a deep, familiar, rolling voice. September leapt up and ran toward it, wheeling around the bramble-wall of the Briary with Iago close behind. The Wyverary stood by the moat bank in a kind of pen, his tail waving back and forth like a dog who has found a stash of bones. A high fence of kimono-silk posts came up to his knee. A-Through-L waved with one foot and then bent to peer into a cage.

The cage was wooden, shabby – a lobster cage, September recognized. The kind lobstermen from far east where Aunt Margaret lived used to drag the creatures off the sea floor. A great many of them lay about, empty, some shattered and broken. Only in one of them, a boy crouched, shivering, his eyes downcast. A boy with dark blue skin and black swirling patterns on his back, curling like waves. He looked up at her, his face drawn and thin, greasy hair tied in a knot on the top of his head. His eyes were huge and black and full of tears.

'Don't let me out,' he whispered. 'I know you'll want to. All good souls want to. But she'll never forgive you.'

Oh, September. Such lonely, lost things you find on your way. It would be easier, if you were the only one lost. But lost children always find each other, in the dark, in the cold. It is as though they are magnetized and can only attract their like. How I would like to lead you to brave, stalwart friends who would protect you and play games with dice and teach you delightful songs that have no sad endings. If you would only leave cages locked and turn away from unloved Wyverns, you could stay Heartless. But you are stubborn and do not listen to your elders.

• • •

September fell to her knees before the lobster cage. 'Oh! But you must be miserable in there!'

'I am,' answered the blue child, 'but you mustn't let me out. I belong to her.'

'Too right he does,' warned the Panther Iago, batting at a little cotton beetle skittering through the dusty pen. 'I wouldn't even consider it if I were you. But then if I were you, I would not be me, and if I were not me, I would not be able to advise you, and if I were unable to advise you, you'd do as you like, so you might as well do as you like and have done with it.'

'Well,' September said slowly, burning to defy the Marquess in something, anything, and make up for her weakness in the Briary. 'This Spoon belonged to her, too, until a few minutes ago.'

'I'm different. I'm a Marid.'

September looked blank. The boy sighed, his tattooed shoulders slumping as if he always suspected the world would be a disappointment.

'Do you know what *djinni* are?' sighed Iago dramatically, as if he could not begin to hear her ignorance.

September shook her head.

'Like genies,' piped up the Wyverary, delighted that he could be helpful, as *djinni* began with D. 'They grant wishes. And wreck things, but mostly grant wishes.'

'Well, he's like a djinn, which is like a . . . genie, like he said.'

'Only I'm not,' said the boy. 'I'm a Marid. Djinni are born in the air. They live in the air. They die in the air. They eat cloud cakes and storm roasts and drink lightning beer. Marids live in the sea. They're born in the sea. They die in the sea. Inside them, the sea is always roaring. Always at high tide. Inside me. And, yes, we grant wishes. And so the Marquess loves us. She has her own burly magic, angry and old. But in the end, she knows she is safe even if her magic should fail, for she has her Marids. We can be made to parcel out her will in wishes.'

'Why don't you just wish your way out of the cage?' asked September, very sensibly.

'It doesn't work like that. I can only grant wishes if I am defeated in battle; if I am hurt nearly to death. I cannot change the rules. When she needs one of us, she beckons. She gives us wooden swords; she is at least sporting.'

'Oh, that's *ghastly,*' breathed September.

'She sends the black cat after us, to the far north where we live. He pounced on my mother, Rabab, and held her still while her fishermen closed me up in a cage. I was small. I could not help her. I wished as hard as I could, but I cannot wrestle myself. I owned a scimitar of frozen salt, and I slashed at the cat with it, but he seized it in his jaws and splintered it, and I shall never see it again, or my mother, or my sisters, or my beautiful, lonely sea, which is so far off I cannot even hear her breathing.'

Iago licked his paw and looked mildly at September. *Go on, little human,* his gaze seemed to say, *tell me I am wicked.*

'But I've heard of Rabab!' said September suddenly. 'I saw her on the newsreel! But she's so young! She's just been married!'

The boy fidgeted. 'Marids . . . are not like others. Our lives are deep, like the sea. We flow in all directions. Everything happens at once, all on top of each other, from the seafloor to the surface. My mother knew it was time to marry because her children had begun to appear, wandering about, grinning at the moon. It's complicated. A Marid might meet her son when she is only twelve and he is twenty-four and spend years searching the deeps for the mate who looks like him, the right mate, the one who was always already her mate. My mother found Ghiyath because he had my eyes.'

'That sounds confusing.'

'Only if you're not a Marid. I knew Rabab as soon as I saw her. She had my nose, and her hair was just the same shade of black as mine. She was walking on the shore; a cloud of mist followed her like a dog. I brought her a flower, a dune daisy. I held it out to her, and we stared at each other for a long time. She said, "Is it time, then?" I said, "Now, we shall play hide and seek." And I ran off down the strand. She still has to have me, of course. It's like a current: We have to go where we're going. There are a great number of us, since we are all forever growing up together and also already grown. As many as sparkles in the sea. We are solitary, though. So as to avoid awkward social situations. But it does mean the Marquess can wrestle us and still have us whole and healthy. We are her cake *and* her having it. I think my older self is already dead.'

'Does that mean you'll never have children or a mate then, if the older you is gone?'

'No, I shall be him presently. I need only wait.'

'You poor thing, how terribly strange your life is! What is your name?'

'Saturday,' the boy said. 'And it is only strange to you.'

'Even so . . . my name is September. And I am not going to let you stay in there, Saturday. Not today, not after everything.'

Now, September might have left well enough alone if she did not feel so terribly guilty about accepting employment with the Marquess. If she were not already thinking of some way to tell the Wyverary (while not looking at his blistered skin under his chain) that they had to go and get a sword for the tyrant. If she did not want to leave some bit of mischief in her wake. She took a step back, drew the Spoon out of her sash, and with a great swing that nearly whacked into Ell's kneecap behind her, she brought the Spoon crashing down on the cage's lock. Splinters of lobster cage flew in a most satisfying fashion.

Saturday crouched back, like a hound certain the dog-catcher is just around the corner. September reached out her hand. The blue boy hesitated.

'Will you beat me if I say no?' he whispered fearfully.

September thought she might cry. 'Oh . . . oh dear. Not all the world is like that. Well. I am not like that.'

The boy took her hand, after all. It was heavier than she expected, as though he were made of sea stone. September was struck by how dark his eyes were, how wide in his thin face. It was like looking into the darkest possible sea, with strange fish at the bottom of it. He stared at her, silent, wild.

'I suppose you fancy yourself brave now, hmmm? A knight?' Iago growled.

'Saturday,' said September, ignoring the Panther. She held the Marid gently around the shoulders. 'Do you think, if I wanted to, could I wish us all away from here and someplace with a warm fire and cider for you and food for all of us and safe harbor and just everything?'

'I told you—'

'No, I know, but we could just pretend to wrestle. And you could give in. That would be all right, wouldn't it?'

Saturday straightened a little. He was taller than September, but not by much. The looping black patterns in his skin made whirlpools on his skinny chest. He wore some sort of sealskin trousers, torn at the knees, worn at the cuffs. 'I cannot cheat. I cannot pretend. And even now, I am strong. I must be made to submit. Like the sea, my grandmother, I cannot be changed – I can only be mastered.' His shoulders slumped. 'But I would rather be gentle. And loved. And never wish for anything, ever.'

'Oh . . . I'm sorry, I didn't mean to offend you.'

'I'm not offended. I'm sorry for you. You will be punished for freeing me. The cat will eat you, probably. Or me. Or both of us. He's very hungry most of the time.'

'He cannot eat Ell. Ell will whack him if he tries, I am sure. And possibly roast him. Come with us, Saturday, come away from Pandemonium. Into the forest, into the wild places where she does not want to go. I am not very tall, but I have a Spoon and a sceptre, and I will protect you if I can.'

The Panther Iago regarded them in a vaguely bored way. 'But I hoped you'd stay for luncheon,' he purred. 'I would have laid my head on your lap.'

'Thank you kindly, but I don't think I'd like that,' said September brightly.

'You're stealing her Marid,' the cat said tonelessly. 'Do you want one of her cannons, too? They're about the same: stupid, dangerous, and useful.'

'He doesn't belong to her!'

'Well, he certainly does.' Iago grinned. His pink tongue flopped out between sharp teeth. 'But I won't tell. Iago won't, no.'

'Why wouldn't you? She's your mistress!'

'Because I'm a cat. A big one, the Panther of Rough Storms, in fact. But still a cat. If there's a saucer of milk to spill, I'd rather spill it than let it lie. If my mistress grows absentminded and leaves a ball of yarn about, I'll bat it between my paws and unravel it. Because it's fun. Because it's what cats do best.' He tried to smile, but his teeth got in the way. 'If I have a mind, I could even help. After all, it would be much more efficient . . . more modern . . . if you could fly to your destination instead of walking all that way. Being a Lieutenant has its small pleasures. Very small, sometimes. I could grant special dispensation to your Wyvern and remove his chains. Temporarily, of course. She would approve of that.'

A-Through-L slowly sat back on his haunches, sending up a cloud of dust.

'I could fly? Really fly? Like when I was small?'

Iago rolled his eyes. 'Yes, like when you were small. Like when you were a wee lizard with nary a care in the world, licking your eyeballs and sucking crows' eggs. Just like life was in that distant Eden of your scaly, wormy youth. How wonderful it will be, I'm sure. Shall I remove them for you?'

Ell looked down at his chains. With his claws, he lifted them in awe and let them fall against his hide. Several times, he opened his mouth to speak, but was overcome. Once, and only once, he allowed himself to look up into the forbidden sky. And at last, he shook his great head. The sun glinted on his horns. 'I . . . I can't,' he said wretchedly. 'Not while my sister M-Through-S can't fly. Not while my brother T-Through-Z can't. Not while my mother wanders on foot. The Marquess is splendid – oh, she is so splendid! If she should appear right this second, I would abase myself in gratitude. But I cannot take her beneficence. I cannot bargain for my own joy alone – no one else gets to fly. Why should I? I am not special, or worthy. If she should appear right this very second, I would beg her, 'Let your magnanimousness find some other soul who longs to fly and unlock her chains.' I will walk wherever it is I wish to go. I will walk to my grandfather the Municipal Library, and he will praise me for my unselfishness. I have walked my whole life. More will not hurt me.'

September's eyes filled with tears. *Why did I not just say no?* She thought wretchedly. But her own voice answered her back: *To save him, so that he could say no if he liked. Glue cannot say yes or no. I did the right thing, I did.*

Iago shrugged his furry shoulders. 'As you like. Saves me the work of picking the lock with my incisor.'

His almond-shaped eyes fixed suddenly on Saturday and narrowed. The Panther padded over to Saturday and sniffed at him. With slinky deliberateness, he licked the boy's face. 'Keep in touch, blueberry-boy. And if you should see my sister again, September, lick her cheek for me.'

Iago strode away, tail held high. The three of them, Ell, September, and Saturday, leaning on September for strength, tried to look as though they belonged and were not doing a thing wrong as they walked quickly to the gate of the Briary, never looking back, not once.

'September,' said the Wyverary wonderingly when the brambles and golden flowers and babbling moat were behind them at last, 'where did you get those shoes?'

CHAPTER X

The Great Velocipede Migration

In Which September, the Wyverary, and Saturday Leave Pandemonium and Make Their Way Across Fairyland by Means of Several Large Bicycles

Well,' said A-Through-L, sniffing hugely through his scarlet nostrils, 'we had better be on our way. *Autumn* begins with A, you know. The Provinces are very far away.'

September stopped in a shadowy alley. On one side of the street rose the toasty-brown woolen wall of a bakery; on the other, the gold lamé of a bank. A Switchpoint on the corner readied its hands, flexing and cracking its hundred bronze fingers.

'Ell, aren't you ashamed of me?' cried September miserably. 'Aren't you going to tell me I'm awful?'

The Wyverary scrunched up his face uncomfortably and hurried on. 'Do you remember where I found you? By the sea? Well, the Autumn Provinces are all the way over by the other sea, on the other side of Fairyland. If I ran dead fast, stopping only to nap and drink, I might make it in something like good time. But you wouldn't. You'd fly right off, or break your bones on my spine as I bounced you!'

'Ell! I'm working for the Marquess! I didn't even stand up to her a little bit! I met the villain – surely, it's obvious she's a villain – and I wasn't brave; I wasn't!'

Ell nuzzled her gently with his enormous head. 'Well, no one expected you to, love. She's a Queen, and Queens have to be obeyed, and even the very bravest aren't brave at all when a Queen tells them they ought to do something. When the lions came to put on my chains, I just sort of lay there and cried. At least you stood on your feet, wee as they are. You said no once – that's more than I've ever done! And for me! To save me! A silly half library lizard. What kind of friend would I be if I scolded you for saving me?' He made a little, weird, wild sound deep in his throat, something like *cluork*.

'When I am weak, when I am poorly, I cannot bear to be scolded. But if it will make you feel loved, I will scold you right proper, I will.'

'And you broke my cage,' added Saturday. 'You didn't have to.' His voice was strange and slushing, as if a crashing wave had stood up and asked after tea. 'The Marquess likes it best when you don't want to do as she says, but you have to do it anyway. That's like . . . a big bowl of soft cream and jam to her.'

'Besides, what's the difference, really, between fetching a Spoon for the witch and fetching a sword for the Marquess? Not much, I'd say.'

September thought about it. 'I suppose it's because I offered to get Goodbye's Spoon for her. I wanted to do it. To make her happy and to do something grand, so that maybe I could be a little grand, too. But the Marquess demanded that I do it, and then she said she'd kill you if I didn't – and me if I didn't do it fast enough. That's not the same thing at all.'

'It's service, though, either way,' said Saturday softly.

'It's *slavery* when you can't say no,' said September, quite sure she was right.

'It's still very far away,' insisted the Wyverary. 'And we haven't any more time than we did a moment ago, indeed, a fair bit less.'

'Why do you keep speaking as if you are coming, Ell? You're here, in Pandemonium! You ought to go to your grandfather and be happy and learned and careful of your fiery breath!'

'Don't be silly, September. I am coming. How could I face my grandfather if he knew I had let a small one go off into dangerous places alone?'

'Not alone,' whispered Saturday.

'How much more lovely would it be to enter the Library with laurels, having accomplished a great deed involving a sword? My grandfather must have hundreds of books praising the deeds of such knights. And we shall all be knights, all three of us! And not punished at all!'

September looked dubiously at him. She neatly tucked her long dark hair behind her ears.

'Please, small friend. Now that I'm here, so close I can smell the glue of his bindings, I am not sure. I am afraid he will not love me. I should feel much better if I had a dashing story to tell him. I should feel much better if I knew you were safe and not crowning the topiaries in the Marquess's garden. I should feel much better if no one could call me a coward. I don't want to be a coward. It is not a nice thing to be.'

September reached up, and the Wyverary dropped his long, curved snout into her hands. She kissed it gently.

'I shall be ever so much more glad if you are with me, Ell.'

Saturday looked away from them, to give them privacy. You could not ask for a more polite Marid, even then, when he was so feral he could only remember to breathe every third breath, polite, and eager to be helpful.

'You're right, of course, the velocipedes *are* running,' he said meekly, as though someone else had suggested it. He was still too shy to suggest anything without wrapping it up tight to keep it safe.

'What a funny, old-fashioned word!' said September, placing her hand on the hilt of the Spoon stuck into her belt. She felt stronger just holding on to it.

'I'm sure you know it means bicycle.' Saturday shifted from one foot to another. September had not thought to find someone more unsure of the world than she. 'I didn't mean to say you didn't know.'

'Oh!' cried Ell. '*Bicycle*! Yes, well, now we're in my section of the alphabet! It's high summer, September! That means the running of the bicycles, and that means Lickety-Split Transportation!'

September looked uncertainly at her denuded sceptre, hanging sadly from Ell's bronze chain. 'I don't think I've anything like enough rubies left to buy bicycles for both of us.'

'Pish! We don't buy; we catch! September, the bicycle

herds, well, I suppose they're called voleries, not herds, right, Saturday? Voleries. Anyhow, their migration path runs though the Meadowflats just east of the City, and if we are lucky and have a bit of rope with us, we can hitch on with them all the way to the Provinces. Or nearly all the way. It's difficult: They're wild beasts, you know. And if I run just as hard as I can, I shall be able to keep up with you, and no one's bones need be smashed or jangled. It goes without saying, I think, that it would be a bit ridiculous for me to ride a highwheel, even a big, brawny bull. Let us go now, right away! I shouldn't want to miss it; we would feel much chagrined, and stuck.'

'September,' pleaded Saturday, his blue eyes growing even wider and darker. 'I have to eat. If I don't eat, I will fall, soon, and not ever get up.'

'Oh, how rude of me!' September had forgotten her own hunger with all the excitement, but now it was back, and all the more insistent. And so, quite without thinking about it, September spent the last of her chipped rubies at a public house called the Toad and the Tabernacle, where the tables and chairs and walls were a deep-black widow's weeds, and the milky yellow light from the silken candelabra made Saturday's skin appear just as black as the ceiling.

'Salt,' whispered the boy regretfully. 'I need salt and stone.'

'Is that what you eat?' September wrinkled her nose.

Saturday drooped in shame. 'It's what the sea eats. When I have been starved, no other food will sustain me. When I am well, I shall have goosefoot tarts and hawthorn custard with you, I'm sure.'

'I didn't mean to hurt your feelings! Please, you mustn't slump so! Besides, I'm not certain I can eat anything here. It's all sure to be Fairy food, and I think I've been reasonable enough about that so far – and safe – but surely eating in a Fairy public house is right out.'

A-Through-L's lips quirked, as if he knew a bit about both Fairies and Food, beginning as they both did with F. But he said nothing. September sat politely and drank a glass of clear water, which was not food in the least and so obviously innocent. She tried to bargain with her stomach not to growl as A-Through-L demolished three plates of radishes and a flagon of genuine Morrowmoss well-water. Saturday gnawed a slab of blue sea-stone and daintily licked a joint of salt. He offered some to her uncertainly, and she demurred politely.

'I have a delicate digestion,' she said. 'I don't think it would bear much stone.'

A platter of painted duck eggs, sweet dense bread, and marshmallow fondue passed by, hoisted on the shoulders of a waiter who might well have been a dwarf. September drank her water vigorously, trying not to look at it. And when all was done and swallowed and September was still hungry but pleased with herself for avoiding temptation, the last of the sceptre went into the toll chest of a much smaller, less splendid ferry. Without incident, its paddle wheel splashed through the other side of the Barleybroom. It took the three of them away from the soft, gleaming spires of Pandemonium and deposited them on a grassy, empty shore.

'It seems so sad to leave,' September remarked mournfully, as she stepped onto the muddy shore, 'when we have only just arrived. How I wish I could get to know Pandemonium a little better!'

September tucked the green smoking jacket under the Wyverary's bronze chain, knotting the sleeves together. The jacket mourned, crying out in silent, emerald-colored consternation. Alas, the ears of folk with legs and noses and eyebrows are not made to hearken to the weeping of those with inseams and buttonholes and lapels. Already, September could hear a kind of thunder in the distance. The Meadowflats stretched long and far around them as they walked: even, well-tempered grass, without tree or welcoming shade or the smallest white flower. If the grass were not so rich and green, she would have called it desolate.

'Remember, they are fast and tall and vicious! Many have

perished or, at least, been roundly dumped off and bruised in the attempt to travel by wild bicycle.' A-Through-L fretted and stamped his great feet in the grass. The thunder grew closer.

September retied the green sash of the smoking jacket around the hilt of the Spoon. No money had remained for proper adventuring equipment, but she was her mother's daughter, always and forever, and felt sure whatever she set her hands to would work. Once, they had spent a whole afternoon fixing Mr Albert's broken-up Model A so that September would not have to walk every day to school, which was several miles away. September would have been happy to watch her mother shoulder-deep in engine grease, but her mother wasn't like that. She made September learn very well how a clutch worked, what to tighten, what to bend, and in the end, September had been so tired, but the car hummed and coughed just like a car ought to. That was what September liked best, now that her mother was not about and she had the freedom to think about her from time to time – to learn things, and her mother knew a great number of them. She never said anything was too hard or too dirty and had never once told September that she would understand when she was older. On account of all of this, September could make a very respectable knot in the sash, and the sash, being part of the jacket, dutifully tightened itself even further and prepared for what was sure to be great discomfort to come. Saturday watched it all with vivid interest but said nothing.

A long, loud horn sounded, and several answering hoots honked into the blazing day.

'They're coming!' shouted Ell excitedly, his wings wobbling under the chains as he leapt up, his tongue lolling like a puppy's. Really, he needn't have said anything. The velocipede volery sent up a choking cloud of dust, and Saturday and September could see quite clearly that as soon as they heard the horns, the bicycles were nearly upon them, a great throng of old-fashioned highwheels, the wheel in front enormous, the wheel behind tiny – though tiny in this case meant somewhat larger than Saturday's whole body. Their seats, borne loftily into the sky, were battered velvet of various motley, dappled shades, their tires spotted like hyenas, their spokes glittering in the naked meadow-flat sun.

'Hold on to me, Saturday!' yelled September. He tucked his arms around her waist, and again she was struck by how heavy he was, when he seemed so small. The horns *sqwonked* again, and as a great, soaring highwheel came roaring by, September threw the Spoon as hard as she could. It flew, far and true, and she clutched the end of the sash, which extended much farther than you might think, so eager was the sash to please its mistress. The Spoon tangled in the spokes of the large wheel, and up they shot into the air, the turning of the wheel pulling them forward. Saturday shut his eyes – but September did not. She laughed as she flew nearer and nearer to the broad speckled orange-and-black seat. She reached out to catch it and just caught her fingers in the copper springs beneath. Her knees banged against the tire and burned against the spinning, bloody and painful – but still, September scrambled up as best she could.

'September! I can't!' Saturday called after her, his blue face contorted with fear and strain as he tried to hold on to her but slipped, more by each minute, until he was only barely clutching her ankle. 'I'll fall!'

September tried to raise her leg and pull him up, but she could not fight the jostling and honking of the velocipede as it angrily tried to dislodge its would-be rider. She hooked her elbow around the musky-smelling seat and reached down as far as she could, her fingers stretched to their limit, to catch him. It was not enough. He could not get hold, and he was so terribly, awfully heavy. September cried out wordlessly as the highwheel reared up, determined to dash her bones against the meadow.

Saturday fell.

He did not shriek. He just looked at September as she

rushed upward, away from him, his dark eyes terribly sad and sorry.

September screamed for him, and the honking horns seemed to laugh in wild victory – at least, one child they could trample underfoot! But Ell came thumping up behind them, his powerful legs knocking weaker, younger velocipedes aside. He caught Saturday by the hair in mid-fall and tossed the Marid up as though he weighed not a thing, bumping him at the last with the tip of his nose so that September could catch his elbow and haul him on to the speckled seat beside her.

He clung to her, shaking a little. September could not make herself let go of the long brass handlebars. Her grip tightened until she could hardly feel her hands, but she bent her head and rubbed her cheek against Saturday's forehead, the way Ell had done with her when she'd been frightened. He seemed to calm a little. Yet still, the noise and dust blew awfully all around them. Ell ran alongside them, whooping and lolling and laughing, as little velocipedes took him for a bull and tried to roll up to ride on his shoulders.

'Excellent save, chickie-dear!' came a hollering voice over the pounding bicycle herd. September looked around and saw on a nearby highwheel a handsome woman with lovely dark-brown skin and wild curly hair. She wore something like a leather bomber jacket with a fleecy collar and a hat with big flopping earflaps. She had on big goggles to keep the dust out of her eyes and thick boots with dozens of buckles over the kind of funny riding pants September had only seen in movies, the kind that bow out on the sides and make one look like one has squirreled away watermelons in one's pockets. Behind her were two delightful things: a pair of iridescent coppery-black wings bound up in a thin chain, and a little girl dressed just the same.

The woman deftly steered her velocipede in and out of the volery to come up alongside them.

'Calpurnia Farthing!' she hollered again over the din. 'And that one's my ward Penny!' The little girl waved cheerfully. She was much younger than September, perhaps only four or five. Her blue-black hair stuck out in tangled pigtails, and she wore a necklace of several bicycle chains which left her neck quite greasy. She wore mary janes like September's old shoes, but the girl's were golden – dirty and muddy, but golden all the same.

'H . . . hello!' answered September, barely holding on.

'You'll get used to it! Gets to be pretty natural after a while, the banging and bedlam! That's quite a cow you've lashed there; she's an alpha and no joking! I'd have tried for one of the milking calves my first time.'

'Beggars can't be—'

'Oh, yes, I'm just congratulating, you know! She's a beaut!'

'Erm, right now, you understand, Miss Farthing, it's hard to carry on a conversation . . .'

'Oh, well, it would be, if you're not accustomed!' Calpurnia Farthing held out her hand. Penny spat a wad of beech-sap gum into it. Calpurnia reached down and wedged the gunk into a broken spoke. Her highwheel screeched, possibly in relief, possibly in indignation at her particular brand of field medicine. 'Well,' she yelled, 'they do stop to drink at night! They've a powerful thirst, you know. Takes hours to slurp their fill!'

'Till then?' said September politely.

'Ayup!' And Calpurnia veered off wildly, with Penny laughing all the way.

The campfire crackled and sparked, sending up smoke into a starry sky. September had never seen so many stars, and Nebraska was never poor in stars. There were so many unfamiliar constellations, spangled with milky galaxies and the occasional wispy comet.

'That's the Lamp,' whispered Saturday, poking the fire with a long stick. He seemed to be most comfortable whispering. 'Up there, with the loopy bit of stars in a circle – that's the handle.'

'Is not,' humphed Ell. 'That's the Wolf's Egg.'

'Wolves don't lay eggs,' said Saturday, staring into the fire.

September looked up in surprise – Saturday had never contradicted anyone yet.

'Well, there's a *story*. I read it when I was a lizard. There's a wolf, a banshee, and a bird of prophecy, and they all make a bet—'

'And the wolf says, "Ain't what's strong, but what's patient,"' said Calpurnia, tossing a palm frond into the fire. Penny threw a clump of grass.

'No, he says, 'Give me that egg, or I'll eat your mother,'' huffed A-Through-L.

'Regional folkloric differences.' Calpurnia shrugged.

The highwheel pilot opened her jacket and pulled out several long strips of dark meat. She passed them around, along with a fancy oakwood flask. Penny gnawed her jerky contentedly.

'What . . . is it?' asked September dubiously.

'What do you think? Dried tire. I share and share alike with fellow velocipeders. Only fair; it's a hard life. Don't turn up your nose at it! It's as good as any other meat. A little gamy, sure, but they're wild. Not all fattened up like mutton. Go on, eat. And drink – that's good axle grease in there. Just as nice as yak blood.'

Ell chomped his and swallowed it right quick. September chewed slowly. This could hardly qualify as food at all, let alone Fairy food. But it wasn't awful, not nearly. And not rubbery in the least. It was as though someone had found an extremely skinny, tough old turkey and burnt it thoroughly in the oven. The flask smelled rich and salty, and when she drank, she came near to spitting it out – or throwing it up – for it was indeed the closest thing to raw blood she had ever tasted. But she felt strength in her afterward, sinewy and springy and warm. Saturday ventured a little tire and a sip of grease but could not stomach it. He nursed a bit of stone he had dug up from the earth instead. Penny stuck out her tongue in disgust.

'That's not nice, love,' admonished Calpurnia. 'Changelings, you know? No manners at all.'

'Is she? Really?'

Penny picked at her golden shoes. *All changelings must wear identifying footwear,* September remembered, as though from a hundred years ago. 'Didn't like the 'chestra,' Penny mumbled. 'Can't play nothin'.'

'She's right. I went to a recital – the poor thing was playing her grummellphone upside down. Fortunate-like, I keep my pockets full of oilcan candy in case I'm in need of bait. I offered her a handful, and she jumped right into my arms. Took to the velos much better – practically born to it, you might say!'

'But a changeling,' said September, 'that's when a Fairy takes a baby and leaves a Fairy in the crib.'

'It's more like . . . a cultural-exchange program,' Calpurnia said, ripping off a chunk of tire in her teeth. Her eyes were wild and golden, and the starlight was all caught up in her wings. September tried not to stare. 'Well, unless they leave a poppet. That's just a bit of a joke. But usually, we swap them out again when they grow up, and everyone's the wiser for solid communication between realms. It's nice. Well, not nice, but fun. I'm not having that for my Penny, though! Princess of the Highwheels, I'll have her up to be!'

'I talk to the little velos,' whispered the child. 'They say, "Penny, where's your seat?" '

'I don't approve of the changeling orchestra. It's not pretty; it's just a zoo, really. For rich Fairies – who are in good with Miss Fancy Curls herself – to peer at. Couldn't bear that for such a sweet thing as Penny. Time was, changelings were the toast of the town, fed with biscuits and new cream and got to dance at the Thistle-Balls in the spring, dance until their shoes wore through and then dance some more—'

'That doesn't sound quite nice either . . .' said September uncertainly.

'Well, it's a certain sight better than being strapped to a grummellphone until your spine grows W-shaped!'

'Grum'phone sounds like a cow chucking, anyway,' Penny groused.

'That's right, chickie-love. And you never have to play one again. Anyway, I don't approve of chamber music in general. It's stuck-up on itself. Much prefer the velo horns.'

'What was her name before?' asked September.

'That's private. No one needs to know that but her.'

'Molly!' piped Penny. 'I was a Molly! And I had a Sarah and a Donald, and they were a sister and a brother. And I had a velo of my own! Only it wasn't wild, and it didn't talk. It was pink, and it had a little bell and three wheels instead of two. But I didn't have a Calpurnia, so I must have been sad. I don't remember, really.'

They were all silent for a while, staring into the fire as those not possessing tires and spokes have done since the dawn of the world. The Wyverary drifted helplessly to sleep, sitting up. He snored lightly; it sounded like pages turning. Calpurnia scratched under her hat

'Where are you lot off to, then? You'll pardon, you don't seem like the lifestyle type. Short-term transport, am I right?'

'The Autumn Provinces,' answered Saturday, his voice echoing low among the snorting, snuffling highwheels as they teemed around their watering hole and spun their spokes in antique mating dances.

September found she did not want to say why they were going. She delicately wrapped the sash of the smoking jacket around her recovered Spoon. Calpurnia whistled.

'Ayup, that's a respectable haul! We ought to make that in a week or two. Hope you brought comestibles of your own!'

'A week or two!' cried September. 'But that's not fast enough! We need to get there and back in seven days.'

Penny giggled. 'Can't do it!'

But Calpurnia was thinking. She scratched her chin with three long brown fingers, then licked them and held them up to the wind. 'Aye, but we might . . . if you think you can handle your alpha. I don't like to do it, but I'm not so dense as to miss that you're running hard, and that almost always means there's a beast behind you.'

September nodded miserably.

'Well, a velo is a lazy thing in the end. They don't like to go as fast as they can go. It suits them just as well to roll along leisurely-like. This is the Great Migration – they're all homebound, to the spoke nests, to mate and die. Some of them feel the mating drive stronger than others. Some only feel the dying drive. Makes them lag. But if you and I apply a bit of encouragement, they'll bear down on the road like it's dinner. And by encouragement I mean whipping of course and I know it's not civilized and I cringe to think of it but sometimes with steeds it's all you can do.'

'Don't want to whip my velos,' Penny whimpered.

'They forget, chickie. They'll all forget.'

'No they won't! They'll whisper, "That Penny, she's naughty and nasty!" '

'Penny, you don't have to do a thing,' said Saturday gently, who knew a thing or two about whipping.

'But Saturday, we've so little time . . .'

Saturday looked at September for a moment, his expression, as always, unreadable. Then he leaned over and rubbed his cheek against her forehead just as she had done to him. The Marid got up and walked away from the fire into the dark and wavering grass and the volerie of snorting, spinning velocipedes.

'Is he yours, then?' Calpurnia asked, draining her wooden flask with relish. She spat into her goggles and rubbed them clean with her fingers.

Mine? No, he's his own.

Calpurnia grunted doubtfully and squinted at the dark.

'Miss Farthing, may I ask you a question?'

'How can I deny such a nicely wrapped request?'

'Are you helping us because you want to? Because you like us, because you're friendly and good-hearted? Or because the Marquess wants you to be nice? Because she'll greenlist you if you're not?'

Calpurnia Farthing looked long and deep into September's eyes. She felt as though she was naked again, as she had been in the bath house. The Fairy's golden gaze seemed heavy and hot.

'What makes you think I'm not already greenlisted, girl? Do you think taking a changeling out of the orchestra comes at no price at all?' She tugged on the flaps of her hat. 'If it will make you feel better, I can lead you to a pit in the forest or steal your breath or whatever it is I might – and I'm not admitting to anything – have done in my profligate youth. These days, I have my highwheels and my girl to look after. Hardly time to go spoiling the barley for beer. Maybe when I retire, I'll go back to it. But if it pleases the Marquess to think that her hoofing list is all that's keeping me in my place, then let her think it. Mainly, I'll help you because lost little human girls are a hobby of mine.' Penny snuggled up to Calpurnia and laid her head on her lap. The Fairy woman stroked her changeling's matted hair. September smiled. She liked them. She felt safe with them near.

Out of the dark, Saturday returned amid much grinding and crushing noises, leading two huge highwheels behind him. They rolled along docilely, each leaning in to nuzzle the other's handlebars occasionally.

'They'll take us as fast as they can – faster, even,' said Saturday firmly. 'They're ready to go home, they don't want to wait. They'll leave right now if we want. They've drunk their fill.'

'Hey! Only I talk to them!' said Penny, hands on her little hips.

Saturday shook his head and crouched next to her, his wild blue hair catching the firelight and blazing orange. 'There's not a creature living that doesn't have wishes, Penny. And I can always hear wishing, even the very quietest kind.' The Marid stood up. 'No whipping,' he said softly, almost embarrassed. 'Not ever. Not even if the whipping would make them do your will as fast as blinking. Especially *if*.'

Calpurnia Farthing held out her hand. Saturday shook it, thought better, and then kissed it in a very courtly way. 'I said I didn't like to whip anyone. They'd have forgiven me. Probably not you, but me, they would have loved again.'

'I know,' whispered Saturday.

Calpurnia slapped her thigh. 'Let's be off then. I'll see you to the edge of the equinox. Leastaways I can do, for such raw wheelers as you and yours.'

Into the silver-spangled night, two great bicycles rolled silently, bearing them all into the dark, so swift the moon never saw them go. A-Through-L ran beside them, his tongue clamped between his teeth, willing his legs to pump faster.

'Calpurnia,' said September, when they had left the last ruddy light of the campfire behind them, 'I thought Fairies danced in reels together and had big families.'

'Ayup, we do.'

'Then why are you alone? And Charlie Crunchcrab, too? Where has everyone gone?'

Calpurnia turned her face away. Her wings fluttered weakly under their iron chain, and September could see where red hives had boiled up under the metal. *It's the iron,* she thought, *Fairies are allergic.*

When Calpurnia Farthing, Queen of the Velocipedes, looked out across the flats again, her face was streaked with silent, stubborn tears.

CHAPTER XI

The Satrap of Autumn

In Which September Finally Eats Fairy Food, Very Nearly Matriculates, and Discovers the Nature of Autumn

I suppose you think you know what autumn looks like. Even if you live in the Los Angeles dreamed of by September's schoolmates, you have surely seen postcards and photographs of the kind of autumn I mean. The trees go all red and blazing orange and gold, and wood fires burn at night so that everything smells of crisp branches. The world rolls about delightedly in a heap of cider and candy and apples and pumpkins, and cold stars rush by through wispy, ragged clouds, past a moon like a bony knee. You have, no doubt, experienced a Halloween or two.

Autumn in Fairyland is all of that, of course. You would never feel cheated by the colors of a Fairyland forest or the morbidity of the Fairyland moon. And the Halloween masks! Oh, how they glitter, how they curl, how their beaks and jaws hook and barb! But to wander through autumn in Fairyland is to look into a murky pool, seeing only a hazy reflection of the Autumn Provinces' eternal fall. And human autumn is but a cast-off photograph of that reflecting pool, half burnt and drifting through the space between us and Fairyland.

And so I may tell you that the leaves began to turn red as September and her friends rushed through the suddenly cold air on their snorting, roaring highwheels, and you might believe me. But no red you have ever seen could touch the crimson bleed of the trees in that place. No oak gone gnarled and orange with October is half as bright as the boughs that bent over September's head, dropping their hard, sweet acorns into her spinning spokes. But you must try as hard as you can. Squeeze your eyes closed, as tight as you can, and think of all your favorite autumns, crisp and perfect, all bound up together like a stack of cards. That is what it is like, the awful, wonderful brightness of Fairy colors. Try to smell the hard, pale wood sending up sharp, green smoke into the afternoon. To feel the mellow, golden sun on your skin, more gentle and cozier and more golden than even the light of your favorite reading nook at the close of the day.

September's orange dress seemed suddenly drab; the Wyverary's scarlet skin looked a bit brown and dull. They could not compete – but they laughed all the same, as leaves drifted slowly from trees and fell into their hair. Penny balanced expertly on her highwheel seat and reached up to catch them out of the air, whooping and giggling.

'Ah, Penny, we'll not go in, though,' sighed Calpurnia Farthing, raising her goggles to drink in the colors of the forest ahead of them, its shady paths, its mournful brown birds.

'Oh, why not, Cal? They're sure to have flapjacks! I'm hungry!'

'We have to bring in the herd, love. The highwheels' home is off farther toward the sea, in the oil tides and the nickel pools. We'll camp, and I'll sing you "The Nobell Lay of the Unicycle and the One-Legged Gyrl" – you like that one! The rest of the velos will catch up, and we'll take them down to the water's edge, and I'll let you have a puff of my pipe.'

'Can't we just stay one night?' Penny pleaded, pulling her pigtails.

Calpurnia shuddered. 'It's best . . . not to go in if you don't have doings there. Autumn has a hungry heart – September is the beginning of death.' The Fairy looked at the earnest girl in the orange dress and laughed shortly, realizing what she had said. 'Well . . . Pan forgives all puns. Be glad autumn is brief, Penny, in our familiars. As for you, September, I feel a powerful urge to tell you to be careful, but I think you've lead ears for such advice. Just remember that autumn is also called *fall,* and some falling places are so deep there's no climbing out.'

'Goodbye, dragon!' chirped Penny, and A-Through-L, still panting from his great exertion across the plains – three days' running with barely a break for napping – did not argue with her but tolerated her smacking a kiss on his toes. 'Goodbye, Saturday!'

Calpurnia Farthing brusquely extended her hand to Saturday, but when he moved to shake it, she grabbed it up and kissed his fingers like a lord kissing a lady's hand. She crouched down to look the boy in the eye. 'I have a thing to tell you, Marid.'

Saturday waited patiently.

'We're not kin, but fey to fey, you'll hark?'

He nodded. She leaned in to whisper in his ear so that September could not hear.

But we have special privileges. I shall tell you what Calpurnia Farthing said. 'The riddle of the Ravished,' she whispered, 'is that they must always go down into the black naked and lonesome. But they cannot come back up into the light alone.'

The light in the Autumn Provinces is always late afternoon light, the golden, perfect kind that slants and sighs, that casts gentle shadows on the earth.

Of course, September had no shadow.

But the shadows of the others walked long and thin through the forest of bloody-bright trees. They were disturbed by their missing compatriot, and pulled away from the place where September's shadow was not. Shadows have a kind of camaraderie. As folk become friends and have adventures, so, too, do their shadows frolick and quaver in fear and emerge triumphant from battles with enemies' shadows, all unknown to us, who think we are the movers of our tales. And so the shadow of the Wyverary mourned the loss of his companion, and the shadow of the Marid caught its black mood.

And yet, none among them could keep from delight as many paths opened up wide and even before them, a bed of crisp brown leaves blowing up in little dervishes and settling again. A few mournful birds sang out. The wind smelled of smoke, and baking bread, and apples. Saturday closed his eyes and breathed through his mouth like a cat to take it all in. A-Through-L fairly skipped.

'Truly, Autumn is my season,' the scarlet beast chortled. 'Spring and Summer and Winter all begin with such late letters! But Autumn and Fall, I have loved best, because they are best to love.'

The three of them might have taken any path through the forest and come upon little but toadstools and acorns. However, on account of the tendencies of Fairy towns to get quite firmly in one's way, they did not. They found themselves striding into the herald's square of a place called Mercurio before they could discuss whether it was nightingales or sparrows that sang so prettily in the woods. That September's shoes were dark and crafty and most certainly knew their way around the world can have had nothing to do with it, I am sure.

I wonder if every city in Fairyland is made of some strange thing? thought September. For some mad baker had built the town of Mercurio from loaves of thick, moist bread shingled with sugar and mortared with butter. Heavy eaves of brown crust shaded sweet little dinner-bun doors. Many of the houses were small. September could reach up her hand and tear off a piece of their roofs to eat if she had had a mind. But many more were enormous, towering up high, cakes piled upon cakes, baked dark and fragrant, up past the tops of the trees. The cobbles of the square were muffin-tops, and all the fountains gushed fresh, sweet milk. It was as though the witch who built the gingerbread house in the story had a great number of friends and had decided to start up a collective.

In the center of the square stood a statue of a lady September knew well by now, patted together from cream-colored crumpets. Below her benevolent gaze, a long table groaned with food: apple dumplings and apple tartlets and candied apples and apple chutney in big crystal bowls, huge roasted geese glistening brown and gold, giant potatoes and turnips split and steaming, rum cakes and blackberry pies, sheafs of toffee bundled together like wheat, squash soup in tureens shaped like stars, golden pancakes, slabs of gingerbread, piles of hazelnuts and walnuts, butter domes carved like pine cones, a stupendous broiled boar with a pear in his mouth and parsley in his hoofs. And pumpkin, pumpkin everywhere: orange pumpkin soup bubbling in hollowed-out gourds, pumpkin bread, pumpkin muffins, frothy pumpkin milk, pumpkin trifles piled up with whipped cream, pumpkin-stuffed quail, and pumpkin pies of every size cooling on the clean tablecloth.

No one ate at the table or guarded the feast. The Wyverary,

the Marid, and the human stared in naked hunger, having had nothing but tire-jerky and axle-whiskey for days. Ell stepped forward but hesitated.

'Surely, it belongs to someone,' he fretted.

'Surely,' agreed Saturday.

'I oughtn't to have any, anyway,' said September mournfully. 'A feast out of nowhere and no one here who might have cooked it or had it cooked for them? That's Fairy food to be sure.'

A little man stepped deftly out from behind the pig, as if he had been there all along, though surely they had seen no feet under the table. His nose curved down: long, skinny, hooked like a bird's beak, the kind meant for fishing beetles out of logs. A pair of square spectacles perched on it, showing large, orange, red-rimmed eyes, as if tired from too much reading. He rubbed his little hands together – they each had only two fingers and a thumb, long and hooked like his nose. His skin was all over deep, baked brown, like good bread. Most odd of all, however, were his clothes: He wore a tweed jacket with velvet elbow patches; a caramel-colored waistcoat; toast-brown plaid trousers; and an oak-leaf ascot, fading from green to brown, full of wispy holes, pinned with an acorn button. Over all this, a white laboratory jacket, gone yellow with age, draped over his hunched shoulders.

'Of course it's Fairy food,' he chuckled. 'Where do you think you are?'

'Well,' September answered, 'I'm not to eat Fairy food. I've been very careful and only eaten witch food, dragon food, dryad food, that sort of thing.'

The little man laughed so loudly a few folk like him poked their heads out of the bread-house windows in curiosity. He held his small paunch and kept giggling.

'Oh, you were being serious!' He tried to look solemn. 'This is *Fairyland,* girl! There is no dragon food or witch food or dryad food. There is only Fairy food – it's all Fairy food. This is Fairy earth that bears it, Fairy hands that carve it and cook it and serve it. I daresay you have quite the bellyful of the stuff. If there's damage to be got from it, I promise it's quite done by now.'

September's mouth dropped open. Her eyes filled up with tears, and now, finally, they spilled over and dropped on to the muffin-stone square. Saturday put his hand on her arm but did not know what to do to comfort her beyond that. This may seem like a silly thing to cry over, but September had suffered so very much in such a very short time, and she was so certain that she had been circumspect with regards to food. She *had* been careful! Even if the Marquess was frightening and Saturday so dear and broken and Ell so devoted – at least, she had thought, she had not eaten Fairy food! At least, she had managed better than most little girls in stories who are *repeatedly* told not to eat the food but do it anyway, being extravagantly silly and stupid!

'What will happen to me?' she wept.

A-Through-L waved his tail in distress. 'We can't say, September. We're not Ravished.'

'But look on the bright side!' cried the little man. 'Eat your fill and have no fear of it now. Fairy food is the best kind – or else no one would have to warn children off it. I think it's very dear of you to have tried to be so . . . abstinent! My name is Doctor Fallow, and I am the Satrap of Autumn. We had word that guests were careening our way.' He bowed at the waist and caught his jacket in the act of slipping off. 'This is a wedding feast for my graduate assistants, and you are most invited.'

September bowed as well. 'These are my friends A-Through-L, who is a Wyvern and not a dragon, and Saturday. My name is September.'

Doctor Fallow beamed. 'What an *excellent* name,' he breathed.

A great, jubilant noise rose up from the southern end of the village, and it became clear in a moment why they had found the square so empty. Everyone who was anyone had been at the party. A throng of creatures like Doctor Fallow, with long skinny noses and dear little clothes, came dancing in with crowns of leaves in their hair – for the leaves of the Autumn Provinces are brighter than any flower. Many wore glittery masks in black and gold and red and silver. Some played delicate twig pipes, some sang rude songs that greatly featured the words *swelling, growing,* and *stretching* in complicated puns.

'I . . . I think they must be spriggans,' said Ell, embarrassed. Naturally, he could offer no further illumination on anything that so rudely insisted on beginning with S.

At the head of the host came a pair of spriggans, looking at each other under the lashes of their eyes, blushing, smiling, laughing. One, a young man, was red from the tips of his hair to the tips of his feet, his skin glowing like an apple, his evening suit crimson from cuff to cuff link. The other, a young girl, was golden from lash to leg, her hair just the exact color of a yellow leaf, her gown butter bright.

'The red fellow is Rubedo,' Doctor Fallow said jovially. 'He specializes in Gross Matter, quite a promising lad, a bit iffy on the mathematics, of course. The doe is Citrinitas, my star pupil. She's at work on the highest alchemical mysteries, all of which must be solved, like a detective solves a dastardly crime. I'm so pleased for them both I could sprout!' He drew a faded orange kerchief from his pocket and dabbed at his eyes.

'Please,' called Citrinitas, her voice ringing out bright and clear as sunlight through the deepening evening. 'Eat! We shall all have bad luck if a single soul goes hungry!'

Ell trodded up to the table, happy as anything. 'I don't suppose you've any radishes, hm?' he asked – and no sooner than he had, a little spriggan lad held up a plate of shining red radishes, so bright they must have been polished. Saturday inched toward the table, looking apologetically back at September.

'Well,' she said, 'if the damage is already done . . . it certainly *does* look delicious. And I have a weakness for pumpkin.' Her mother often liked to say she had a weakness for things: for hot cocoa, for exciting novels, for mechanics' magazines, for her father. September felt it quite a grown-up thing to say.

Let it be said that no other child has ever eaten as September did that night. She tasted a bit of everything – some things more than others, for Fairy food is a most adventurous cuisine, complex and daring. She even sipped the hazelnut beer and slurped at the cauliflower ice cream. Together, she and Saturday took on the challenge of a Gagana's Egg, which was not really an egg at all, he explained, but a sugar-glazed shell of many colors containing a whole meal. Saturday deftly placed eight bone cups around a massive copper-rose globe. Saturday pierced the egg with an ice pick (thoughtfully provided) in eight places and let the steaming liquid spill into the little cups in eight different colors. September delighted in each one: the violet brew that tasted of roasted chestnuts and honey; the bloody red one that tasted like fig pastry; the creamy pink one, a kind of limy rosewater treacle. Saturday drank, too, always after her. His stomach was still weary from starving, and he would have preferred a nice salt lick and a lump of schist, but for her, he would eat any sugar, drink any red draught. When September finished the cups, Saturday showed her how to pierce the top hemisphere of the egg four more times so that the top of the shell could be lifted away whole and filled with water to steep into a sort of gooseberry-tasting tea. Inside the egg, a golden broiled bird nestled next to oil-soaked bread, brandied clams, and several fiery, spicy fruits September could not name but which quite took her breath away.

Indeed, by the end of the feast, she was only sorry to have waited so long to gorge herself on Fairy food.

Doctor Fallow belched loudly. 'Have you strength in you still to see my offices? I think you'd find them most interesting.' The spriggan's eyes flashed like a wolf's in the candlelight, for it was now quite dark. The stars of autumn wheeled overhead, hard and bright and cold. A lonely wind began to pick up outside the warm, ruddy village. 'Rubedo and Citrinitas must come along, too, of course.'

'But it's their wedding night!' protested September. 'Surely, they would like to retire with milk and a nice book!'

Ell snorted. Bits of radish remained in his whiskers. In the firelight, his eyes seemed crinkly and soft. September remembered what he said, that they belonged to each other. She rather liked to think that. She felt it was a thing she might take out and look at when all was dark and cold, and it might warm her.

Doctor Fallow waved his hand. 'Rubbish. Every night is their wedding. Every night is their feast. Tomorrow, too, they will be married with just as much pomp and song, and we will eat just as well and then go to my offices, for work must be done even on wedding nights. And then we will do it all over again. How wonderful is ritual, what a comfort in dark times!'

September remembered what the Marquess had said: *'A place where it is always autumn, where there is always cider and pumpkin pie, where leaves are always orange and fresh-cut wood is always burning, and it is always, just* always *Halloween.'* And so it was – so many of the spriggans wore masks and danced wildly and leapt out from the shadows to spook one another.

'You may as well come along, September. You were expected, and the expected ought to do what they're told. It's only manners.'

'But the casket in the woods . . . I don't have much time. . . . It took so long to get here!'

'All that tomorrow, my dear! You can't worry on a full stomach!'

The whole colorful throng of them, Rubedo and Citrinitas arm in arm, A-Through-L prickly and guarded, Saturday walking silently just behind September, his eyes huge and wary, September herself, and Doctor Fallow leading the way, crossed the square to one of the largest buildings. Thready clouds hid its roof up above the crowns of the trees. It seemed far too big for the little folk.

Doctor Fallow waggled his bushy eyebrows, winked twice, pinched his long nose, puffed out his cheeks, and spun around on one foot. Rubedo and Citrinitas did the same – and all three of them sprouted up like nothing you've seen: swelled, grew, stretched, until they were taller than A-Through-L and of a perfect size to enter the huge building.

'I . . . don't think I'm of a girth to walk comfortably in there,' sighed Ell. 'Though I'm certainly of a height. I shall wait outside. If anything proves wonderful there, do yell out the window.' He settled down, heavy with radishes, to nap in the courtyard of Doctor Fallow's office.

• • •

As they passed through doors and down hallways, the spriggans swelled up and shrunk down to fit each passageway. September and Saturday sometimes had to crawl on their bellies and sometimes could not even see the top of the door frames above them, and they had to scale the staircases like mountain climbers. The building could only be comfortable to a spriggan. Finally, the spriggans settled into something smaller than they had been when they entered – but taller than they had been at the feast – and opened the door to a great laboratory full of bubbling things.

'The heart of our university,' said Doctor Fallow expansively. 'Only *broadly* speaking a university, of course.'

'We don't have classes, really,' said Rubedo.

'Or exams,' said Citrinitas.

'And we're the only students,' they said together.

'But no work is more important than ours,' finished Rubedo.

'You're . . . alchemists, right?' said September shyly. She remembered, *'The practice of alchemy is forbidden to all except young ladies born on Tuesdays'* and spriggans, who were exempt from everything, if the Green Wind was to be believed.

'Exact as an *equation*!' crowed Doctor Fallow.

'Then I should tell you I was born on a Tuesday.'

'How *marvelous*!' exclaimed Citrinitas. 'I am so weary of running all the student committees myself.'

'And what use I could make of an assistant! The volume of papers is monstrous,' said Rubedo ruefully, glaring at his wife.

'Now, now, let's not be hasty,' said Doctor Fallow, raising his hands for silence. 'The young lady can have no more than the most rudimentary understanding of the Noble Science. Perhaps she would rather be a rutabaga farmer. I hear the market is very good this year.'

'It's . . . turning lead to gold, right?' said September.

All three spriggans laughed uproariously. Saturday flinched – he did not like people laughing at September.

'Oh, we solved that *long* ago!' Rubedo chuckled. 'I believe that was Greengallows, Henrik Greengallows? Is that right, my love? Ancient history has never been my subject. A famous case study even reported a method for turning straw into gold! The young lady who discovered it wrote a really rather thin paper – but she toured the lecture circuit for years! Her firstborn refined it, so that she could make *straw* from gold and solve the terrible problem of housing for destitute brownies.'

'*Hedwig* Greengallows, my dear,' mused Citrinitas. 'Henrik was just her mercurer. Men are so awfully fond of attributing women's work to their brothers! But, September, you have no idea how freed we all felt by Hedwig's breakthrough. It is tedious to spend centuries on one problem. Now, we have several departments. Rubedo labors at the task of turning gold to bread, so that we may eat our abundance, while I am writing my dissertation on the Elixir Mortis – the Elixir of Death.'

'It seems to me,' said Saturday shyly, 'that the country of Autumn is a strange place to conduct experiments. Nothing here changes, yet alchemy is the science of change.'

'What a well-spoken boy!' exclaimed Doctor Fallow. 'But truly, the Autumn Provinces provide the most ideal situation for our program. Autumn is the very soul of metamorphosis, a time when the world is poised at the door of winter – which is the door of death – but has not yet fallen. It is a world of contradictions: a time of harvest and plenty but also of cold and hardship. Here we dwell in the midst of life, but we know most keenly that all things must pass away and shrivel. Autumn turns the world from one thing into another. The year is seasoned and wise but not yet decrepit or senile. If you wrote a letter of requisition, you could ask for no better place to practise alchemy.'

'What is the Elixir of Death?' asked September, running her fingers along several strange instruments: a scalpel with a bit of mercury clinging to it, scissors with a great mass of golden hair caught in the shears, a jar full of thick liquid that shifted back and forth from yellow to red.

Citrinitas brightened – if that were possible. She clutched her three-fingered hands to her breast. 'Oh, nothing could be more fascinating! The Elixir of Life, as you will certainly know, is produced via the *Chymical* Wedding, a most secret process. The resulting stuff makes one immortal. The Elixir of Death, more rare by far, returns the dead to life. I expect you've heard the tale of the boy and the wolf? No? Well, it was terrible: The boy's brothers betrayed him and cut him all up, but his friend the wolf got himself a vial of the water of Death and fixed him right up. It's quite a famous story. Death herself produces the Elixir, when she is moved to weep – not a frequent occurrence, I assure you! I am trying to synthesize it from less . . . esoteric ingredients.'

'And the casket in the Worsted Wood? Where does that fit in to all these strange studies?' said September shrewdly.

'Well,' said Rubedo uncertainly, 'the Worsted Wood lies at the heart of the Autumn country. None of us go in. The geese here, they migrate each evening, and one of them said a girl was on her way who would want to enter the woods, and we felt sorry for her.'

'You are certainly welcome to, though none of us can

truly recommend it,' said Doctor Fallow, rushing his words. 'We confess – we made the casket. One of my undergraduate projects, I'm afraid! *Quite* a long time ago. You're the first to show any interest in it since, oh, since Queen Mallow claimed her sword here, I expect.'

September started. 'It's Queen Mallow's sword?'

'No, no, I didn't say that, did I, girl? I said she claimed it. You can't claim something that's already yours. If it's yours, it's yours, eh? The casket is really quite clever. I received first marks for it. How shall I explain? It is both empty and full until one opens it. For when a box is shut, you cannot tell what it might contain, so you might as well say it contains everything, because, really, it could contain anything, see? But when you open it, you affect what is inside. Observing something changes it, that's a law, nothing to be done. Oh, you'll see in the morning! How splendid you will find it!'

'But, September,' said Citrinitas sadly, 'these sorts of things, well . . . they're always guarded, aren't they? It might be best to enroll with us now and worry about the casket when you've progressed in your studies a bit.'

'I can't! I haven't time. I must open the casket tomorrow, or I shan't have time to get back before the Marquess has my head!'

'September,' whispered Saturday.

'Perhaps you'd like to decide on your class schedule now, then? I have room in my morning Hermetics lecture, and I expect Citrinitas will be happy to get you up to speed in Elemental Affinities.'

'September!' Saturday said, more loudly, but the spriggans were exclaiming and pulling at her, and she could not hear him.

'We've even a free space on the squash team! How fortunate!' cried Rubedo, clapping his ruddy hands.

'September!' wailed Saturday, tugging at her sleeve. Finally, she turned to him, flustered by all the yelling.

'What?' she said, shaken.

'Your hair is turning red,' Saturday said softly, embarrassed to have all the attention suddenly on him.

September looked down at her long, dark hair. One curl had indeed turned blazing scarlet, terribly bright against the rest of her. She touched it, amazed, and as her fingers brushed the red lock, it broke off and drifted off on an unseen wind, for all the world like an autumn leaf wafting away.

CHAPTER XII

The Mother's Sword

In Which September Enters the Worsted Wood, Loses All Her Hair, Meets Her Death, and Sings It to Sleep

'It's because I ate the food,' sniffed September miserably, hiding her face in the Wyverary's chest. A-Through-L lay on the leafy ground like a Sphinx, nuzzling her hair with his nose. He stopped that right quick, though, as more of it broke off and sailed away into the night.

'Don't be silly,' he said. 'We ate it, too!'

'What's happening to me?' September wept.

Her hair shone, bright red, curling up at the edges in pretty shapes. She had already lost much of it. The spriggans looked discomfited but they tried to be cheery.

'I think it's rather nice!' chirped Doctor Fallow. 'An improvement, I declare!'

'You *do* match me, now,' said Ell, trying to be helpful and optimistic.

September rolled back the sleeve of the green smoking jacket, which was terribly chagrined and tried to keep covering her to protect her, but in the end, she wrestled the sleeve up to her elbow and waved her hand for the doctor to see. The skin there, once the same warm brown as her father's, had gone hoary and rough, tinged with gray and green, like bark.

'Is this an improvement?' she cried.

'Well, this sort of thing happens. We must be adaptable. Autumn is the kingdom where everything changes. When you leave, it'll be all right, probably. If you haven't put down roots yet.'

'Still, about my syllabus . . .' insisted Rubedo. Citrinitas elbowed him roughly.

September rubbed her eyes with the heels of her hands, which had begun to grow a healthy bit of silver moss. 'Fine,' she said shortly. 'Fine. I shall go now, then, to the woods, and get this awful business over with before I turn into an elm.'

'I think you're a bit more birch-y,' said Doctor Fallow contemplatively.

'Not helping!' snapped Ell. 'You *could* help if you had some medicine for her in your weird, ugly tower.'

'Medicine's not our business,' said Citrinitas helplessly. 'And besides . . . change is the blessing of Autumn. She should feel lucky.'

Ell, as September had never seen him do before, spat a lick of fire at her. Not enough to scorch, but enough to singe her hair. Citrinitas yelped and leapt back, batting at her curls. The Wyverary curled closer around September.

'Well, you can't go with her, so you might as well stop smothering,' huffed Doctor Fallow. 'This is strictly a lone-knight situation.'

'Then she isn't going! I shan't let her go anywhere without something large and fire-breathing and double smart behind her! Since I don't see a flaming burp between the three of you, I suggest you leave us alone!'

'Ell, if that's how it's done, you can't bellow it into doing it differently,' sighed September. She stood up and disentangled herself from her friend. Blazing curls of her hair fluttered to the ground.

'I can try!' Ell insisted.

'No, I shall go alone. I always thought I would be going alone. I shall be back presently, I promise. Say you'll wait for me, you and Saturday, that you won't go anywhere without me, that when I come out of those woods I shall see a red face and a blue one smiling!'

Ell's eyes filled with panicked turquoise tears. He promised, his wings jangling his chains fretfully.

Saturday did not say anything. He bent and tore the cuff from one leg of his trousers. The cuff was blue and ragged and not a bit muddy with velocipede-grease. The Marid tied it around September's arm. His fingers trembled a bit. The green jacket introduced itself politely but coolly to the cuff. Just so long as the cuff knew who came first.

'What is this?' said September, confused.

'It's . . . a favor,' answered Saturday. 'My favor. In battle . . . knights oughtn't be without one.'

September reached up and touched his face gently to thank him. Her fingers grazed his cheek. They had shriveled into thin, bare, dry branches, bundled together at the wrist.

As September walked through the starry, misty night, trying not to look at her ruined hand, she realised that she had not traveled alone in days. She missed Ell immediately, who would be telling her all sorts of things to keep her from being afraid, and Saturday, who would be quiet and steadfast and dear at her side.

She shivered and whispered to herself to keep from shivering: 'Bathtub, Bathysphere, Barometer, Bear, Bliss, Bandit . . .'

Gradually, the trees turned from wood and leaf to something altogether stranger: tall black distaffs wound around with fuzzy silk and wool and fleeces September could not name. They were all colored as autumn woods are colored, red and gold and brown and pale white. They crowded close together, fat and full, shaped more or less like pine trees. She could just see the sharp distaff jutting out of the wispy top of one great red beast of a tree. *This must be where they get the stuff to build Pandemonium!* September thought suddenly. *Instead of cutting down a forest, they weave it!*

The moon peeked out of the clouds, too shy to show herself fully. September came, by and by, to a little clearing where several parchment-colored distaffs had left their fibers all over the forest floor like pine needles. In the corner of the clearing sat a lady. September brought her hand to her mouth, so surprised and shaken was she, forgetting that her fingers were only branches now.

The lady sat on a throne of mushrooms. Chanterelles and portobellos and oysters and wild crimson forest mushrooms piled up high around her, fanning out around her head – for the lady, too, was primarily made of mushrooms, lovely cream-yellow ones opening up like a dress collar around her brown face, lacy bits of fungus trailing from her every finger and toe. She looked off into the distance, her pale eyes a pair of tiny button mushrooms.

'Good evening, my lady,' said September, curtsying as best she knew how.

The mushroom queen said nothing. Her expression did not change.

'I have come for the casket in the wood.'

A little wind picked up, ruffling the shiitakes at the lady's feet.

'I do hope I've not offended, it's only that I haven't much time, and I seem to be coming all over tree.'

The lady's jaw sagged open. Bits of dirt fell out.

'Don't mind her,' came a tiny, breathy voice behind her. September whirled.

A tiny brown creature stood at her feet, barely a finger high. She was brown all over, the color of a nut-husk. Only her lips were red. Her hair was long, covering most of her body like bark. She seemed very young. She wore a smart [illegible]

'She's just for show,' breathed the wee thing.

'Who are you?'

'I am Death,' said the creature. 'I thought that was obvious.'

'But you're so small!'

'Only because you are small. You are young and far from your Death, September, so I seem as anything would seem if you saw it from a long way off – very small, very harmless. But I am always closer than I appear. As you grow, I shall grow with you, until at the end, I shall loom huge and dark over your bed, and you will shut your eyes so as not to see me.'

'Then who is she?'

'She is . . .' Death turned her head, considering. 'She is like a party dress I wear when I want to impress visiting dignitaries. Like your friend Betsy, I, too, am a Terrible Engine. I, too, have occasional need of awe. But between us, I think, there is no need for finery.'

'But if we are so far apart, why are you here?'

'Because Autumn is the beginning of my country. And because there is a small chance that you may die sooner than I anticipated, that I shall need to grow very fast very soon.'

Death looked meaningfully at September's hand. Within the green jacket, her arm had now shrunk into one long, knobbed branch from shoulder to fingertip.

'Is that why the Worsted Wood is forbidden? Because Death lives here?'

'And also Hamadryads. They are very boring to listen to.'

'Then the Marquess sent me here to die.'

'I do not make such judgments, child. I only take what is offered me, in the dark, in the forest.'

September crumpled to the ground. She stared at the winter branches of her hand. A great orange tuft of her hair flew off – she was nearly bald now, only a few wisps of curls clinging to her head. She sniffed and cried – or tried to cry, but her eyes were dry as old seeds, and she could not.

'Death, I don't know what to do.'

Death climbed up into her lap, sitting primly on her knee, which had already begun to darken and wither.

'It's very brave of you to admit that. Most knightly folk I happen by bluster and force me to play chess with them. I don't even like chess! For strategy Wrackglummer and even Go are much superior. And it's the wrong metaphor entirely. Death is not a checkmate . . . it is more like a carnival trick. You cannot win, no matter how you move your Queen.'

'I've only ever played chess with my mother. I wouldn't feel right, playing with you.'

'I cheat, anyway. When their backs are turned, I move the pieces.'

Slowly, a hole opened up in September's cheek, just a tiny one. She rubbed at it absently, and it widened. She felt it widening, stretching, and was so terribly afraid. She trembled, and her toes felt awfully cold in the mushroomy mud. Beneath her skin, twigs and leaves had begun to show. Death frowned.

'September, if you do not pay attention, you will never get out of this wood! You are closer than you think, human girl. I guard the casket.' Death's tiny eyes wrinkled kindly. 'All caskets are within my power. Of course they are.'

September yawned. She didn't mean to. She couldn't help it. A twig in her cheek popped, turning to dust.

'Are you sleepy? That's to be expected. In Autumn, trees sleep like bears. The whole world pulls on its nightclothes and snuggles in to sleep through all of winter. Except for me. I never sleep.'

Death climbed up on to her knee, looking up at her with hard acorny eyes. September tried very hard to listen to her Death, instead of the sound of her slowly opening cheek. 'I have terrible nightmares, you know,' Death said confidentially. 'Every night, when I come home from a long day's dying, I take off my skin and lay it nicely on my armoire. I take off my bones and hang them up on the hat stand. I set my scythe to washing on the old stove. I eat a nice supper of mouse-and-myrrh soup. Some nights, I drink off a nice red wine. White does not agree with me. I lay myself down on a bed of lilies, and still, I cannot sleep.'

September did not want to know. The moon moved silently overhead, making gape-faces at them.

'I cannot sleep because I have nightmares. I dream all the things the dead wish they had done differently. It is dreadful! Do all creatures dream so?'

'I don't think so . . . I dream sometimes that my father has come home, or that I have done well on my math exams, or that my mother's hair is all made of candy canes and we live on a river of cocoa on a marshmallow island. My mother sings me to sleep, and only once in a while do I dream of awful things.'

'Perhaps it is because I have no one to sing me to sleep. I am so tired. All the world earns its sleep but me.'

September felt sure that she was meant to do something. That, like Latitude and Longitude, the Worsted Wood was a kind of puzzle, and if she only knew how the pieces were shaped, she could manage the whole thing handily. Lost in thought and terror at her own nightmares, September's Death curled, small and feral, on her knee, her cloak of barkish hair wrapping her like a blanket. With her good hand – a relative thing, really, since it was blackened and rough as a hawthorn branch already, and showing sap under the fingernails, September gathered up her Death and laid it in the crook of her arm. She did not quite know what to do. September had never had a brother or a sister to rock to sleep. She could only remember how her mother had sung to her. She felt as though she were in a dream. But she brushed Death's hair gently from her face and sang from memory, softly, hoarsely, for her throat had gone rough and dry:

Go to sleep, little skylark,
Fly up to the moon
In a biplane of paper and ink.
Your wings creak and croon,
borne aloft by balloons,
And your engine is singing for you.
Go to sleep, little skylark, do.

Go to sleep, little skylark,
Fly up past the stars
In a biplane of sunshine and ice,
Past comets and cars, past Neptune and Mars
Still your engine is singing for you.
Go to sleep, little skylark, do.

Go to sleep, little skylark,
Drift down through the night
In your biplane of silver and sighs,

Slip under the light,
come down from the heights
For your mother is singing for you.
Go to sleep, little skylark, do.

September reached the end of the song and began again, for Death's eyes were sliding just the littlest bit closed. Her mother had sung that song, not since she was small, but since her father had left. When she sang it, she curled September in her arms just as September now curled Death and sang it close to her ear so that her long black hair fell over September's brow just as the remains of September's hair now fell on Death's brow. She remembered her mother's smell, the comfort of it, even though she mainly smelled of diesel oil. She loved that smell. Had learned to love it and settle into it like a blanket. When September got to the part about Neptune and Mars again, Death relaxed in her arms, her bark-brown hair falling delicately over September's elbow. She kept singing, though it hurt her, her throat was so shriveled and sore. And as she sang, an extraordinary thing happened:

Death grew.

Death stretched and lengthened and grew broader and heavier. Her hair curled and spread, and her arms grew to the size of September's own arms, and her legs grew to the size of

September's own legs, and in no time at all, Death was the size of a real child, and September held her still in her arms, slumped, sleeping, still.

Oh no! thought September. *What have I done? If my Death has grown so big surely I am doomed!*

But Death moaned in her sleep, and September saw, glinting in her mouth, something bright and hard. Death opened her mouth, yawning in her sleep. *Be bold,* September told herself. *An irascible child should be bold.* Gently, she put her blackened, sappy fingers into Death's mouth.

'No!' cried Death dreaming. September snatched her hand back. 'She loved you all those years; it was only that you couldn't see it!'

September tried again, just grazing the thing with her fingertips.

'No!' cried Death, dreaming. September snapped back. 'If you had gone right instead of left, you would have met an old man in overalls, and he would have taught you blacksmithing!'

September tried one more time, sneaking her fingers past Death's teeth.

'No!' cried Death, dreaming. September recoiled. 'If you had only given your son pencils instead of swords!'

September stopped. She felt hot all over, and the hole in her cheek itched, as though there were leaves crinkling in at its edges. She breathed deeply. September smoothed Death's hair with her ruined hand, which was sprouting new branches even now. She bent and kissed Death's burning brow. And then she began to sing again, softly:

'Go to sleep, little skylark . . .' She caught the edge of the thing.

'Fly up to the moon . . .' It was slippery and sharp, like glass.

'In a biplane of paper and ink . . .' September pulled. Death groaned. Birds flew up from the night forest, spooked.

'Your wings creak and croon, borne up by balloons . . .' There was a terrible creaking, crooning sound as the thing in Death's throat came free. Death's mouth opened horribly wide, bending back and back and back, and her whole body *folded* strangely back around itself as the thing emerged, so that just as September pulled it out entirely, Death vanished with a little sound like the snapping of a twig.

'And your engine is singing for you,' September finished quietly, almost whispering. In her arms, she cradled a smoky glass casket, just the size of a child. It was hung with red silk ropes and bells, and on its face was a little gold plaque. It read,

WILL HILT TO HAND YET BE RESTORED?
TAKE ME UP, THY MOTHER'S SWORD.

September ran her hands over it. She did not understand. But given a magical box, no child will leave it shut. She fumbled with the knots and rang the bells a great many times with her twiggy hands, but finally, under all that blood-colored silk was a little glass latch. September wedged her woody thumb underneath it, and all the forest echoed as it popped free.

One by one, the mushrooms that made up the Lady's face began to peel off and float away, until September was surrounded by a gentle whirlwind of delicate, lacy mushrooms and the last curls of her own hair, gone red as knots of silk. She lifted the casket lid.

Inside was a long, sturdy wrench.

CHAPTER XIII

Autumn is the Kingdom Where Everything Changes

In Which Our Heroine Succumbs to Autumn, Saturday and the Wyverary are Abducted, and September Has a Rather Odd Dream

September ran.

The sky behind her had gone an icy, lemony-cream color, pushing the deep blue night aside. Dew and frost sparkled on the Worsted Wood, clinging to the silken puffs like stitched diamonds. Her breath fogged. Leaves crushed and rustled beneath her feet. She ran so fast, so terribly fast – but she feared not fast enough. With every step, she could feel her legs getting skinnier and harder, like the trunks of saplings. With every step, she thought they might break. In the Marquess's shoes, her toes rasped and cracked. She had no hair left, and though she could not see it, she knew her skull was turning into a thatch of bare, autumnal branches. Like Death's skull. She had so little time.

When they are in a great hurry, little girls rarely look behind them. Especially those who are even a little heartless, though we may be quite certain by now that September's heart had grown heavier than she'd expected when she climbed out of her window that long-ago morning. Because she did not look behind, September did not see the smoky-glass casket close itself primly up again. She did not see it bend in half until it cracked and Death hop up again, quite well, quite awake, and quite small once more. She certainly did not see Death stand on her tiptoes and blow a kiss after her, a kiss that rushed through all the frosted leaves of the autumnal forest but could not quite catch a child running as fast as she could. As all mothers know, children travel faster than kisses. The speed of kisses is, in fact, what Doctor Fallow would call a cosmic constant. The speed of children has no limits.

Up ahead of her, September could see Mercurio, the spriggans' village, nestled in the flaming orange trees, loaf chimneys smoking cozily, the smell of breakfast, pumpkin flapjacks, and chestnut tea floating over the forest to her shriveled nose. September tried to call out. Red leaves burst from her mouth in a scarlet puff and drifted away. She gasped, something between a sob and an exhausted wracking cough. *I've lost my voice after all,* she thought. She clutched the wrench to her chest, hooking it through her twiggy elbow, which had grown soft sticky buds, like rosehips. The wrench gleamed in the dawn, burnished copper, its head shaped and carved into a graceful hand, ready to clutch a bolt in its grip. Everything shimmered with morning wetness.

A-Through-L yawned in the town square, his huge neck shining as he stretched it up and out. As September burst into the square, she saw the Wyverary playing some kind of checkers with Saturday, using raisiny cupcakes for pieces. Doctor Fallow sat back in a rich, padded chair, smoking a churchwarden pipe with satisfaction. They looked up joyfully to greet her. She tried to smile and open up her arms to hug them. But September could not fault them for the shock and dismay on their faces as they saw her ruined body stumble on to the bread bricks. She wondered if she still had her eyes left. If they were still brown and warm or dried up seedpods.

September could hardly breathe. Branches poked and stabbed at her as she gasped after her breath. The green smoking jacket despaired. If it had hands, it would have wrung them; if a mouth, it would have wept. It cinched itself closer to her waist – only a cluster of maple branches now – trying to stay close to her.

'September!' cried A-Through-L. Saturday leapt to his feet, upsetting the cupcake checkers.

Saturday gasped, 'Oh, no, no . . . are you all right?'

September sank to her knees, shaking her head. Saturday put his thin blue arms around her. He was not sure it was allowed, but he could not bear not to. He held her, gingerly, much as she had held Death. Saturday had never had anyone to cradle and protect before, either.

Saturday, September tried to say, *I understand now.* But red leaves puffed from her mouth, branches ground on branches in her throat, and no words came. Rubedo and Citrinitas peeked out of one of the low, round houses, clucking piteously. Rubedo stroked his wan crimson face. Citrinitas nervously tied knots in her golden hair. But Doctor Fallow kept smoking his pipe, smacking his lips and blowing rings.

Ell! The Marquess needed me because of my mother! Golden leaves dribbled on to the square. Saturday stroked September's brow, and she had a moment, only a moment, to be amazed that he did not think her ugly, that he was not afraid to touch her.

Because she fixes engines, Ell. So this is her sword. *Do you understand? If it had been anyone else, it would have been something else. Like, for you, it might have been a book. For Saturday, a raincloud. If only I knew what she needed a magic wrench for! I am sure if we think hard on it, all three of us, we shall be able to figure it out.* A torrent of orange leaves vomited up from her dry brown mouth. September laughed. More leaves flew. She was probably the only girl in all of Fairyland who could have pulled a wrench, of all the ridiculous things, out of that casket. Whose mother here could have wielded such a weapon? The Wyverary and the Marid exchanged miserable looks.

'We must get her out,' Citrinitas said. 'How could this have happened so fast?'

'Does it happen *often*?' snapped Saturday, quite beside himself. A-Through-L's eyes rimmed slowly with turquoise tears. One fell with a plop on to September's poor bald head.

'Well, no . . . but then, we don't have many human visitors . . .' Rubedo swallowed wretchedly.

'Autumn,' said Doctor Fallow, the [illegible], the Department Head, 'changes everything. If she could only relax, she could be happy. She might even bear fruit, given a few years' careful pruning. One must accept the way of the world, for it will always have its way, one way or another.'

'But everything doesn't change,' said A-Through-L. 'They have their wedding, every night, just the same. Because every day is harvest and feasting! I may not know Winter or Spring or Summer, but I know my Autumn, I know my *Fall,* that's A and that's F, Doctor Fallow! September is the only thing changing here! Winter never comes. It will never snow. The leaves never die and fall off; they stay red and golden forever. Why not her? Why must she wither all up? What have you done? We only have a few days left to get back to the Marquess . . .'

Saturday was shaking his head back and forth like a little bull. His face darkened, as though clouds moved beneath his skin. 'Did the Marquess tell you to do this to her?' he said coldly.

'Oh, no!' cried Citrinitas. 'No, it's only that she's Ravished and human, and it's all so unpredictable, the chymical processes that occur in Autumn . . .'

'But she probably knew,' mumbled Rubedo. 'She could have guessed what might have happened. She could have hoped.'

Doctor Fallow smoked his pipe and sat back, his expression unreadable.

A terrible sound broke through the morning, like a tuba being crushed with iron hammers. The sound shook Doctor Fallow from his chair. Saturday laughed cruelly at him, but his laughter caught itself and crawled away as the sound grew only louder. September found she could not get up, her knees had locked into sapling trunks. They no longer moved at all. Rubedo and Citrinitas shrieked together and dashed into their house, bolting the door. Doctor Fallow squeaked and abruptly shrank to the size of an insect. He scurried away between their feet. September, Ell, and Saturday were left alone, clinging to each other, Ell trying to shelter the little ones with his bound wings, when the lions came.

They pounced with a horrible silence, their paws landing softly. There were two of them, each nearly as big as the Wyverary. Their fur shone deep blue, deeper than Saturday's skin, the color of the loneliest winter night, and all through their manes and tails silver stars shone and burned. They roared together; the terrible tuba sound blared once more. Saturday screamed, and if she could have put out an arm to comfort him, September would have. But it all happened faster than she could understand. One lion snatched up Saturday in his jaws. Drops of Marid blood, the color of seawater, spilled on to the square. But he did not scream when the lion's teeth clamped on him. The boy only closed his eyes and reached out for September, imploring, even though he knew it to be useless. The second lion slashed Ell's face with his claws, leaving a long gash in his red scales. There must have been a treacly-dark poison in those claws, for the great red Wyverary tottered and fell with a crash down to the forest floor in a deep sleep. The starry lion grabbed Ell by the scruff and began dragging him away. Neither of them paid the slightest bit of attention to September.

No! cried September. But only leaves fell out of her mouth, and she could not move. *No!*

But even if she could have spoken loud and true, it would have been no help. The lions' eyes were shut. The Marquess's lions slept, and dreamed, even as they did their work, and carried off their prizes into the bright, clear day.

September screamed without a sound and cried bitterly and beat her twig-hands against the ground. Her heart ached as though a knife had quietly slipped between her ribs. She looked up to the cheerful sun, as ever unimpressed by little girls' sorrows, and tears of amber maple sap squeezed out of her eyes.

September finally fell backward, quite out of herself, and the world slid away, for a little while.

September dreamed. She knew she was dreaming, but she could not help it. She was quite well and whole and sitting at a very fine table with a lace tablecloth draped over it. On the table lay several greasy, grimy iron gears and a great number of mismatched nuts and bolts. September did not know what they were for, but she felt certain that if she could fit them together as they were meant to go, everything would suddenly become clear.

'Shall I serve?' said Saturday. He sat primly across from her, dressed in a fine Sunday suit, with a high collar and cuff links. His hair was neatly combed; his face, scrubbed clean. The Marid took up one of the gears and scraped it with a butter knife. He handed it back to September.

'It's getting very late, November,' said a young man. He sat very near to her and held her hand. September felt certain she had never seen him before. He had dark red hair and oddly golden skin. His eyes were big and blue. They swam with turquoise tears.

'My name is September . . .' she said softly. Her voice was weak, as it often is in dreams.

'Of course, October,' said the young man. 'You must speak twice as loudly just to be heard in the land of dreams. It is something to do with physicks. But then, what isn't? Dreams begin with D, and therefore, I can help you. To be heard.'

'Ell? Where is your tail? Your wings?'

'It is mating season,' the Wyverary said, straightening his lapels. 'We must all look our best, January.'

'She wouldn't know a thing about that,' said Saturday reproachfully. September saw suddenly that Saturday had a purring cat in his lap. The cat's fur was blue, and in his bushy tail was a single, glowing star. 'Such a lazy girl. Lax in her studies. If only she'd kept up with her physicks homework, we'd all be safe and sound and eating pound cake.'

'I'm not lazy! I tried!' September looked down at the buttered gear in her hand. It was smeared with Marid blood, like seawater.

'Mary, Mary, Morning Bell,' sang a third voice. September turned to see a little girl sitting next to her, swinging her legs under her chair. The girl looked terribly familiar, but September could not think where she could have met her before. She had dull blondish hair bobbed short around her chin, and her face was a bit muddy. She had on a farmer's daughter kind of dress, gray and dusty, with a yellowish lace at the hem. She rubbed at her nose.

'All praise and glory to the Marquess,' said Saturday reverentially, passing a thick iron gear to the girl. The child accepted it and allowed him to kiss her dusty hand.

'Dances in her garden dell!' she sang. The blonde child giggled and swung her legs harder.

'Please, oh, please, start making sense!' cried September.

'I always make perfect sense, December,' said Ell, smoothing pomade into his hair. 'You know that.'

The dream-Saturday held up his hands. They were chained in ivory manacles. 'Did it mean me, do you think?' he said. 'When it said you'd lose your heart?'

'But when the night comes rushing on,' sang the girl, laughing uncontrollably. She took a bite out of her iron bolt. It crumbled like cake in her mouth. 'Down falls Mary, dead and gone!' The girl smiled. Her teeth were full of black oil.

And for a moment, just a moment, September saw them all: Saturday, Ell, and the strange blonde girl, bound and bolted and chained in a dreary, wet cell, sleeping, skeletal, dead.

CHAPTER XIV

In a Ship of Her Own Making

In Which September Leaves Autumn for Winter, Meets a Certain Gentleman of Means, and Considers the Problem of Nautical Engineering

September woke to the sound of the snow falling. Hoarowls cried overhead: *'Hoomaroo! Hoomaroo!'* The sun burned white and soft behind long clouds. A cold, piney wind blew over her skin.

She opened her eyes – and she had eyes! She had skin! She could even shiver! September lay on a makeshift stretcher, a piece of piebald hide stretched between long poles. Her hands – and she had hands! – were folded neatly over her chest, and her hair flowed over her shoulders and down to the sash of the exultant green smoking jacket, dark brown and familiar and dry and clean. She was well again and whole.

And alone. It all came rushing back to her: the sleeping blue lions, Saturday and A-Through-L, all of it. And the dream, too, still clinging to her like old clothes.

Mary, Mary, Morning Bell.

In a panic, she reached for her sword – and felt the copper wrench safely beside her on the piebald hide. The Spoon still rested snugly in her sash. Saturday's favor was gone, though, lost to the woods. September sat up, her head heavy and sick. A wood spread out around her, and it appeared long past autumn, the trees black and stark, snow glittering on everything, softening every edge to exquisite, perfect white. The green smoking jacket busily puffed up to keep out the gently blowing snow.

'You see? You're quite well again. I promised you would be.' Citrinitas sat a little ways away, as though afraid to come too near. The little spriggan clutched her three-fingered hands together miserably. She scratched her long yellow nose and pulled up a great yellow hood over her head. She snapped her fingers, and a little golden fire burned before her, floating above the snow. Citrinitas sheepishly fished a marshmallow out of her pocket and speared it on her thumbnail to roast.

'Where are my friends?' September demanded, happy to find she had her voice back, strong and loud, echoing in the empty wood.

'I didn't have to bring you out, you know. I could have left you there, and it would have been a good bit less trouble than dragging you out across the Winter Treaty. So close to Spring! It doesn't sit right with the stomach. Rubedo didn't even want to come. And he so longs to travel! Doctor Fallow is a bit of a coward – he hid when the lions came. Eventually, we'll find him, though. I think he's angry with you – you might have at least matriculated before turning all . . . tree-ish. And now I've missed our wedding, *thank you very much.*'

'You'll have another tomorrow! And, anyway, if it's so much bother, why didn't you just grow and cover the distance in three steps?'

'Well,' Citrinitas blushed deep ochre, 'I did. But that's not the point. The point is *gratitude,* and how you ought to have it.'

September gritted her teeth. She liked the feeling of it – of having teeth. 'Where are my friends?' she repeated icily.

'Oh, how should *I* know? We were only told to feed you up and send you into the woods. No one tells us anything unless it's "Mix up Life-in-a-Flask for me, Citrinitas!" "Bake me a Cake of Youth, Trinny!" "Grade these papers!" "Watch that beaker!" "A monograph on the nature of goblins' riddles, Ci-ci!" I swear to you, I am *finished* with postdoctoral work!'

The golden spriggan struck her bony knee with her fist. As she spoke, her voice got higher and higher until it squeaked like a teakettle.

'Anyway, it's no use interrogating *me.* I don't know. But I've brought you to the snow, and the snow is the beginning and the end of everything, everyone knows that. I've brought you to the snow and the Ministry, and the clerk will . . . well, mainly he'll say "*Ffitthit*" at you. But I expect they're in the Lonely Gaol, you know, since that's where the lions take people usually, and that's far, oh so awfully far, and it won't do you any good, anyway. Parole was outlawed years ago. And the Gaol is guarded by the Very Unpleasant Man, and you're *just a little girl.*'

September's face burned. She got up and marched over to Citrinitas and crouched next to her. And maybe Lye's bath, oh so terribly long ago now, really had given her a red, frothy draught of courage, because otherwise she could not imagine where she might have found the gall to hiss at the miserable spriggan, 'I am *not* just a little girl.' Then September straightened up, scowling at the alchemist. 'I can get bigger, just like you. Only . . . it just takes me a little longer.' She turned on her heel, seized her copper wrench, and began to walk over the crystal snow drifts to a little hut nestled between two great yew trees, which could only be the Ministry, or at least, she hoped it was the Ministry, because otherwise she would suddenly look very foolish. She did not look back.

'I'm sorry!' cried Citrinitas after her. 'I am! Alchemy really is lovely, once you get past the alchemists . . .'

September ignored her and walked up the hill, the snow swallowing up the spriggan's voice.

September breathed relief. The Marquess's lovely black shoes had gotten soaked with snowmelt. A pleasant sign, freshly painted black and red, rose up out of a snow drift:

THE MARVELOUS MINISTRY OF MR MAP
(YULETIDE DIVISION)

The hut was covered in white furs and bits of holly, but the bits were placed rather haphazardly, as if someone meant to be festive but got bored and gave up instead. The door was a sturdy thing with a compass rose stamped rudely into the wood. September knocked politely.

'Ffitthit!' came the answer from within. It was an odd sound, like someone spitting and coughing and growling and asking after one's relations all at once.

'Excuse me! Citrinitas sent me! Please let me in, Sir Map!'

The door cracked.

'It's *mister*, kitten. MISTER. Do you see an Order of the Green Kirtle on my chest? Eh? A Crystal Cross? It'd be news to me. Call me by my proper name, good grief and all gallows!'

An old man peered down at her, the bags under his eyes wrinkled like old paper, his hair and long corkscrewed mustache not even white, but the color of old, stained parchment. His skin was lined and brown, and his neatly brushed hair curled in a stately fashion, tied up in a black ribbon, like the old portraits of presidents in September's schoolbooks. He had a pleasant, jolly belly and broad cheeks – and fat, furry wolf's ears with a great deal of gray fur in them. He wore a bright blue suit with the cuffs rolled up over impressive forearms, so bright it startled in the midst of the white woods. His forearms were covered in sailors' tattoos. For a moment, he and September just stared at one another, waiting for the other to speak first.

'Your suit . . . it's lovely . . .' murmured September, suddenly shy.

Mr Map shrugged. 'Well,' he said, as though it were perfectly logical, 'world's mostly water. Why pretend it's not?'

September leaned in close, rather closer than is courteous.

She saw that his suit was a map, with little lines and bits of writing on it. The buttons of his blazer and his cuff links were green islands, as was his belt buckle, an enormous, sparkling gem, the biggest island of all. September recognized the shape of the buckle. She had seen it, oh so briefly, as she fell from the customs office in the sky. *That's Fairyland,* she thought.

Mr Map left the doorway and went back to his work. September followed him inside. A great easel dominated the little room, on which Mr Map had been busy painting a sea serpent in a wild ocean bordering a small island chain. Maps covered and cluttered every surface of the hut, topographical maps, geological maps, submarine maps, population-density maps, artistic maps and scribbled-over wartime maps. The maps left room for only a single chair, the easel, and a table groaning with paints and pens. September shut the door gently behind her. It latched, and somewhere deep in the woods, a lock spun.

'Excuse me, Mr Map, but the lady alchemist said you'd know where to find my friends?'

'Now why would I know that?' Mr Map licked his pen – his tongue was all black with ink, and the pen's bristles filled up with it. He returned to his map. 'Seems to me a friend knows best where friends are.'

'They . . . were taken. By two lions, the Marquess's lions.

She said their strength came from sleeping, but I didn't understand . . . I guess I understand now.'

'Do you know where I learned my Art?' Mr Map said nonchalantly, sipping a hot brandy, which seemed to materialize in his hand. September could swear she had not seen him pick up a snifter from his side table. *'Ffitthiiit!'* sighed Mr Map slowly, smacking his lips. 'I promise, I waste nothing in asking. Like a ship, I always come round again to where I started.'

'No, Mister. I don't know.'

'In prison, my kit, my cub! Where one learns anything worth knowing. In prison there is nothing but time, time, time. Time goes on just positively forever. You could master Wrackglummer, or learn Sanskrit, or memorize every poem ever written about ravens (there are exactly seven thousand ninety-four at current count, but a no-talent rat down in the city keeps spoiling my count), and still you'd have so much time on your hands you'd be bored sleepless.'

'Why were you in prison?'

Mr Map sipped his brandy again. He shut his eyes and shook his glossy curls. He offered his drink to September, who, having given up all pretence of carefulness, took a big gulp. It tasted like burnt walnuts and hot sugar, and she coughed.

'That's what happens to the old guard, my pup. You can always count on it. We who serve, we who make the world run. When the world changes, it stashes us away where we can't make it run the other way again.' Mr Map opened his eyes. He smiled sadly. 'Which is to say I once stood at the side of Queen Mallow, and loved her.'

'You were a soldier?'

'I didn't say that. I said I stood at her side.' Mr Map blushed. It looked like ink spreading under his skin. His wolfy ears flicked back and forth in embarrassment. 'You're young, little fawn, but surely you catch my meaning. Once, you might have called me "Sir" and no one would have corrected you.'

'Oh!' breathed September.

'Fftthit!' spat Mr Map. 'All done now – and gone, gone to old songs and older wine. History. She's just another in a list of Queens to be memorized now.'

'My friend the Wyverary . . . the Wyvern said some people think she's still alive, down in the cellars, or wherever the Marquess keeps folk . . .'

Mr Map glanced at her, and his eyes drooped sadly. He tried a smile, but it did not quite work out.

'I met a lady in prison,' he went on, as though September hadn't spoken. 'A Järlhopp. They keep their memories in a necklace and wear it always and forever. Since her memory is so safe, she never forgets anything she's seen, and the Järlhopp – her name was Leef, and how furry and sleek were her long ears! – Leef taught me to copy out my own memories on to parchment, to paint a perfect path . . . a path back to the things I loved, the things I knew when I was young. That's what a map is, you know. Just a memory. Just a wish to go back home – someday, somehow. Leef kept hers in that jewel at her throat; I kept mine on paper, endless paper, endless time, until the Marquess had need of me, until she sent me away to the wilds of the Winter Treaty, where nothing happens, where I cannot possibly cause trouble, where no one lives. And where there are no kind Järlhoppes to comfort me, or folk who might need maps to find their way.'

September looked at her feet. At the elegant, glittering shoes. The brandy warmed her all over. 'I . . . I need to find my way,' she said.

'I know, little cub. And I'm telling you your way. The way to the bottom of the world, to the Lonely Gaol, where the lions take all the souls the Marquess hates.' Mr Map leaned forward, licked his pen until it was full of ink, and wedged a jeweler's glass into his eye so that he could brush in tiny details on the little island map. 'You see, September, Fairyland is an island, and the sea that borders it only flows one way. It has always been so, and must always be. The sea cannot be changed in its course. If the Gaol were but offshore from us here in this land, you could not get there by sailing straight.

The current does not move that way. You can only reach it by circumnavigating Fairyland entirely, and that is not a small task.'

'You know my name.'

'I know quite a number of things, you'll find.'

'But surely, there is some place from which it is a short distance! If one could only get on the right side of it.'

'Surely. But I will not take you there.'

'Why ever not?'

Mr Map looked grieved again. *'Ffitthit,'* he said softly. 'We all have our masters.'

September clenched her fists. She could not bear to think of her friends in a wet, dreary prison. 'It's not fair! I could have gotten her this wretched thing in seven days! She didn't even give me a chance!'

'September, my calf, my chick, seven days were never seven. They were three, or eight, or one, or whatever she wished them to be. If she wants you at the Lonely Gaol, she has a reason, and you could never have gone anywhere else. And I suspect' – he looked at the copper wrench, twisting his mustache in one great hand – 'that she has devised some work for you to do there, with your fell blade. Hello, old friend,' he greeted it, 'how strange for us to meet again, like this, with the snow blowing so outside.'

'You know my . . . my wrench?'

'Of course I know it. It was not a wrench when we were last acquainted, but one's friends may change clothes and still one knows them.'

'Why does she need me to go all the way to her horrid old Gaol? I have the sword! The lions could have taken it and left us alone!'

'September, these things have their rhythms, their ways. Once the sword is taken up, none but the hand that won it can brandish it true. She cannot touch the sword, not for all the power in both her hands. But you can. And both your hands called it forth, gave it shape, gave it life.'

'I'm really very tired, Mr Map. Ever so much more tired than I thought I could be.'

Mr Map signed his parchment with a flourish.

'*Ffitthit,* sweet kitten. So it always goes.'

September turned to go. Her feet felt heavy. She turned the knob of the great door and listened to the lock whir in the woods. When she opened it, no winter wood glittered outside, but a long shore and a bright sea. Gillybirds cried overhead, wrestling over bits of fish. The tide flowed out [illegible] from a silver beach, the very opposite from the one she had arrived on. Here, the sand was all manner of silver coins and crowns and sceptres and bars, filigreed diadems and long necklaces set with pearls, and chandeliers glittering with glass. The violet-green sea – the Perverse and Perilous Sea, she reminded herself – beat huge waves against the strand.

'What is a map,' said Mr Map, 'but a thing that gets you where you're going?'

'The sword,' September whispered, her eyes all full of the sea. 'Who had it before me?'

'I think you know. My Lady Mallow kept it.'

'And what was it, when she had it?'

Mr Map cocked his head to one side. He drank off the last of his hot brandy.

'A needle,' he said softly.

September stepped out of the hut and on to the silver beach.

September could see the current Mr Map had meant. The sea flowed just offshore, a deeper violet amid the violet waves, fast and cold and deep. She could see it – but she was still only September, and she could not swim all the way around Fairyland. The empty beach stretched far and long, and nowhere hulked a broken ship or raft for her to climb aboard. She had come so far, and for lack of a boat, her friends suffered in who knew what dark place. And Saturday, especially, had such a horror of being closed up and trapped. And Ell! Sweet, enormous Ell! At least, Gaol begins with G— or J, she was not exactly sure. What awful cell could they devise to contain her beast?

She could not leave them there to wait for the Marquess to get angry enough to deal with them. She did not think they would get cozy government posts in the winter wilds. She would simply have to think, and think quickly.

September began to walk through the jeweled, silver beach, searching desperately for real wood, something that might float. *But,* she thought suddenly, *it was all wood once, on the other beach! Wood and flowers and chestnuts and acorns! It's not really silver or gold at all! The wairwulf said it was Fairy gold! Like in stories when you wake up after selling your soul for a chest of pearls, and it's all full of mud and sticks!* September scrabbled in the flotsam and drew up a huge silver rod tipped in sapphire, something like her long-ago spent sceptre if it had been made by a giant's hand. She tugged it down to the shoreline and tossed it on to the waves experimentally.

It floated, bobbing happily in the surf.

September yelped in victory and set about hauling several of the log-size sceptres together and lining them up side by side. By the time she had finished, the sun was very high, and she was all sweat from scalp to sole. *But how shall I ever lash it together?* she despaired. There was no silver rope or filigree wire to be had on all the beach. The distant dune grasses were short and sharp and furry and would never do. *Oh, but I've just gotten it back,* September thought. *Surely I could use something else.* As if to answer her, September's hand fell upon the handles of a pair of silver scissors.

Well. If that's the way of it, that's the way of it.

She held out the length of her hair, heavy and thick and not red at all, not falling away bit by bit. She did not want to sniffle – what was a little hair? She had already lost it once after all. But that was magic, which could be undone, and this was scissors, which could not. And so, as the scissors sliced smoothly through her hair, she cried a little. Just a tear or two, rolling slowly down her cheek. Somehow, she had thought it would hurt, even though that was silly. She wiped her face clean. September braided her hair into many thin, strong ropes and knotted the sceptres together into a very serviceable raft. She wedged the witch's Spoon into the center of it as a makeshift mast.

'Now, I really am terribly sorry, Smoking Jacket. You've been a loyal friend to me, but I'm afraid you'll get quite wet, and I must ask you to excuse my using you so.' September sadly secured the mast with the long green sash, and stuffed the jacket into a gap where seawater might come in. The jacket did not mind. It had been wet before. And it liked very much being asked pardon.

Finally, it was all finished. September was quite proud of herself, and we may be proud of her, too, for certainly I have never made a boat so quickly, and I daresay only one or two of you have ever pulled off such a trick. All she lacked was a sail. September thought for a good while, considering what Lye, the soap golem, had said: *'Even if you've taken off every stitch of clothing, you still have your secrets, your history, your true name. It's hard to be really naked. You have to work hard at it. Just getting into a bath isn't being naked, not really. It's just showing skin. And foxes and bears have skin, too, so I shan't be ashamed if they're not.'*

'Well, I shan't be! My dress, my sail!' cried September aloud, and wriggled out of her orange dress. She tied the sleeves to the top of the mast and the tips of the skirt to the bottom. The wind puffed it out obligingly. She took off the Marquess's dreadful shoes and wedged them between the sceptres. There she stood, her newly shorn hair flying in every direction, naked and fierce, with the tide coming in. She shoved the raft out to sea and leapt on, nearly tipping the thing over, clutching her wrench and using it as a rudder to steer her way. She would not have known to call it a rudder, really, but she needed something to push on and direct herself, and the wrench was all she had left. The wind caught her little orange sail and the current caught the little ship, and soon enough, she was sweeping along the shoreline in a whipping breeze. Her skin pricked and she shivered, but she would bear it. With clenched teeth and goose bumps.

I did it! I figured it out myself, with no Fairy or spriggan or even a Wyverary to tell me how! Of course, she would have preferred to have a Wyverary to show her, to be a great red ship for her to whoop and ride upon. But he was not here, and she was hoisted on the bursting, splashing waves by a ship of her own making – her hair, her Spoon, her dress, and her loyal jacket, who rejoiced, quietly, with her – as the gillybirds shrieked and sang.

The moon rose slim and horned that night. All the stars flashed and wiggled in the sky, so many constellations September could not name. One looked a bit like a book, and she named it Ell's Father. Another looked something like a spotted cat with big glowing red stars for eyes. She named that one My Leopard. Still, another looked like a rainstorm, and as she watched, falling stars twinkled through it, like real rain.

'And that's Saturday's Home,' September whispered to herself.

The night wind blew warm, and she stretched out beneath the orange sail, watching the distant, shadowy shore slowly slip by. She had not really considered the problem of food – *silly girl, after all the trouble over it!* And in the dark, she loosened seven or eight strands of hair from the raft and tied them to the wrench, hoping to catch a fish for her supper. Even September did not quite think this was going to work. She had some idea about fishing, since her mother and grandfather had taken her to catch minnows in the pond one summer or another. But they always cast for her, and baited the hook – *ah, a hook.* That was a bother. And no bait, either. Still, she had little enough choice, and sunk the length of hair into the lapping sea.

Despite everything, despite being terribly afraid for her friends and not having the first idea how far the Gaol might be, September had to admit that sailing at night by one's lonesome was so awfully pleasant she could hardly bear it. That stirring, which had fluttered in her on first glimpsing the sea, that stirring landlocked children know so well – moved in her now, with the golden stars overhead and the green fireflies glinting on the wooded shore. She carefully unfolded the stirring that she had so tightly packed away. It billowed out like a sail, and she laughed, despite herself, despite hunger and hard things ahead.

Somewhere toward dawn, September fell asleep, her wrench curled tightly against her, her hair still trailing in the surf, catching no fish at all.

INTERLUDE

In Which We Return to the Jeweled Key and Its Progress

Now, what, you have every right to ask, *has happened to our erstwhile friend the jeweled Key all this while as such awful and marvelous events have befallen September?*

I shall tell you. I live to please.

The Key finally entered Pandemonium and immediately knew the city to be beautiful, rich, delicious – and empty of a little girl named September. It drooped despondently and peeked through organdy alleys – abandoned, but not hopeless. It did not follow her scent, but her memory, which left a curling green trail visible only to lonely animated objects and a certain ophthalmologist's patients, which doctor it would be poor form to mention here. Finally, the wreckage of Saturday's lobster cage informed the Key in a breathy, splintered voice that the whole troupe had left for the Autumn Provinces some time back. The Key's little jeweled breast swelled with renewed purpose, and it flew out over the Barleybroom and across the Meadowflats as fast as it could, a little blur of orange in the air, no more than a marigold petal.

It saw the dust cloud of the velocipedes running but could not catch them. The Key wheezed and cried sorrow to the heavens, but Keys have a certain upper speed limit, and even in love our gentle-hearted brooch could not exceed it. Calpurnia Farthing glimpsed the rushing Key on her return from the borders of Autumn and thought it curious. Penny squealed and begged to catch and keep it, but Calpurnia would not allow it, pets being a nuisance to traveling folk. Calpurnia squinted through her goggles and thought to herself, *That is a Key. Where there is a Key, there is yet hope.*

The Key entered the Autumn Provinces far too late but followed the trail of September's memory into the Worsted Wood. There, it met with the Death of Keys, which is a thing I may not describe to you. It is true that novelists are shameless and obey no decent law, and they are not to be trusted on any account, but some Mysteries even they must honor.

Much shaken, the Key returned to see the ruined

September, her wracked body all branches and leaves and buds, being carried by Citrinitas in three long strides so far from itself that the Key fell to the forest floor and did not move for a long while.

But move, at last, it did. What if September came upon a lock and was lost without her Key? What if she were imprisoned? What if she were lonely, with all her friends snatched away? No. The Key would not abandon her. It set out, after her curling, spiraling green trail, all the way to the hut of Mr Map, who gave it a cup of fortifying tea and showed it the way to the sea, placing a gentle kiss upon the Key's clasp before it went.

The Key blushed and set out over the Perverse and Perilous Sea, full of purpose, sure that soon – oh, so very soon! – September would be near.

CHAPTER XV

The Island of the Nasnas

In Which September Runs Aground, Learns of the Vulnerabilities of Folklore, and Is Half Tempted

It was not so much that September came upon an island as that she had a bit of an accident with an island. She cannot be entirely blamed. The current ran right into the little isle, and even if she had been awake and at the tiller, she might not have been able to avoid it. As things stood, September awoke with her ship tangled in a bramble of lilies and seagrass and spiky cream-colored flowers she could not name. It was not the collision that had woken her, but all the perfume of that thin beach, drifting out with the tide. Her mouth was thick and dry, her belly empty, and the sun beat at her head. The violet salt of the sea caked her arms and cheeks. She looked, in fact, entirely a mess.

If there are folk here, I ought to make myself fit for company, September thought, and she set about taking down her sail, which was by now quite sodden with seawater and not at all nice to wear. She shook out her green smoking jacket and tied it on, and lastly, with much frowning, slid the Marquess's shoes back on her feet, though she did not like doing so. But roses have thorns and girls have feet, and the two do not get along. September still felt wet and sore, but she thought she might be more or less respectable-looking. She bent in the flowery shore and searched for berries, any sort that might make a breakfast. She found a few round hard pinkish things that tasted a bit of salt and grapefruit rind. *Can't ask them all to taste of blueberry cream and be knocked off a tree by a Wyverary for me,* she thought, and with the thought of Ell, slumped.

'I'm alone again,' she whispered. 'Just me and the sea and not much of anything else. Oh, how I wish my friends were here! I am coming, I promise, it's only that I must eat something and drink fresh water, or I shall not make it round the horn of Fairyland at all.'

'N' whol al,' said a quiet voice. September started and looked round.

A lady stood uncertainly by, looking as if she might run at any moment – if indeed she could run, for the lady was truly only half a lady. She was cleanly cut in half lengthwise, having only one eye, one ear, half a mouth, half a nose. It did not seem to trouble her any. Her clothes had been made to fit her shape, lavender silk trousers with only one leg, a pale blue doublet – or singlet – with only one padded sleeve. Half a head of hair tumbled down her side, colored like night.

'What?' said September. The one-legged woman flushed and hopped backward a little, ducking her half face into a high yellow collar.

'Oh, I don't mean to be rude – I didn't understand you, is all!'

'Ot ly one,' tried the lady again, and then leapt away on her one leg, bounding up the beach and over a tangled heath that led into the center of the island. She hopped gracefully, as if it were the most natural way of moving invented. Little black flowers wavered in her wake.

Now, September knew she ought to stay straight on course and never turn aside until she reached the Lonely Gaol. But one cannot simply say mysterious things and then run off! That's practically begging to be followed. September's feet were already scrambling up through the heath before her mind could worry about her little ship or what terrible clock might be ticking toward a miserable prison at the bottom of the world. She was off and running, calling after the half-lady, so thirsty she thought her throat might catch on fire. We must simply count ourselves lucky that she remembered her wrench and did not leave it to be carried off by some enterprising turtle.

The island was not great or broad, and September might well have caught the lady, but that both of them ran right into the center of a village before a victor could be declared in their race. September understood immediately that the strange creature was home – all the houses were cut neatly in half. Arranged in a gentle half circle, each sweet, small green-grass house had half windows and half doors and half roofs of coral tile, each and everything precisely and deliberately built for half a soul. Half a great edifice stood at one end of the long village green, with half pillars and half stairs all of silver. The lady ran full tilt toward a young man, tall and half formed just as she was. His trousers, too, were silk and purple, his collar yellow and high. The two joined – smack! – at the seam, and she turned to face September. A glowing line ran down their bodies where the join had been made.

'Not wholly alone,' said the creature, in a voice neither male nor female. 'That's what I said. You are not wholly alone.'

'Oh!' said September simply, and sat down on the smooth green. Now that she had run all that way, she was quite beside herself with tiredness and strangeness. If only she could get a drink of water! She would not mind half a glass . . .

'When I am myself, I cannot speak as you would understand me. I can only say half my words. I need my twin to speak to outsiders – not that you are an outsider!'

'I rather think I am!'

'All things being equal,' the half-lady continued in her same soft voice, 'outsiders are to keep to the outside. But we can see you are one of us.'

'One of . . . who?'

'The Nasnas. The half-a-whole, whom the gods saw fit to bisect. I am Nor. My brother is Neither.' The two of them bowed in perfect unison, the glowing line between them intact.

'My name is September, but I'm not a . . . a Nasnas.'

'And yet you've been cut in half.'

'But I haven't!' September clutched at her chest to be sure.

'You have no shadow,' said Neither/Nor, wandering away up toward the great silver half-palace. 'Half of you is gone,' she called over her shoulder.

September scrambled after her.

'It's no bother to me not to have a shadow,' she panted, trying to keep up with the hopping Neither/Nor as she bounded over a tangled heath. 'But it must be terribly difficult to live without a left part!'

'All Nasnas are twins. I have a left part. It is only that he is not attached to me. Much as your shadow is not attached to you, but off and having its own adventures, singing its own shadow songs, eating feasts of shade and gloam. It's still your shadow, even if you are not bound to it. And, perhaps, it is a bother to *it,* to be separated from you. One must always be considerate of one's other half.'

Nor shuddered, and the glowing seam between her and her brother went dim. She leapt away from him and caught the hand of a passing girl, spinning her like a dance partner. The two leapt up and joined as Nor and her brother had done. 'Not!' the new creature cried to itself. 'It's been too long!' A new Nor turned toward September, almost a normal woman, but for the seam in her face. Her voice was different, too, higher, more musical.

'Of course, one may have a number of other halves,' Nor said with a grin. 'We have always felt sorry for those who are forced to be only one person, forever and ever until they die. My brother and I are Neither/Nor, my sister and I are Not/Nor, and on and on the combinations go, sharing dreams and labor and life. We are halves, but we make an infinite whole.'

'I'm . . . not like that,' whispered September. She could

not say why they frightened her, but the Nasnas lady and her many siblings made her feel more unsure and unsettled than even Death had. 'Why are you like that?'

'Why do you have two legs? Why is your hair brown?'

September remembered Charlie Crunchcrab, the ferryman. 'Evolution, I guess.'

'Well, we guess, too.'

'But don't you have stories? About yourself. About why the world is the way it is.'

'You mean folklore?'

September shrugged uncertainly.

Not/Nor scratched her chin. 'I think we had a folklore once. I seem to remember. We locked it up in a vault to keep it safe. Or a library. Terribly similar. But bandits, you know. Bandits, bandits, always about! Wearing masks and carrying sacks. I'm afraid there was a break-in. They left a few crumbs – bandits are slovenly. I think I recall something about "Cosmic Scissors", and "Entropy", and "Where Love Comes From". But no one remembers more, and the police don't visit the hinterlands much.'

'I'm sorry for your loss.'

'And I for yours! I was born half, but to lose yourself in the prime of life! What a trauma!'

'Honestly, I hadn't really thought about it much. It hurt

while the Glashtyn cut it away, but I'm not sick or anything.'

'What do you suppose your shadow is doing without you? She might be ill with pining!'

September thought back to her shadow's vicious smile, dancing on the shoulders of the horse-headed Glashtyn. 'I don't think so,' she said and, for the first time, felt it had been a bit shabby of her to have cast off her shadow so quickly and not to have written to it or asked after it at all.

'I have to go to work now, little girl. Not's shift is already done, and I'm keeping her from roast fish and nap.'

'What sort of shift do you have?' said September curiously. 'And mightn't there be some water there?' She knew about shifts, of course, because her mother had them. Shifts were the suns and moons of her old world, dividing everything into times when her mother was there and when she was not.

'I work at the shoe factory, girl! We all do; it's what we do. Why, before the Marquess came, we just lay about on beaches and ate mangoes and drank coconut milk and knew nothing about industry whatever! How gladsome we are, now that she has shown us our laziness! Now we know the satisfaction of a full day's labor, of punchcards and taxable income.'

September bit her lip. She wondered if the Marquess had happened by around the time their folklore had been stolen. 'I like mangoes,' she said glumly.

'We make the changelings' shoes,' continued Not/Nor, striding toward the silver half-palace that September now understood was a factory.

'That's all? No shoes for anyone else?'

'Well, there are rather a lot of changelings. Bandits, again. Always about. Besides, it's quite hard, to make the sorts of shoes changelings wear.'

September waited. She long ago learned that if she waited and blinked and behaved like a pupil, eventually someone would lecture her on something.

'It's why we're best suited, you know. Being this far southerly. It's all magnetized, see. If we didn't make the shoes, why, changelings would just float away back to their own world, and where would that leave all the honest folk who stole them fair and square?'

'I haven't floated away.'

'You're not a changeling! There's no poppet or goblin in your bed, taking your place at supper. There's more than one way between your world and ours. There's the changeling road, and there's Ravishing, and there's those that Stumble through a gap in the hedgerows or a mushroom ring or a tornado or a wardrobe full of winter coats. It's all dangerous, but changelings are terrible hard to keep track of. Someone's always trying to capture them back or pull them off their horses during dress parade. The shoes, though, the shoes keep them here. Otherwise they'd just . . . *fwoop*! Like balloons. I make right-foot shoes. With iron in the soles. Iron won't go through, see. Fairyland's allergic. So am I, of course, but I take my pills like the Marquess taught us.'

'What about the Ravished? How do they get home?' September realized that she was considering how to get home for the first time.

Not/Nor grinned. She had sharp, wolfish teeth. 'Can't say, can I? Or won't say, won't I? But it's better to Stumble, really, if you've a heart set on home.'

At the factory door, Not/Nor gathered up a great deal of leather into the crook of her arm. She pointed with her eyebrows at a communal well just outside the gate. September fell upon a copper ladle and drank deep. As she slurped, the Nasnas scratched her chin again. 'I might could make you a pair that works the other way,' she said finally. 'Reverse engineering, and all? A pair that would take you home.'

'Really? You could do that?'

'Shoes are funny beasts. You think they're just clothes, but really, they're alive. They want things. Fancy ones with gems want to go to balls, big boots want to go to work, slippers want to dance. Or sleep. Shoes make the path you're on. Change your shoes, change the path.' Not/Nor looked meaningfully at the Marquess's dandied black shoes. September wished she'd gone barefoot. 'Changeling shoes want to stay here. I wager I can make a pair who want to go to the place you come from. Bit of old mud on the heel, bit of devil's salt in the buckle, bit of growing up hammered in. You'll wake up, as if it were a dream. It will *have been* a dream. No worries, no faults, no blame. Off to school with you and your peanut-butter sandwich, too!'

September squeezed back tears. She suddenly missed her mother, and she'd lost her shadow and her hair, and salt creaked in her elbows, and she was so awfully tired, and really, she hadn't counted on adventures being so exhausting. She was hungry, still, and she missed her Wyverary so! And how could she know how much farther there was to go? September still did not think herself terribly brave, and she trembled when she thought of the thirst of the sea and the possibility – even probability – of sharks and other terrible things. When the stars were out and the night warm and Mr Map's brandy had been hot in her belly, it had been all right, even wonderful. But now her knees hurt – and her fingers – and she was lonely. September shivered in her wet, salt-crusted dress. And she hated her cursed shoes, hated them wholly and utterly.

'I can't,' she squeaked finally. 'I can't. My friends are not dreams. They need me.' And she remembered the awful dream and little Saturday chained up again on the floor of that dark cell. 'Who else will come for them if I don't?'

'What a dear heart you have, girl,' said Not/Nor. 'Of course, that's how she'll catch you, in the end.'

'How did you—'

'I know shoes, little one. And I know *those* shoes.' The Nasnas shrugged helplessly. 'I can't be late to work, you know. Other beasts in the world have troubles.'

Nor slid her fingers into the glowing seam between her and Not, and the two popped apart. Not bowed to her sister and bounded away. Nor punched her card in the machine near the silver door of the factory.

September let the half-lady go. She walked back over the heath where the little black flowers waved. Down at the beach, she wriggled out of her dress again and strung up her sail. She pushed off with her wrench into the current and watched the island dwindle.

'I'm not one of them,' she said to herself. 'No matter what they say. I don't work at some awful old factory, and my shadow isn't half myself.'

But she thought of Ell and Saturday, lost at the bottom of the world, bound up in the dark. And some part of her hurt, a part which had been joined to them as if along a glowing seam.

CHAPTER XVI
Until We Stop

In Which September Feeds Herself by Gruesome Means

I *shall* catch a fish, just see how I do!' cried September to no one but the moon. The moon, for his part, smiled behind one white hand and tried to look very serious.

But September had been thinking about the problem of a hook, and when she had her lock of hair tied up to the wrench again, she suddenly seized the hilt of the wrench and brought it banging down on the curlicued head of one of the silver sceptres. The wrench, eager for something to do, quite crushed the wand's head, and bits of metal flew over the deck of the raft. September picked out a likely shard and knotted it into her long, braided strands of hair.

'Now for bait,' she said, 'which I've none of *at all*.'

September suddenly cursed herself for not having thought to save a few berries from the beach.

'No points for ought to have,' she sighed.

September pushed the makeshift hook into the pad of her thumb until she could not help but yelp in pain. Blood welled up, and she rubbed the hook in it, all over, until it shone red. Her eyes watered, but she did not cry. The sound of her stomach was louder than the pain of her thumb. Slowly, she sunk the bloody hook into the water, and waited.

Fishing, as many of you know, is a very tedious activity. Fish are stubborn and do not like to be killed and eaten. One has to stay very still, so still one almost falls asleep, and even then no fish might come. Even the moon busied himself elsewhere, watching a pine forest full of martens and Harpies chase each other round in circles. The stars moved overhead, racing on their long silver track, and still, September sat, her line in the water, patient as death.

Finally, the line went taut and tugged beneath the mild waves. September leapt up. 'What have I caught?' she cried with excitement. 'What will it be? Why, this is like Christmas, when you've no idea what might be in the packages!'

September hauled hard on the wrench and fell backward as her prize flew up onto the deck. It was pink, the very color of a pink crayon, and its eyes bulged huge and emerald. It gaped pitifully, suddenly forced to contend with air instead of water. September felt sorry for it, all in a rush.

'I know you don't want to be eaten,' she said wretchedly. 'And I don't want to eat you! But it's been two days now, and I must have something!'

The fish gaped.

'If only you were a magic fish, you could grant a wish, and I could have more of the lovely spriggans' feast – or Ell's radishes.'

The fish sucked at the air but found no sea to breathe there.

'I am so sorry,' she whispered finally. 'I don't want to chew up another creature just to keep on for another day! You're alive. But I'm alive, too! Alive doesn't much care about anything but staying that way. Just like you meant to eat my blood, and that's why you were caught. I suppose I ought to stop talking. I don't think you are a magic fish.'

September did not know anything about killing fish, really. Her mother and grandfather usually did that part. But she could think logically enough. She brought the hilt of the wrench down hard on the pink fish's head. She shut her eyes at the last moment, though, and missed. Twice more and she had it, though she quite wished she hadn't. However, September knew that was not the worst part. You couldn't just bite into a fish. The guts had to come out. Wincing, not wanting to watch what her hands were doing, September took up the hook and brought it down on the fish's soft pink belly. The skin was tougher than she thought, and she had to saw at it. Her hands got quite soaked in blood, which looked black in the moonlight. Finally, she got the belly open and reached inside, where it was warm and slimy, and she was crying by then, big, hot tears rolling down her face and into the ruined fish. With one pull, she hauled the fish's organ parts out and threw them overboard, sobbing on her knees over her supper.

You mustn't think poorly of her for crying. Up until that moment, fish had mainly come into her life filleted, cooked, and salted with lemon juice on top. It is a hard thing to be starving and alone with no one to show you how to do it right. She got such sprays of blood on her face and on her knees.

September had no way to cook it. The sodden smoking jacket wanted to make fire for her, but that was beyond its power. The moon wished her a hearth but had to content himself with watching the young girl, kneeling on her raft as the sea rushed by around her and she pulled raw fish from the bone in strips. September ate slowly, deliberately. Some instinct told her that she had to have the blood, too, for at sea water is so scarce. It took her until morning to eat the fish. She wept all the while, a terrible circuit, all the water she drank from the fish pouring out again.

Just before dawn, September spied the shark's fin. Something deep in the ancestral memories of humans quakes in sight of a shark's fin, even if that human grew up in Omaha and never saw a shark in all her days. It rose dark and sharp in the pearly gloaming just before the sun peeked up. The fin made a long, lazy circle around September's raft. The wind was utterly calm. September's dress hung slack on the Spoon-mast. Little ripples glinted in the water, and the current moved her along, but it had been slow going for several hours, and September had slept. But now she was awake, and the stars were winking out one by one, and in the distance, the unmistakable triangle of a shark's head circled slowly, unconcerned.

This sort of thing happens in pirate stories, September remembered. *As soon as someone goes overboard, voilà! Sharks. But I am not a pirate. But then, pirates are often eaten by sharks. So perhaps I shall not have a pirate's luck with them if I do not have a cutlass or a feathered hat?*

It circled closer, and September could see its shadow in the water. It did not seem *huge,* but certainly big enough. Perhaps it was a baby and would leave her alone.

It circled still closer. September scrunched up into the center of the raft, as far as she could get from water on all sides, which was not very far at all. Finally, it circled so close to the raft that it jostled the sceptres, and September cried out fearfully. She held the wrench ready to whack the shark as hard as she might, her knuckles white on the handle. *If they all want to call it a sword,* she thought, *I'll use it as one!* She was quite wild with terror.

'Please,' she whispered. 'Don't eat me. I'm sorry I ate the fish.'

The shark swam lazily around the raft. It rolled up a little, showing its black belly – for the shark was all black, with a few wild golden stripes running down the side, and its eyes were golden, too, rolling up out of the water to stare mercilessly at September.

'Why are you sorry?' it said softly, its voice rasping and rough. 'I eat fish. That's what fish are for.'

'I daresay you think that's what little girls are for, too.'

The shark blinked. 'Some of them.'

'And who eats you?'

'Bigger fish.'

The shark kept swimming around the raft, rolling up toward the breaking surf to speak.

'Are you going to eat me?'

'You ought to stop talking about eating. It's making me hungry.'

September shut her mouth with a little snap. 'You're making me dizzy with all your swimming in circles,' she whispered.

'I can't stop,' the shark rasped. 'If I stop, I shall sink and die. That's the way I'm made. I have to keep going always, and even when I get where I'm going, I'll have to keep on. That's living.'

'Is it?'

'If you're a shark.'

September rubbed at the blood on her knee. 'Am I a shark?' she said faintly.

'You don't look like one, but I'm not a scientist.'

'Am I dreaming? This feels like a dream.'

'I don't think so. I could bite you, to see if it hurts.'

'No, thank you.' September looked out at the flat gray water, all severe and stark in the sunrise. 'I have to keep going,' she whispered.

'Yes.'

'I have to keep going, so that I can keep going after that, forever and ever.'

'Not forever.'

'Why haven't you eaten me, shark? I ate the fish; I ought to be eaten.'

'It doesn't work like that.'

'But you're a shark. Eating is what you do.'

'No. I swim. I roar. I race. I sleep. I dream. I know what Fairyland looks like from underneath, all her dark places. And I have a daughter. Who might have died, but for a girl in an orange dress who traded away her shadow. A shadow who might have known not to mourn over fish.'

September stared. 'The Pooka girl?'

The shark rolled over entirely in the water, her huge fin rearing up out of the waves and slicing down again. 'We all just keep moving, September. We keep moving until we stop.' The shark broke off and ploughed through a sudden, heavy swell that soaked September in its crashing. Just as she dove under the surf, September could see the great black tail shiver into legs, disappearing beneath the violet sea.

CHAPTER XVII

One Hundred Years Old

In Which September Discovers a Great Amount of Old Furniture and Finds Herself in a Very Dark Place with Only a Little Light

This time, September saw the island coming. It glimmered on the edge of the horizon, fitfully green and golden. In the evening of her fifth day at sea, September steered her raft toward it. She longed to feel land beneath her again, to drink real water, to eat bread. She fell gratefully on to warm sand, rolling in it like a puppy for pleasure. She found several coconuts strewn over the beach and cracked one in a single blow against a stone.

The sea makes a girl strong, you know.

Slurping the watery juice and crunching the meat of it, September dismantled her raft and dressed, making sure to tie the sash of the smoking jacket tight around her waist. She began to walk inland in hopes of better food. Surely she was near the Lonely Gaol by now. Surely she could spare a moment for lunch if it meant not having to go through the dreadful ordeal of fishing again.

But there was no village in the interior of that grassy little island. No sweet houses, their chimneys smoking away. No herald's square, no ringing churchbell. All she found was junk.

The beach sand gave way to long, whispering sea grass and in that long meadow lay a tremendous number of odd things, as though it were a garbage yard. Old sandals, teakettles, broken umbrellas, clay jars, torn silk screens, cowboy spurs, smashed clocks, lanterns, rosaries, rusted swords.

'Hello?' September called. The wind answered, buffeting the grass, but no one else.

'What a lonely place! I believe someone has forgotten to clean up after himself . . . for a good while, I suppose. Ah, well, perhaps I shall find a new pair of shoes . . .'

'I think *not*!'

September jumped half out of her skin, quite ready to run back to her raft and never make eyes at an island again. But her curiosity defeated her good sense. She peered over the grass to see who the voice might belong to. All she could see was an old pair of straw sandals with a bit of leather wrapped around the sole.

As she tiptoed over to get a better look, two old yellow eyes opened in the heels of the shoes.

'Who said you could have me? Not me, and *I* say whose feet I have to smush up against all day, I should rightly think!'

'I . . . I beg your pardon! I didn't know you were alive!'

'Well, that's folk with feet for you. Always thinking of themselves.'

Some of the other bits of junk crept closer to September: the swords unfolded long steely arms, and the jars sprouted thick, muscled feet. The silk screens accordioned their way to her, the teakettles turned their spouts toward the earth and spat steam until they popped upward. A great orange lantern floated on the wind, glowing slightly, and from beneath it, a green tassel hung, fluttering. A great clatter sounded as the garbage gathered around.

'Mr Shoes . . .'

'My name is Hannibal, if you don't mind.'

'Hannibal . . . I have read a great many books, and I have met spriggans and Pookas and even a Wyverary, but I cannot begin to imagine what you are!'

'WHO!' bellowed the shoes, hopping upright, straps flapping in indignation. '*What* is an *indirect dative* reserved for *things.* I am alive! I am a WHO. Or a *whom,* if you must. And we are Tsukumogami.'

September smiled uncertainly. The word meant no more to her than Mr Map's *ffitthit.* A pair of spurs whirred and clicked on spindly spidery legs.

'We're a hundred years old,' they said, as though that explained it all.

The great orange lantern, which September could not help comparing to a pumpkin, flashed briefly for attention. Slowly, gracefully, golden, fiery letters began to write themselves on the papery surface of the lamp:

You use the things in your house
and think nothing of them. It leaves us bitter.

September put her hands on her hips. 'I'm sorry! I didn't know! If a couch just sits there, looking like a couch, I can't be expected to know it isn't one.'

That's the trouble.
But when a household object turns one hundred years old, it wakes up. It becomes alive. It gets a name and griefs and ambitions and unhappy love affairs. It is not always a good bargain. Sometimes, we cannot forget the sorrows and joys of the house we lived in.
Sometimes, we cannot remember them.
Tsukumogami are one hundred years old. They are awake.

'All my house . . . just sleeping until their birthdays?' September bit her lip and looked out at the lonely grass. 'That's strange and sad. I often lose things, and break them, long before they turn one hundred. But . . . why haven't you any houses of your own? Or a village?'

We spent a century closed up within four walls and a roof.
We are claustrophobic.
We prefer the sun and the wind and the sea,
though it bites some of us,
who are made of metal, and tears papery hearts.

'How old are you?' snorted Hannibal, the pair of straw sandals.

'I'm twelve, Sir.'

A great consternation went up: kettles shrieked, swords rattled, shoes stomped.

'Well, that's no good *at all*!' Hannibal yelled. 'Never trust anyone under one hundred!' The throng of Tsukumogami rustled agreement. 'I'm afraid you'll have to leave. Folk under one hundred can't be borne – they're not mature enough. Not seasoned. They haven't seen grandchildren come and go or been left to gather dust in the winter while their family swans off to the sea for holiday! They're unpredictable! They could go off at any second! All caught up in *walking around* and *doing things*!'

'Twelve!' sniffed the spurs. 'Why, that's barely fifty!'

'It's not fifty at all,' snapped a silk screen. 'It's not even twenty. She might be a revolutionary! Young people go in for that sort of thing.'

The orange lantern flashed:

If she were a revolutionary,
I think she would have a rifle . . .

No one paid the lantern any attention.

'I certainly don't want to be a bother,' demurred September. 'I'll go, I will. Only, I wonder if you might have something I could eat? It is a harsh life at sea.'

'No!' snapped Hannibal, snapping his straps. 'Get out! Young cretin!'

September knew when she was not wanted. At least, when someone hollered at her to get out, she could guess as much. But she was wounded – so many folk had been so kind to her in Fairyland. Her cheeks burned under the gaze of the cast-off furniture. But then, perhaps, in the hinterlands, in the wild islands, the Marquess had not yet had a chance to force niceness upon them. She turned to go – and oh, she oughtn't to have turned her back on them! But perhaps it was not her fault. Perhaps it was the sudden trouble-making breeze that came along and drew aside the tall grass, just far enough that the flash of September's black shoes shone through the blades.

Several broken bells clanged an alarm, and Hannibal stomped after her like a musk ox. He tackled her, the soft smack of straw sandals slapping her back and knocking her forward.

'Shoes!' he crowed from atop September's body. 'Black shoes, ahoy!'

'Get off me!' yelled September, struggling under the sandals and trying to grab at them.

'Told you, told you! Even ninety-niners are suspect. Twelve? Why, that's as good as saying, "wicked and up to no good!"'

'I'm *not* up to no good! I'm trying to rescue my friends!'

'Don't care, don't care!' howled the sandals. 'Grab her, Swords! Don't be too careful with your blades, either! Down the well she goes!'

Cold, sharp hands grabbed her arms. Kettle steam scalded her feet until she screamed, scrambling to get up. The swords' grip cut into her arms. They hauled her over the grass while Hannibal giggled and sang along with his compatriots.

'She'll reward us, you'll see!' he assured them. 'We'll have our own young kettles for tea and not have to brew up the Earl Grey in Mildred anymore!'

'She?' cried September. 'Who told you to do this? Was it the Marquess?'

'We don't share state secrets with youngsters!'

The throng stopped suddenly short as a black hole opened up in the earth. It was lined with stone, all the way down. September could not see its bottom, but she thought she could hear the sea down there, splashing darkly.

'No!' she wept, trying to tear away from that terrible darkness. The swords cut deeper, and pain flooded her vision. Her skin was slippery with blood.

The orange lantern bobbed in front of her, just over the pit. The lovely handwriting flowed over its face.

The Marquess said to look for a girl wearing beautiful black shoes. I'm sorry.

'And do what?' shrieked September.

Kill her.

The swords threw September down into the black.

She fell a long way.

At first, September was not sure she was awake. She saw no difference, whether she opened her eyes or not. Slowly, she felt the cold wetness of sitting in several inches of seawater. Her bleeding, she thought, had stopped, at least, mostly stopped. But she could not move her arms, and she suspected her leg was broken. It surely was not supposed to bend that way beneath her. The cold water numbed her all over, and softly, quietly, September cried in the dark.

'I want to go home,' she said shakily to the dark. And she meant it, for the first time. Not as the lie that had gotten her into Fairyland, but the real and honest truth. Her lips trembled. Her teeth chattered. 'It's all so scary here, Mom,' she whispered. 'I miss you.'

September put her cheek to the cold stone wall. It was

fuzzy and wet with slime. She tried to think of Saturday, pressing his cheek against a dire wall like this one, waiting for her, believing she would come for him and smash his cage as she had before. She tried to think of Ell's warm bulk, curled against her in the dark.

'Help!' she yelled hoarsely. 'Oh, help . . .'

But no help came. September saw the day come pale and blue over the rim of the well. It seemed very far away. But the thin sunlight gave some courage. She tried to fill her mind with the scent of Lye's golden bath, fireplaces crackling and warm cinnamon and autumn leaves crunching underfoot. She put all of her weight on to her good leg, and pushed up out of the water – only her body buckled underneath her, and she fell back down, gasping for air.

Some time later, a soft thing brushed her face. September could not tell time at the bottom of the well, but it must have been night, because she could not see what it was. Blindly, she reached out. Orange light flooded the well. Sinking down to her came the lantern, beautiful and round as a pumpkin. Its tassel hung down below it and tied to the tassel was a huge green fruit. September snatched at it and tore it open with her teeth, slurping the pink juice and devouring the meat. She did not say thank you – she was quite beyond manners. The lantern watched her eat. When she had finished, September panted with the exertion of eating, looking wildly about.

Very slowly and gingerly, as though it was afraid to be caught at the deed, a slim hand rose up out of the top of the lantern. And then another. The pale greenish hands clutched the lantern sides and pulled up the orange globe – so that two girl's legs could stretch out beneath it. September waited, but no head came.

'Please help me get out,' whispered September.

Golden writing spooled out across the surface of the lamp.

I cannot.
They would tear me in half.

But the orange lantern wrapped her arms around September, and her legs, too, and held the little girl in the dark, stroking her hair. If September had looked up, she might have seen a gentle lullaby writing itself across the Tsukumogami's face.

Go to sleep, little firefly,
Float down to the earth . . .

But she did not look up, and very soon, September was asleep.

When she woke, the lantern had gone. The seawater had risen slightly. No day peeped through the top of the well. September screamed in frustration, kicking the wall with her good leg.

'I shan't make it to one hundred, you know!' she hollered up angrily. 'People don't live that long with *broken legs* in the *dark*!'

September screamed again, wordlessly. The cold seeped in, unmoved. She shoved her hands in her apologetic smoking-jacket pockets to keep warm – and what was there but the glass globe the Green Wind had given her? September seized it and threw it hard against the opposite wall in a fit of rage and frustration. She felt a little better. Breaking things heals a great many hurts. This is why children do it so often.

The green leaf that had been caught inside the crystal drifted down to the stagnant seawater and spun a bit on the surface of it, like a camping compass.

September felt something heavy and furred settle to rest on her lap. The well filled with a deep, profound purring.

'Oh . . .' choked September. 'It can't be. I must be dreaming. It just can't.'

September stroked a huge head nestled against her. Even in the dark, she knew it was spotted. She could feel whiskers prickling her arms.

'How would you like to come away with me, September?' said a familiar voice. The scent of green things filled the well: mint and grass and rosemary and fresh water, frogs and leaves and hay. September threw up her arms in the dark, knowing they would settle on broad shoulders. Her tears wet the cheek of the Green Wind, and he chuckled in her embrace.

'Oh, my little rolling hazelnut, where have you lost yourself?'

'Green! Green! You came! It was all going so well, and then the Marquess said she'd turn Ell to glue and I stole her Marid and we rode bicycles and I tried so hard to be brave, and irascible, and ill-tempered, but then they were gone, all of them, and I had to build a raft and I cut my hair off and my shadow's gone and I think my leg's broken, and I'm so scared! And I got a wrench! But I don't know what I'm meant to do with it and in the stories none of the heroes ever broke their legs and it's all on account of my shoes somehow, but that means the Marquess must have known, all along, that I'd come here, and I just want to go home.'

'Really? That's all? I can take you home just now,' murmured the Green Wind. 'If that's all you want. Nothing but a blink, and we're in Omaha, no harm done, all well and ending well. There, there. No need of crying.'

September's leg burned, and her arms felt so heavy. 'No,

but . . . my friends . . . they're locked away and they need me . . .'

'Well, it's all a dream, no worries about that. I'm sure it'll all work itself out. Dreams have a way of doing that.'

'Is it a dream?'

'I don't know, what do you think? It certainly *seems* like a dream. I mean, talking Leopards! My *stars*.'

September squeezed her fists in the dark.

'No,' she whispered. 'It's not. Or if it is, I don't care. They need me.'

'Good girl,' chuffed the Green Wind. 'When little ones say they want to go home, they almost never mean it. They mean they are tired of this particular game and would like to start another.'

'Yes, please, I would like to start another.'

'That's not a magic I have, love. You're in this story. You must get out on your own if you are to get out at all.'

'But how does this story end?'

The Green Wind shrugged. 'I don't know. It seems familiar to me so far. A child whisked off to a foreign land beset by a wicked ruler, sent to find a sword . . .'

'Am I to save Fairyland, then? Did you choose me to do that? Am I a chosen one, like all those heroes whose legs were never broken?'

The Green Wind stroked her hair. She could not see his face, but she knew it was grave.

'Of course not. No one is chosen. Not ever. Not in the real world. You chose to climb out of your window and ride on a Leopard. You chose to get a witch's Spoon back and to make friends with a Wyvern. You chose to trade your shadow for a child's life. You chose not to let the Marquess hurt your friend – you chose to smash her cages! You chose to face your own death, not to balk at a great sea to cross and no ship to cross it in. And twice now, you have chosen not to go home when you might have, if only you abandoned your friends. You are not the chosen one, September. Fairyland did not choose you – you chose yourself. You could have had a lovely holiday in Fairyland and never met the Marquess, never worried yourself with local politics, had a romp with a few brownies and gone home with enough memories for a lifetime's worth of novels. But you didn't. You chose. You chose it all. Just like you chose your path on the beach: to lose your heart is not a path for the faint and fainting.'

'I cannot just *choose* to get out of a well, though.'

The Green Wind laughed. 'No, no, you can't. But, September, my sparrow, my pigeon . . . I am still not allowed in Fairyland.'

'But you're here!'

'Technically speaking, I am *below* Fairyland. It's these little loopholes that make cheating so pleasurable. I mean to say, I can push you up – oh, any Wind can with half a mind. But I can't go with you. I can't help you anymore. Until the great doors swing open, I cannot enter.'

The Green Wind bent his head and blew gently upon September's mangled leg. September grimaced – it was rather a horrid feeling, being forcibly healed all at once, bones shoving together, muscles righting themselves. She groaned as the Leopard of Little Breezes lifted her head and licked roughly at the wounds on her arms until they vanished.

But still, September clung to the Green Wind, her safety, her protector. 'I had to kill a fish,' she whispered finally, as though confessing a great sin.

'I forgive you,' the Green Wind said softly, and dissolved in her arms with one great final purr from the Leopard. In his place, a whirlwind spun and spat, catching September up and pushing her into the air, up and out of the well.

It was night, and the stars were going about their shimmering business in the sky. The Tsukumogami slept in their warm field. The last of the Green Wind dissipated in a rustle of dry grass.

'Goodbye,' said September quietly. 'I wish you could stay.'

September crept along the field as silently as she could. The Spoon-mast of her little ship bobbed into view, and she nearly whooped for joy, but caught herself in time – for the orange lantern floated expectantly next to the raft, her green tassel hanging still.

'Please don't cry out,' whispered September. 'You brought me food; I know you don't think I'm wicked. Don't give me away, please!'

The orange lantern glowed warmly, beaming reassurance. Golden writing looped and swooped over her face.

Take me with you.

'What? Why? Don't you want to stay here? I'm only twelve, what am I to you?'

I'm only one hundred and twelve.
I wish to see the world. I am brave. I am strong.
They used to unpack me for festivals,
and I kept the night at bay.
When you get lost in dark places, I can show the way.
And you must admit, getting lost is likely,
and where one is lost, it is likely to be dark.

'I'm afraid I'm not much of a tour guide. I'm going to rescue my friends from the Lonely Gaol, and very terrible things will almost certainly happen.'

I will not disappoint you, I promise.
My name is Gleam. Take me with you.
I held you in the dark.
I defied straw sandals to bring you sunfruit.
I am worth something.
One hundred and twelve years is worth something.

September shrugged off her jacket and dress. She looked down at her shoes, the beautiful, shining, glittering black shoes. Slowly, she took them off, one by one, and set them on the sand. September looked at them for a long time, shining blackly on the beach. Finally she picked them up and threw them as hard and as far as she could into the sea. They bobbed for a moment, then sank.

'There,' September said. 'That's better.' She smiled at the orange lantern. 'Oh, Gleam, do you know? I forgot to tell the Leopard that I met her brother the Panther . . .'

September pushed her raft into the bouncing waves. Gleam followed quickly behind, lighting up the night like a tiny autumn moon.

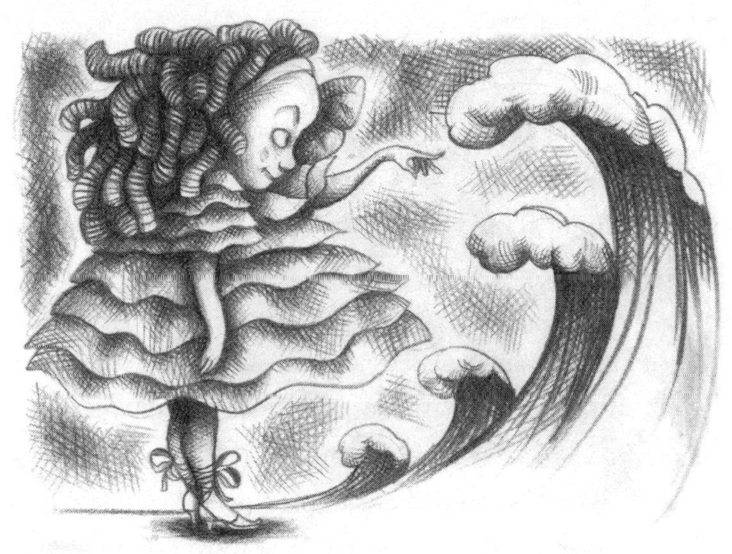

CHAPTER XVIII

The Lonely Gaol

In Which September Arrives at Last at the Bottom of the World, but Is Unexpectedly Expected

A ring of blue storms dance around the Lonely Gaol. They are on social terms with one another – the storms hold cotillions in the spring and harvest dances in the fall. If one has the right wind speed and precipitation, one can attend storm weddings, storm funerals, storm christenings. It is a happy life for a storm. None think of travel, nor sailing the free ocean, nor venturing into foreign lands of any sort. They do not know why they stay, huddled up tight at the bottom of the world, only that they have always lived there. These were their parents' and grandparents' stomping grounds, too, all the way down to the single primordial storm that in days of old covered the whole of the continent.

But I am a sly and wicked narrator. If there is a secret to be plumbed for your benefit, Dear Reader, I shall strap on a headlamp and a pickaxe and have at it.

The current of Fairyland circles the Lonely Gaol. It sluices in through holes in the base of the great towers and emerges on the other side, to begin once more its long journey around the horn of Fairyland. This unstoppable circulation kicks up storms the way you kick up dust when you run very fast down a dirt road. It cannot be helped. Somewhere deep down there in the roots of the Lonely Gaol lives a hoary old beast, something like a dragon, something like a fish, something like a mountain rill. She is older than the Gaol and the sluicing of the water – older, perhaps, than Fairyland. When she breathes in, she sucks up crystal from the stones of the earth. When she breathes out, she blows bubbles in the crystal, so that it swells up in great lumps and heaps. The sea splashes and cools the glass, and it grows and grows. Perhaps, she is sleeping. Perhaps, she is too big and too old to do much but breathe. But this is how the Lonely Gaol, which was not always a gaol at all, grew out of the sea in the first place. If you squint just so, you can see the red flares of her breath between the roaring waves, blinking on and off like a dock light.

September could see it. She did not know what it was she saw. That is the disadvantage of being a heroine, rather than a narrator. She knew only that a red light glowed and went dark, glowed and went dark. In the shrieking whirl of the storms, she clung to her copper wrench and steered toward the light. Rain slashed at her face. Her skin had long ago gone numb and half blue. Everything ached from wrestling the raft to stay on course. Gleam bobbed and floated up ahead, valiantly trying to show the way, but the storm air was so awfully dark and thick. Lightning turned the world white – when she could see again, September looked up and glimpsed huge holes tearing open in her orange dress. A whip of wind lashed out and finished the job: The dress ripped along the sleeves and shot off into the dark. The storm ate up September's cry of despair, delighted at its mischief, as all storms are.

Gleam flashed several times up ahead, her orange paper soaked and ragged.

Look!

At first, September could not see what the lantern meant. Before her lay only shadows within shadows. The red light sighed faithfully, off and on, off and on. But one shadow grew greater and blacker than the others as she strained to peer through the violet and violent clouds. It soared lumpish and huge, towering up in gargantuan humps, boulders, misshapen domes. Pale fires lit windows far up the sides of the towers. In flashes of lightning, September could see that mold and moss and lichen covered the lower domes, slurping upward toward the peaks. But the high towers were all of glass, and storms showed through, roiling and purple.

A sickening crack shuddered through the raft – they had run aground. A spear of glassy rock spurted through the silver sceptres, just barely missing September's leg. The rain hissed and fell, and for once, September was glad she had cut off her hair, for if she still had it, she would surely be unable to see a thing for all its flapping in her face. Shaking and tired, she pulled up the sodden green smoking jacket from its place, wedged in between cracks in the raft. Oh, how the jacket wanted to hug her and reassure her that a little rain was not so terribly bad! Having no dress now, September pulled the emerald jacket over her sore body. She untied the sash from the Spoon, which had served so well and loyally as a mast, and knotted it tight round her waist. The smoking jacket rushed to lengthen and broaden into a dress for her, and tried its best to radiate warmth. September slung the Spoon and the Wrench through the sash on either side of her hips, like a cowboy's guns.

Gleam extended a long, pale green arm from the base of the lantern. September took it and began hauling herself up the slippery glass humps of the Lonely Gaol.

Far below, the creature who was neither a dragon, nor a fish, nor a mountain rill, breathed in and out, in and out.

'Gleam,' September whispered. 'Can you fly away up to the top of the towers and see whether a red Wyvern or a blue Marid is there to be seen?'

Gleam brightened a little and disappeared like an orange arrow, darting up through the howling storm. September watched her go, crouching behind a slime-slathered boulder. She did not want to think about the door. All prisons have their gates, and all prison gates are guarded. The gate of the Lonely Gaol glimmered faintly in the storm light, bolted with iron.

To keep them in, September thought. *For iron hurts them so.*

The two Blue Lions flanked the door, their manes waving and curling slowly as though they were underwater, silver stars gleaming in their tails, their fur. Still, they slept, but

September remembered that even sleeping they had stolen her friends away in half a blink. Certainly, she would be no work at all for them.

September thought furiously. She could not possibly fight the lions – they were the size of houses! If Ell could not fight them, she had no hope. All she had was the Spoon and the Wrench and a very wet jacket. *And really, I oughtn't to use the Spoon. It's not mine. I've no idea about how witchcraft is done. Might as well ask me to make a pie out here. With ice cream on top.*

And yet, the Spoon loomed large in her mind, as if offering its services. September peered around her and spied a little tide pool. She crept along the rocks and stuck her hand into the cold water. She could feel a few stubborn mussels clinging to the glass along with a great deal of dead kelp and mud. Well, it was a *kind* of soup, wasn't it? September blindly scraped at the glass lumps around her, gathering lichen and moss and unnameable gunk into the pool, trying to look like a brave, resourceful witch who knew just *exactly* what she was doing. She took up the Spoon and slid it into the pool, stirring counterclockwise, which is to say, *widdershins.*

'Please,' September whispered, squeezing her eyes shut as if wishing. 'Show me a future when I have already gotten through the door, and how I did it.'

For a long while, the pool stayed black and murky. The storm laughed at her, throwing out a few more lightning bolts for good measure. September stirred harder. She did not know what else a witch was meant to do. Perhaps, it would not work, since she did not have a hat and was not at all dressed well. *'We have to dress well or the future will not take us seriously,'* Goodbye had said. Well, certainly the soupy pool had no reason to take September seriously. She didn't even have shoes anymore.

Slowly, the pool began to quiver. *Oh, please!* September thought desperately. A fuzzy, warped image flickered on the surface of the water, like a broken movie reel. September watched a small version of the iron gate coalesce, with two small lions on either side. They were not really blue, but sort of green and wriggly, like mold. A tiny green something walked up to the lions. Behind the tiny green something floated an even tinier round light, like a Will-o'-the-wisp. September turned her head to one side, trying to see what was happening in the tide pool. The tiny green somethings, which were surely herself and Gleam, walked boldly up to the gate. Herself took something out of her coat and held it up high. After a moment, the lions lay down before the tiny green September and put their paws over their eyes.

The Wrench, September thought. *They recognize the Wrench!*

Of course, they do: It's Queen Mallow's sword! They must still be bound by some feline fealty to it, even if she is gone.

Just then, Gleam came spiraling back down the rain-slick towers. She tucked in behind the boulders and kept her golden letters dampened and dim.

Your friends are in the highest cell.
I think the red one is sick.

'Oh, Ell! I'm coming!' September whispered.

Together, September and Gleam approached the gate. September tried to be as bold as the little green version of herself in the tide pool. But of course, tide-pool girls don't sweat and breathe very fast and worry about their Wyveraries. The lions were ever so much bigger than she remembered. A line of silver light shone under their furry blue eyelids. September wondered if they were always on the verge of waking if they ever did wake, and if, perhaps, they were kind and dear when they did, and not vicious at all. She held up the copper Wrench, and it flashed in the lightning-shadows. The waiting was horrible – September winced, prepared for the blow of a great paw. But they lay down gently, the left one first, then the right. They put their paws over their eyes.

September ran at the door and hauled it open, her bare feet

slipping in the rain. She slipped inside, and Gleam behind her, chased by three thunderclaps, all in a row: *crash, boom, crack.*

Warm firelight turned the Lonely Gaol cheerful and ruddy. A great white hearth crackled and snapped with fresh logs. Filigree silver torches shone on the walls. A long, rich rug of every possible color swept over the grand floor. The lumpy glass walls showed the storm still raging outside, but instead of a terror, it had the effect of a beautiful painting hung in a fine hall. The boiling clouds were quiet and brilliant, blue and violet and pale gold all bleeding into one another. Rain spattered the buttresses and left sparkling drops like cast-off diamonds. A few stars even peeked through the ceiling, their light filtering down through many thin, spiral staircases.

A door at the far end of the hall burst open. September started and steeled herself to fight if she had to. All that mattered was getting up the staircase and finding Saturday and Ell, whoever she had to go through to do it.

A peal of delighted laughter echoed through the glass room, and a little girl in a frilly white dress ran full tilt across the many-colored rug, her golden curls bouncing. She embraced September like a long-lost sister, still laughing and exclaiming with joy.

'Oh, September, you're safe! I'm so happy you've come,

finally, and not a scratch on you!' The Marquess pulled away and cupped September's face in her hands. 'What fun we are going to have!' she exclaimed.

'Fun?' September cried, still dripping, sopping wet. '*Fun?* You stole my friends and set the Tsukumogami after me! I broke my leg, and I almost died, and I almost froze in the storm! And you *cheated*! I could have gotten the Wrench back to you in seven days and none of this would have happened! And now Ell is sick and he needs me and this is *fun*?'

September could not help it. Before she even knew she had done it, she slapped the Marquess across the face. But the Marquess's hair flushed pale blue, and she just laughed again. She used her laugh like a little knife. September's handprint flushed on her face.

'Of course I cheated. Why wouldn't I cheat? If I hadn't cheated, you would have brought me the sword like a good little questing knight, and it would have been of no use to me whatsoever. I can't touch the ridiculous thing. I needed you. Here, in this place, with your loyal blade at your side.'

'Then why tell all that furniture to kill me?'

The Marquess cocked her head to one side. Her black hat bobbed merrily.

'September, I had to make it look real. Otherwise, you would have suspected that you were doing my work all along.

Oh, just *everyone* has told you what a wicked beast I am – you're quite biased against me. And more importantly, you had to see how dangerous Fairyland can be. How quickly these darling little creatures with their funny habits can turn on you and destroy you. Otherwise, you might not do my work. I am not really wicked at all. *They* are nasty and cruel. But I can be so terribly kind, September.'

September looked into the Marquess's shining blue eyes. 'But I would have. To save my friends. I would have done whatever you asked.'

'No,' answered the Marquess ruefully. 'Not this. Not even to save them. Believe me, September, I have thought on these matters a great deal. I have made calculations that would beggar your soul. What is it that villains always say at the end of stories? "You and I are more alike than you think." Well' – the Marquess took September's hand in hers and very gently kissed it – 'we are. Oh, how alike we are! I feel very warmly toward you, and I only want to protect you, as I wish someone had protected me. Come, September, look out the window with me. It's not a difficult thing. A show of faith, let's call it.'

September allowed herself to be led to one of the sheer crystal walls. Gleam followed silently, flashing with anxiety. Below them, the sea crashed away, sending up spray and spume. The Marquess held up her hand – and the sea calmed, drew aside, all in a moment. The sky cleared in a widening circle, like an iris. Stars beamed through – and half a moon. And where the sea had been were huge stone shapes in the water, turning at a creeping pace. *Click*. The shapes had wide square teeth like gears. Gears of ancient stone, enormous and inexorable. *Click*. They turned against one another. *Click*.

'What are they?' September asked.

'The Gears of the World. We are within the secret heart of Fairyland, September. The current that moves through the sea begins and ends here. And more than that – so much more.'

The Marquess raised her hand again, and the sea drew farther away. September watched as the stone gears ground into something else – iron gears, more deliberately made, sharper.

'This is the place where your world joins ours. Where the human world touches Fairyland, just for a moment. This place is all that allows folk to travel – only occasionally and by strange roads – from one place to another. The touch of the iron makes Fairies weaker, so that they cannot storm over your world and subdue it. The stone keeps humans at bay. But some can pass through. Without that brief kiss of iron and stone, the worlds would uncouple and separate entirely. No one would ever get trapped here or in the human world. No child could be stolen and replaced with a goblin, or worse, replaced with nothing and her mother left to mourn. No one would ever get lost.'

'Oh . . .'

'You see, don't you? What you have to do.'

'I don't want to.'

'But it is the right thing. Take up thy mother's sword, September, the only girl in Fairyland who could have pulled a wrench from that casket, whose mother could have known and loved machines, engines, tools. As soon as you told me about her, I knew, I just knew that we were meant to find one another, here, at the end of everything. Uncouple the worlds, September. Tear them apart so that no one can ever again drag a poor, lost child across the boundaries and abandon them here without a friend in the world.'

CHAPTER XIX

Clocks

In Which All Is Revealed

'Surely the Wrench is too small,' said September.

'I told you,' coaxed the Marquess, her hair full of storm colors, violet and gray. 'It is not a wrench. It is a sword, impossibly old. It will be whatever size you need it to be.'

'But . . . then there would be no more adventures. No more Fairies in my world to tell stories about, and no humans here to know what a Wyvern looks like. No more fairy tales at all, for where would they come from?'

'No more Fairies making mischief, spoiling beer and cream, stealing children, eating souls. No more humans meddling with Fairyland, mucking up its politics and tracking mud all over the floor.'

'And I should not ever be able to go home.'

'That is why I had to go to such lengths to bring you here, to show you Fairyland as it really is. It is a sacrifice I ask of you, September. A very great one, I know. But you must do it, for all the other children to come.' The Marquess's hair seeped indigo. 'Besides, it shouldn't be that hard. You didn't even wave goodbye to your father, shooting at people in some awful battlefield! You didn't think of your mother at all! You don't *want* to go home, not really. Stay here and play with me. I will let your friends free, and we can all dance together through the snow and the storm. I know such wonderful games.'

September might have cried a week ago, ashamed at how she had treated her mother and father. But she was wrung dry of tears now.

'I won't,' she said firmly. 'It was wrong of me not to say goodbye. That does not mean it is right to put an end to everything. How awful it would be to say that no other child should ever get to see what I have seen. To ride on a Wyvern and a highwheel, to meet a witch.'

The Marquess frowned. Her hair shivered into a frosty white. 'I suspected you would say that. You are selfish, after all, and heartless, like all children. But allow me to make my argument?'

Iago, the Panther of Rough Storms, appeared silently at her side as though he had always been there. He purred.

September, her skin finally and slowly warming in the hall, allowed the Marquess to pull her on to Iago's back, where an onyx saddle bore her up. She could not help but think of the Leopard and the Green Wind as the monarch of Fairyland settled in behind her and put her arms around September's waist.

Gleam hesitated:

She will lie to you.

'I know,' September sighed. 'But how else will Saturday see the sun again? Or Ell?'

I am one hundred and twelve years old.
That is a long time. I know her—

With a singing snap, a silver arrow pierced Gleam's papery skin, and she dropped to the floor in mid-sentence. September whirled in the saddle. The Marquess tucked her iceleaf bow behind her back, where it disappeared like vapor, the thorny branch of it still quivering slightly as it dissolved.

'Old folk are so terribly annoying, don't you agree? Always trying to spoil our fun with their incessant babbling about bygone days!'

Before September could protest, Iago leapt into the air, soaring up into the towers of the Lonely Gaol, leaving the ruin of a paper lantern behind them.

A pale-green hand crept out of the top of the lantern, covered with blood. After a while, it was still.

Everywhere she looked, September was surrounded by clocks. In a tiny room at the top of a bulbous tower, the Marquess, Iago, and September crowded in, nearly squeezed out by the volume of clocks: grandfather clocks and bedside alarm clocks and dear little Swiss cuckoo clocks with golden birds in them, pocket watches and pendulum clocks and water clocks and sundials. The ticking went on and on, like heartbeats. Under each clock was a little brass plaque, and on each plaque was a name. September did not recognize any of them.

'This is a very secret place, September. And a very sad one. Each of these clocks belongs to a child who has come to Fairyland. When it chimes midnight, the child is sent home

– all in a huff, whether she asked to go or not! Some clocks run fast, so fast a boy might dwell in Fairyland for no more than an hour. He wakes up, and what a lovely dream he had! Some run slow, and a girl might spend her whole life in Fairyland, years upon years, until she is snapped horribly back home to mourn her loss for the rest of her days. You can never know how your clock runs. But it does run – and always faster than you think.'

The Marquess leaned forward, her hair shining redder than any apple. She smoothed the dust from a plaque under a particular clock: a milky pink-gold one, cut out of a whole, enormous pearl. Its hands stood golden and motionless at ten minutes to midnight.

The plaque beneath the clock read, SEPTEMBER.

'You see?' crooned the Marquess. 'You have so little time left. Just enough to fly down to the seaside with Iago and do as I ask. Or else you will be snatched back, and your friends stuck here with me. I promise, I will take out my frustration upon them. Don't be stubborn! Just a little turn of your Wrench, and all will be well. You can eat lemon ices and ride highwheels to your heart's content, and your boys safe beside you.'

September touched the face of the pearly clock. She picked it up, marveling at it. She was so tired. All she wanted was to sleep, and wake up to steaming cocoa, then sleep again.

If Saturday and Ell were safe, she could sleep. She tried not to think about Gleam. It would be wonderful, really, to live in Fairyland forever. Isn't that what anyone would wish for? Isn't that what she herself had wished for, so often? To fly and leap and know magic and eat Gagana's Eggs and meet Fairies? September closed her eyes: She saw her mother there, on the backs of her eyelids. Crying on the edge of her bed. Because September had not left a note. Had not even waved goodbye.

When she opened them again, her eyes fell on the little brass plaque: SEPTEMBER. Furtively, so that the Marquess might miss her doing it, she glanced at the other plaques. They said things like, GREGORY ANTONIO BELLANCA and HARRIET MARIE SEAGRAVES and DIANA PENELOPE KINCAID. But hers just said, SEPTEMBER. And didn't it look a little tacked on? Was there – possibly – just the shadow of something else behind it? September bent her head and picked at the bottom corner of the plaque with her thumb.

'What are you doing?' the Marquess said sharply.

September ignored her. The plaque gave a little – she pried it out with her fingernails. It clattered to the floor. Behind it was a much older plaque, gone green with verdigris. It read,

MAUD ELIZABETH SMYTHE

'True names,' said September wonderingly. 'These are all true names. Like, when your parents call you to dinner and you don't come, and they call again but you still don't come, and they call you by all your names together, and then, of course, you have to come, and right quick. Because true names have power, like Lye said. But I never told anyone my true name. The Green Wind told me not to. I didn't understand what he meant, but I do now.' September looked up. Iago watched her with his round, calm eyes. He flicked his gaze toward the Marquess, and all of the sudden September knew; she knew it, though she could not say, not exactly, how she could possibly have known. 'This is *your* clock!' she cried, brandishing it. 'And it's stopped!'

The Marquess's hair went black with rage. Her face flushed and Iago growled under his breath. But finally, she gave out a long sigh and simply took off her hat. She lay it gently on the gable of a cuckoo clock. She ran her hands through her hair – it faded to a plain, dull blonde. She ran her hands over her dress – it became a gray farmer's daughter's dress with old yellow lace at the collar.

'I dreamed about you!' cried September.

'We are alike, I said. It would break your heart, September, how alike we are. This is what I looked like when I was twelve and lived on my father's farm. We grew more tomatoes than any other farm in Ontario. Just acres of them. But we weren't rich. My father drank most anything we earned. My mother was a seamstress – she took in all the mending from the neighbors. She died when I was eight, and I took up the mending after that, so that I could eat some and have a Sunday dress after the harvest was in and the whiskey house closed down. I always smelled like tomatoes. And then one day, when I couldn't bear the mules and the chores and the horrid, horrid tomatoes any longer, I hid in the attic until my father gave up looking for me and went to work the fields with his hands. I had a splendid day up there, rooting around among all the old things my mother had left behind, and her mother before that. Of course, you can imagine what happened. There was an old armoire, covered in a drop cloth. I pulled down the cloth, and when I opened the door of the armoire, it was so deep and dark in there that I couldn't see a thing. So I climbed inside. And the door closed so fast behind me. And I kept walking, until somehow the sun was shining again and I was standing in a field of the greenest grass and the prettiest red flowers you ever saw. And right there in front of me was a Leopard, as big as life.' The Marquess's eyes filled with tears. 'I Stumbled, September, into Fairyland. I didn't know what I'd done, only that it was so beautiful, and the wind was so sweet, and there were no tomatoes anywhere. I certainly didn't know I had a clock. I had such adventures, oh, so many! I grew up a bit and was so glad to grow up a bit and not be small and gray any longer. I learned such things – I met a young sorcerer with funny old wolf ears, and he let me read all of his books. Can you imagine? A farmer's daughter, being allowed to sit and read all day with no one to bother her? I thought I would die with the pleasure of it. And every day, the sorcerer would ask my name, but I was ashamed to tell him. Maud is so ugly and plain, and everyone here was named something marvelous. But one day, we were working the garden. The sorcerer was showing me how to harvest a particular root to make a kind of candy that might – if you boiled it just right – turn your hair all manner of colors.' The Marquess looked up at September, tears streaking her face. She spread out her hands, trembling. 'I took his hand in mine, and I said, "You can call me Mallow."'

September's mouth dropped open.

'The days went by like dreams, September. Before I knew it, I had a sword and I'd faced down King Goldmouth and his army of clouds, and I was Queen. I ruled long and well and wisely. Anyone will tell you. I married my sorcerer. We were happy. Fairyland prospered, and I could hardly remember what a tomato was anymore. My Leopard played at my side. I discovered, by and by, that I was with child. I had not told my sorcerer yet. I was enjoying my secret, lying on the broad lawn outside my palace and drifting off into sleep, my head propped up on my Leopard's flank.

'I think, well, when I remember it now, I think I can remember the tick. The last tick of my clock. With one awful ticking, I was swept out of Fairyland as though I had never been there. I woke up in my father's house, curled up inside the armoire, as though no time at all had passed. No Leopard. No sorcerer. No child. I was twelve again and hungry, and my father was just getting home from his day's work. He bellowed up to me, his voice thick with liquor. But oh, how I remembered it all! I remembered it fiercely, my whole life in Fairyland, taken away in an instant! Because a *clock* ran out! September, surely, you can feel in your bones the unfairness of it! The loss! I screamed in the armoire. I kicked the wooden walls in, trying to get back. I cried as though I were dying. My father found me and gave me a good thrashing for sneaking around where I oughtn't. I tasted blood in my mouth.'

The Marquess sank to her knees. Iago pressed his silky black head against her cheek.

'How . . . how did you get back?' September said softly.

'I clawed my way back, September. I would have broken the world open to crawl back in. I searched every scrap of furniture in that attic for another way. But the armoire was just an armoire, and the closet just a closet, and the jewelry box just a jewelry box. I read newspapers ravenously, looking for missing children, begging my father to take me to the places where they'd vanished. He refused. He got a new wife, and she sent me away to school, to be rid of me. I didn't care – I was glad to be rid of them! My new school was old and creaky, with dusty corners and draughty halls. Just the sort of place that might conceal a door to Fairyland in a story. And one morning, just walking to geometry class, I took one step on those dirty cobblestones and took the next one in a broad golden field full of glowerwheat. It was a hard passage – blood shot out of my nose, and I think I probably fainted. We aren't meant to come that way, so harshly. But it was the only way.'

'What was?' September was almost afraid to know.

'The clock, September. The clock is all. It is the only arbiter. What I needed was a man on the inside. Someone in Fairyland, a friend. Not a husband or a Leopard. Someone whose loyalty and love for me was greater than any law, any boundary, stronger than blood or reason or cat or man. Someone I had made with my own hands, who loved only me, who could not bear to be parted from me.'

'Lye!'

'Yes, Lye, my poor golem. She risked her whole being to come here, where the water is relentless and wore so much of her away. She battled the guards, who in those days were bear-wights, and gained entrance to this little room. She set my clock going backward and pulled me back into this world by the scruff of my neck. I didn't know that then. It was only later, when I came here myself, that I discovered her tracks. Standing in her soapy footprints, I stopped my clock, so that it could never snatch me back out of my own life again. I was a child once more, but I was home. Time is a mystery here. Only a year back home, and everyone I knew here in my life as Mallow had grown old or died. No one remembered what I looked like as a child. I told them I'd killed her. I tore down her banners and broke her throne. And so I had my revenge.'

'But why? You could have ruled well again and been loved! Maybe your time was done, maybe defeating King Goldmouth and restoring Fairyland was your destiny, and when it was finished . . .'

The Marquess grimaced. She ran her hands back over her hair – the black curls returned. She ran her hands over her dress – black crinoline flowed over her, and lace, and jewels. She placed her hat firmly back on her head and dried her eyes.

'I am not a toy, September! Fairyland cannot just cast me aside when it's finished playing with me! If this place could steal my life from me, well, I, too, can steal. I know how the world works – the real world. I brought it all back with me

– taxes and customs and laws and the Greenlist. If they wanted to just *drop* me back in the human world, I can drop the human world into theirs, every bit of it. I punished them all! I bound down their wings, and I set the lions on them if they squeaked about it. I made Fairyland *nice* for the children who come over the gears, I made it *safe*. I did it for every child before me who had a life here, who was happy here! Don't you see, September? *No one should have to go back.* Not ever. We can fix this world, you and I. Uncouple the gears and save us both! Let this be a place where no one has to be dragged home, screaming, to a field full of tomatoes and a father's fists!'

September reeled. She had thought she was done with crying, but she could not bear the Marquess's tale. Tears flowed hot and frightened and bitter. Iago howled, mourning for Mallow or the Marquess or Fairyland, September could not be sure.

'I'm sorry, Mallow . . .'

'Don't call me that,' the Marquess snapped.

'Maud, then. I'm so sorry.'

'Are you going to tell me how wicked I am?'

'No.'

'Good. Now do as I say, little girl, or I shall throttle your friends in front of you and let Iago have the meat of them.'

Iago grimaced a little.

September still clutched the pearly clock to her breast. She could not imagine it – living a whole life here and then, suddenly, horribly, being a lost child again, all of everything gone. It was too awful to think of. Gently, September turned the clock over in her hands. But the Marquess, poor Maud, was broken now, and she wanted to break Fairyland, too, to make it like her, sad and bitter and coiled up like a snake, ready to strike at anyone, friend or foe. September slid her fingernail under the latch. The door of the clock's workings sprang free. What if it had been September, and she had lived here so long that she forgot home?

September's hands found the stopped gears. She knew she could do it. Clocks were easy. Her mother had taught her about clocks ages ago. *Even if it were me,* she thought, *I could not chain Ell's wings like that.*

September drew the Wrench from her side. It was huge and long, its copper hand shining brightly.

'It will be as big as I need it to be,' she murmured.

And the Wrench sighed. It melted in her hand like a popsicle in the summertime, until it was delicate and tiny, a jeweler's tool. Before the Marquess could tell her not to, September gripped the offending wheel within the heart of Maud Elizabeth Smythe's clock with her Wrench and pulled at it.

'Don't you dare!' cried the Marquess. She ran her hand along Iago's black spine. He just looked up at her, his emerald eyes sad.

'Mallow . . .' he whispered. 'I'm tired.'

'Please! I can't go back!' The Marquess snatched September's hand, squeezing it horribly tight.

'Don't you touch me!' cried September. 'I'm not like you!'

The Marquess laughed her knifelike laugh again. 'Do you think Fairyland loves you? That it will keep you close and dear, because you are a good girl and I am not? Fairyland loves no one. It has no heart. It doesn't care. It will spit you back out just like it did me.'

September nodded miserably. They were both crying, struggling with the Wrench. September plunged her fingers into the clock, desperately trying to turn the wheel on her own. The gears cut her chilled hands and soaked the clock's innards with blood.

'No, no, I won't let you! I won't go home!' The Marquess sobbed. And then she did an extraordinary thing.

She let September go. The Marquess took a step back, as big a step as she could manage in that tiny place. The storm flashed lightning and rain behind her. 'I won't let you. Either of you. Not you, not Fairyland. I won't let you win.' She put her hand on her chest. 'I have magic yet. If you will set the clock working again, then I must be still. I have read quite as many stories as you, September. More, no doubt. And I know a secret you do not: I am not the villain. I am no dark lord. I am the princess in this tale. I am the maiden with her kingdom stolen away. And how may a princess remain safe and protected through centuries, no matter who may assail her? She sleeps. For a hundred years, for a thousand. Until her enemies have all perished and the sun rises over her perfect, innocent face once more.'

The Marquess fell down. It was so fast – one moment, she stood; the next, she had dropped like a flower snapped in half. She lay perfectly still on the floor, her eyes shut, serene.

September turned the wheel with her tiny wrench. The hands moved, slowly at first, and then whirred faster and faster.

In the room, suddenly, a soft alarm bell began to ring.

CHAPTER XX

Saturday's Wish

In Which Escapes Are Made, a Great Wrestling Match Occurs, and a Stranger Appears

'Is she dead?' whispered Iago.

The Marquess breathed deep and even. The Panther of Rough Storms bent his ponderous black head and bit her experimentally, the way one pinches oneself to test whether one is dreaming. She did not move.

'I don't think so . . .' said September fearfully.

'I ought to take her away somewhere. Somewhere quiet. I

think a bier of some kind is traditional in these cases.'

'Shouldn't she . . . go back now? That the clock is working?'

'I'm not an expert. Maybe she is back. Maybe she is dreaming of tomatoes and her father. I hope not.' The Panther meowed horribly. 'I did love her. In her sleep, she looked so like Mallow. I kept thinking, *One day, she'll wake up, and it'll be like it once was, and we shall all have a nice cake and laugh about how silly things got.*'

A distant shatter and crash echoed through the Lonely Gaol.

Iago looked up, unconcerned. 'She held half this world together with her will. It will all come apart now. I wonder what we shall all look like without her?'

'I have to get my friends out! Help me, Iago, please, I can't get to them by myself!'

'Oh . . . well, I suppose someone ought to have a good ending, out of all of us.' The Panther's eyes were glassy and faraway. 'She fed me fish,' he whispered. 'And blackberry jam.'

'Not together, I hope,' said September, trying to make him laugh as she climbed into his saddle. A great tear splashed on to the Marquess's sleeping cheek as Iago rose up and away from his still, cold mistress.

• • •

'Oh, Saturday . . .'

The Marid lay on the floor of a cell, his hands bound behind his back, his mouth gagged. Terrible bruises bloomed purple and black where the lion had bitten him. His eyes were sunken and sallow.

'Wake up, Saturday . . .'

He groaned in his sleep. A savage crack appeared in the tower wall behind him, squeaking and shrieking as if about to burst.

'Saturday!' September cried. She took her Wrench by the hilt – it grew huge again in her hand. She swung it with all her might against the moss-slimed glass door of Saturday's cell. The door shattered, shards tinkling to the floor. September pried the manacles open with the hooked hand of her Wrench and pulled Saturday's gag away. She held him for a moment, stroking his hair. Slowly, his eyes opened.

'September!' he croaked.

'Can you walk? We have to go: The Gaol is breaking!'

'It will be all right – the dragon will build it up again . . .'

'What? We're up so high, we'll be killed!'

'Well, she's not really a dragon, but . . .'

'Saturday! Pay attention! Where is Ell?'

The Marid gestured weakly toward the next cell. Iago glanced inside.

'He's really rather poorly, that one. I don't think you'll get him out.'

September lay Saturday gently down and went to Ell's cell. The Wyverary lay curled up on the floor, huge, crimson, and fast asleep. Ugly green gashes ripped through his scales, still oozing blood. Dried turquoise tears stained his dear face.

'Oh, Ell! No, no, don't be dead, please!'

'Why not?' said Iago. 'That's what happens to friends, eventually. They leave you. It's practically what they're for.'

September brought the Wrench crashing down on Ell's door, but the beast did not move. Outside the glass walls, September saw the towers' tips begin to break off and tumble toward the raging sea.

'Iago, I'll never move him!'

'Probably not.'

'Help me!'

'I can fly. That's all. I'm not omnipotent.'

The ceiling exploded in a shower of glass. Blood welled up along September's arms. Rain poured in.

'Please!' she screamed.

'Someone here is, though,' the great cat said. 'Omnipotent. Or nearly so.

September stared numbly for a moment and then scrambled away from Ell.

'Saturday!' she cried. 'Saturday, wake up!'

'Hm? Sort of a fish, but not really . . .' the Marid murmured.

'You have to wrestle me!' September laughed wildly as she said it, half out of her mind with terror.

'What? The dragon *hates* wrestling . . . and *I* . . . I couldn't wrestle a mouse . . .'

'Good! Then it won't be so hard for me to beat you.'

Saturday quailed.

'Don't you see?' said September. 'I can wish us all away and safe! Only you have to wrestle me. *You told me how to do this.* A Marid can grant any wish, so long as he's beaten in a wrestling match.'

Saturday's face colored and blanched as he slowly understood her. He rose up, shakily. The crack behind him grew, grinding, shrieking.

'I can't hold back,' he warned.

'I know,' September said, and darted at him, meaning to tackle him by the knees, to take him by surprise.

Saturday stepped nimbly away. She lunged at him again and he caught her, thrown back against the glass wall, which shattered noisily, dropping them both into the night air. They landed with a shower of glass like snow several storeys below. Saturday broke September's fall, but suddenly, in her arms, his grip tightened. His eyes flashed feral in the storm light. The wish had woken in him the Marid blood, sea-bright and stormy. It would not let his wounded body lose, even now, even when he needed to lose most.

Saturday hit September's chest with both fists. She held on – but just barely. Saturday snarled, his lips curling back. His face was unrecognizable. He tore away from her and scrambled up on to a glass staircase. September ran after him, knocking him down from behind. She shut her eyes as she struck out at him – she didn't want to see herself hurt him. Her fists connected with the blue muscles of his back, and he howled in pain, turning on her and pulling her hair savagely. September screamed and whipped back around to claw him with her fingernails. They separated, panting, bloody, two feuding jackals. Saturday started after her, but the weight of them was too much for the staircase – it shivered and broke, and beneath it the floor. They fell again, this time on to hard stone as the cliffs began to mingle with the glass of the Lonely Gaol. Once again, Saturday took the worst of it. He moaned. September drew away.

'Are you all right?'

The Marid raked her face with his claws, his eyes gone narrow and dark with the strength of the wish in him, trying desperately not to get out. September grasped him around the waist and hurled him back with all her strength. They grappled, breathing hard and shoving each other, gaining an inch here, an inch there. September knew that if he were well, she would be no match. She bit him cruelly on the neck and he recoiled, knocking into a half-shattered wall and sprawling out on to the stone floor of one of the Gears of the World that the Marquess prized so. Rain poured over him. September threw herself against him once more, and they tumbled back over the stone.

Just a little farther, she thought. *Just a little more.*

She no longer even tried to hit him, though his great blows landed on her shoulders, her ribs. Blood trickled into her eye. Relentlessly, she threw herself against his body again and again, pushing him back, farther and farther, until suddenly, it happened.

Saturday fell off of the stone gear of Fairyland and on to the iron gear of her own world. He landed on his back and immediately howled in agony. Sores rose up on his arms as he touched the poisonous iron. Saturday wept and thrashed. September climbed down to him. She sat astride the sobbing Marid. She wanted to stop and hold him and make him well. Instead, she pinned his arms down and hit him again.

'Yield!' she screamed over the storm.

Saturday screeched rage and defeat. September nearly let

him go to clap hands over her ears, so piercing was the sound. But she held on. And Saturday went slack beneath her. Something had passed out of him, and he was quiet again.

'I yield to you, September.'

September collapsed against him, rain pounding at her, blood mingling between them. He gave a tiny sob, and shut his eyes against her skin.

'I wish that we were all of us away from here,' she whispered in his ear, 'and Ell and Gleam and all of us were warm and safe.'

She let him up then, holding out her hand to help him. He took it. They stood together in the storm, smiling.

'Hello,' came a small voice.

September whirled around. Up on the stone gear, far above them, a small child stood, looking down, blinking in the rain. Her skin was blue, though not so blue as Saturday's, and she had long, dark hair. She had a mole on her left cheek, and her feet were very large and ungainly. The child looked quite solemn – and then suddenly, she smiled.

'Now, we shall play hide-and-seek!' she yelled down at them.

Saturday's eyes widened with understanding. He looked at September, dumbfounded.

Then, they both disappeared, quick as a thought.

CHAPTER XXI

Did You See Her?

In Which All Is Reasonably Well, but Time Is Short

The sun fell golden and warm on to a field of gleaming wheat – just a touch blue around the edges and rosy in the middle, as is the way with glowerwheat. Broad trees full of gleaming fruit shaded four bodies. They lay in the grass as though dreaming. A girl in a green smoking jacket with long, curling dark hair and a high, healthy blush in her cheeks rested with her hands closed over her chest. A boy with blue skin and rich, thick hair gathered up on top of his head slept curled next to her, with no bruises at all on his chest. A little ways away a great red Wyvern snored pleasantly, his red scales whole and unbroken.

Near his tail an orange lantern glowed dimly.

September rose up and stretched her arms, yawning. Then she touched her hair, and it all came back to her: the Marquess, the Lonely Gaol, the awful storm. She looked down at Saturday, sleeping sweetly. She moved over to him and lay very close, and then she cried, quietly, so that he couldn't see. All the ache and horror of it, the sea and the fish and the sadness of Queen Mallow and Iago and all of them, poured out of her into the grass, into the day. Finally, she touched Saturday's blue back ever so gently, with the tips of her fingers.

'Saturday,' she whispered, wiping her eyes. 'It worked. I think it worked, anyway.'

His eyes slid open.

September pulled at her curls. 'How did my hair grow back?'

Saturday rolled over in the long grass. 'You wished for everyone to be whole and well again,' he said softly.

September crept over to Ell. She could hardly breathe for

hope. Slowly, she touched his huge face, his broad cheeks, his soft nose.

'Oh, Ell, do wake up. Do be well.'

One great orange eye creaked open.

'Did I miss something?' A-Through-L yawned prodigiously.

September squealed in delight and threw her arms around the Wyverary's nose.

'And Gleam! Gleam, you're back!'

Golden writing looped across her face:

Paper can be patched.

September hugged the lantern, though this was a bit of an awkward operation. Pale green arms reached up out of the paper and embraced September but vanished quickly, as though Gleam was embarrassed of her limbs, as if they were a secret, just between September and herself. Still, if she could have smiled, Gleam would have beamed like Christmas.

'Hallloooo!' came a bellowing, booming voice out of the sky. The four of them looked up to see a Leopard swooping and leaping down to them, and none on her back but the Green Wind, in his green jodhpurs and green snowshoes, his green-gold hair flying.

September thought she would burst. She lost count of the hugs and cat-lickings and tumbling about.

'But how can you be here? I thought you weren't allowed!'

The Green Wind grinned broadly. 'The Marquess's rules are done with! No chain could keep me from you now, my little chestnut. And I have brought gifts!'

The Green Wind snapped off his green cape and lay it on the ground with a flourish. Immediately, it covered itself in every delightful green thing one can eat: pistachio ice cream and mint jelly and spinach pies and apples and olives and rich herby bread – and several huge, deep green radishes.

The Leopard paced nervously, however.

'Has my brother come with you?' she growled. 'I do not see him.'

September's face fell.

'You did not wish for him,' Saturday whispered fretfully.

The Leopard gave a little cry, quite like a kitten who has lost her litter mate. 'It is all right. He would have gone back for her. I'm sure of it. For that which was Mallow still, whom we both loved. And he was always good in a storm.'

'She is only sleeping, Green,' said September slowly. 'Might she come back someday?'

'One can never be sure,' the Green Wind sighed. 'There

is always the danger of kisses where sleeping maids are concerned. But you are safe now, and for a while yet, and why worry about a thing that may never come to pass? Do not ruin today with mourning tomorrow.'

September looked at her hands. She did not know quite how to ask what she needed to know.

'Green,' she said, her voice trembling. 'I know it was not my clock the Marquess showed me. But . . . where is my clock? How much time do I have left?'

The Green Wind laughed. A few fruit fell from the trees with the boom of it. 'You don't have one, love! The Marquess knew it, too, which is why she tried to trick you with hers. The Stumbled have clocks. It is their tragedy. But no one has quite the same tragedy. Changelings can't leave without help. And the Ravished . . .' The Green Wind pulled an hourglass from his coat. It was filled with deep red sand, the color of wine. On its ebony base was a little brass plaque. It read,

SEPTEMBER MORNING BELL

The upper bell of the hourglass was almost empty.

'That's still a clock,' Saturday pointed out.

'True. But the Ravished have their own miseries. The Stumbled cannot stay – the Ravished cannot leave.'

'What?' cried September.

'September, do you remember your big orange book that you like so much, full of old stories and tales? And do you remember a certain girl in that book, who went underground and spent the whole winter there, so that the world mourned and snowed and withered and got all covered in ice? And because she ate six pomegranate seeds, she had to stay there in the winter and could only come home in the springtime?'

'Yes,' said September slowly.

'That is what it means to be Ravished. When the sand runs out, you must go home, just like poor Mallow. But when spring comes again, so will you, and the hourglass will turn over again. It will all begin anew. You are bound to us now, but you will never live fully here, nor fully there. Ravished means you cannot stay and you cannot go. You ate heartily in Fairyland, and I am so terribly glad you did, even though it was certainly naughty of me to have tricked you so. But I do think I warned you not to eat, so you cannot bring suit against me.'

September laughed. 'You did warn me.' She thought of her mother, of leaving her every spring. But then, hadn't the Marquess said that when you go home, it's just as though you never left? Maybe her mother would not miss her. Maybe it would be like dreaming.

A-Through-L tucked his huge head against September's little neck, nuzzling her.

'When spring comes, I shall meet you at the Municipal Library, and you will see how much I've learned! You'll be so proud of me and love me so!'

'Oh, Ell, but I do love you! Right now!'

'One can always bear more love,' the Wyverary purred.

Suddenly, September thought of something that had, excusably, escaped her until this moment.

'Green! If the old laws are all broken, then Ell's wings needn't be chained down anymore!'

'Certainly not!'

September ran to the great bronze chains – they were still bound with a great padlock, and no amount of rattling budged them.

'Oh, if only I knew how to pick a lock!' sighed September. 'I've turned out to be no kind of thief at all!'

You and I may imagine this simple plea floating up and out of the golden field and up into the sky, winding and wending toward our stalwart friend, the jeweled Key, which had sought September through all of her adventures. We cannot fully understand the joy that exploded in the heart of the Key as it heard September's cry, and how fast it flew, knowing she needed it, knowing its girl cried out for it.

Winking down out of the sun, the Key fell like a firefly. It flashed and sparkled, a glittering dart, and came to rest just where September longed for it to be – nestled in the lock of the Wyverary's chains. It glittered with the shock of arriving just when it was called for, the pleasure and surprise of it. With a click, the Key turned. Peace and contentment flooded through its tiny body. The padlock fell away; the chains slid to the earth. A-Through-L, for the first time since he was a tiny lizard at his mother's side, spread his wings.

The great scarlet things cast them all in shade and kicked up warm winds as he flapped them once, twice, and lifted uncertainly into the air. Ell choked, tears welling in his eyes.

'Did you know I could fly, September? I can! I can!' The Wyverary soared up, whooping, spitting joyful fire into the clouds.

'Oh, I did know, Ell,' September whispered as her friend looped and did somersaults in the sky. 'I did.'

September looked down at the Key, finally. Her Key, with which she had unlocked the puzzle of the world. It basked in her gaze.

'Have you followed me all this way?' she gasped.

It spun around, terribly pleased.

'Oh, Key, how extraordinary!'

The Key thought it might die of the sound of her voice.

September gathered it up in her hand, and it felt it must die all over again, for the touch of her fingers.

'Will you do something for me?'

It would do anything, of course it would.

'Go and unlock the others. All over Fairyland, everyone chained and unable to fly freely. When you're done, it will be spring and time for me to come back, and then we shall not be parted again, and you shall ride on my lapel, and we will share jokes in the moonlight and look very fine on parade.'

It bowed to her, not a little puffed up. Then the Key rose up and flew away out of sight, twinkling like a tiny star.

'It's almost time,' said the Green Wind gently. The wine-colored sand was nearly spent.

'I understand now,' September said ruefully.

'What?' said Saturday.

'What the sign meant. To lose your heart. When I go home, I shall leave mine here, and I don't think I shall ever have it back.'

'I will keep it safe for you,' Saturday whispered, barely brave enough to say it.

'Will you see the witch Goodbye gets her Spoon, Green?'

'Of course, my lambswool.'

'And you'll show Gleam Pandemonium and the sea and

the highwheels and all sorts of things, Ell? Like she wanted, to see the world.'

Above them, the Wyverary laughed. 'If the Library gives me weekend liberty, I shall!'

The orange lantern bounced and shone.

September turned to Saturday.

'Did you see her?' the Marid said nervously, looking at her with great dark eyes. 'Our daughter. Standing on the Gear. Did you see her?'

'What?' said September – and then she winked out, like someone blowing out a candle, and all the field was still.

CHAPTER XXII

Ravished Means You Cannot Stay

In Which September Returns Home

Evening was just beginning to peep through the windows of September's little house, glowing blue and rose. September found herself at the kitchen sink, with her hands deep in soapy water that had long gone cold, a pink-and-yellow teacup still clutched in her hand. Behind her, a small, amiable dog yapped away at nothing. September looked down – her lonely mary jane, which had missed all the adventures, lay cast off and forgotten on the parquet floor. Her feet were bare.

'Mama won't be home yet!' she said suddenly. 'Oh, how glad I shall be to see her!'

September put on a kettle of tea for her mother and set out a clean little plate with an orange on it. She opened all the windows to let fresh air in. She even let the small dog kiss her nose. September got a blanket out of the closet and curled up in her father's big, threadbare armchair just by the door, so the first thing her mother saw when she came home would be her girl, safe and sound. Besides, September felt as though she could sleep for a century. She pulled the woolen blanket up around her chin as the dog chewed its own tail at the foot of the chair.

'I wonder what did happen to the Fairies after all?' she said to the dog, who wagged his tail, pleased to be paid attention to. 'When I get back, that will be the first thing I shall ask Ell about! After all, *Fairy* begins with F! And when spring comes again, I shall be sure to leave Mother a note and a nice glass of milk.'

September drifted off to sleep in her armchair, her long hair wrapped around her. When her mother came home from a long shift at the factory, she smiled and bundled her girl off to bed, snug and whole and warm.

She didn't notice. Of course, she didn't. Who would, after a long graveyard shift and with her back so sore? A mother cannot see every little thing – and glad we may be that she could not – as it would have caused a great deal of trouble September would never have been able to explain. All stories must end so, with the next tale winking out of the corners of the last pages, promising more, promising moonlight and dancing and revels, if only you will come back when spring comes again.

For when she lifted her daughter up out of the threadbare couch, September cast no shadow at all.